T0088980

PASSAGE
TO PEACE

PASSAGE TO PEACE

A journey of forgiveness

Norman O'Banyon

iUniverse, Inc.
New York   Bloomington

Passage to Peace
A journey of forgiveness

Copyright © 2009 Norman O'Banyon

All rights reserved. No part of this book may be used or reproduced by any means, graphic, electronic, or mechanical, including photocopying, recording, taping or by any information storage retrieval system without the written permission of the publisher except in the case of brief quotations embodied in critical articles and reviews.

This is a work of fiction. All of the characters, names, incidents, organizations, and dialogue in this novel are either the products of the author's imagination or are used fictitiously.

iUniverse books may be ordered through booksellers or by contacting:

iUniverse
1663 Liberty Drive
Bloomington, IN 47403
www.iuniverse.com
1-800-Authors (1-800-288-4677)

Because of the dynamic nature of the Internet, any Web addresses or links contained in this book may have changed since publication and may no longer be valid. The views expressed in this work are solely those of the author and do not necessarily reflect the views of the publisher, and the publisher hereby disclaims any responsibility for them.

ISBN: 978-1-4401-7001-0 (sc)
ISBN: 978-1-4401-7002-7 (ebk)

Printed in the United States of America

iUniverse rev. date: 09/22/2009

Contents

CHAPTER ONE
An introduction to forgiveness

The adventure began with a phone call.

"Hi dad, it's Bruce. Are you having a good day?"

"Hi Bud. Yeah, it's always a great day when I hear from you. What's up?" He held his breath, waiting for the request for assistance that had become customary with these surprise conversations. His son had a way of remembering him when there was some need to be met.

"I was just talking to Gram. She told me you are going to spend a few days on *Dreamer*. Where are you planning to go?" The Hunter 41 foot sloop had been a favorite sailing opportunity since his college days.

"I've wanted to revisit Desolation Sound. It seems a good idea to do it before school's out, and families fill the place." The phone conversation lacked the usual warmth of a dad talking with his only son. "Tell me what's on your mind."

A warm chuckle suggested that indeed there was another agenda. "You are pretty good at getting through to the other stuff, aren't you?" He replayed the planned conversation before he asked, "I'm wondering if you'd like to have some help moving the boat up to Anacortes. I sure liked the last time we did that together."

The father's heart wanted to believe the offer, but his suspicion was still alert for the request for a loan. He decided to accept the offer as genuine and very welcome. Somehow there still seemed to be more to this call. He decided to go along with the mood of it. "You're darned right I'd like to have you come along! Have you got a spare day soon?"

"Yeah, my division just finished a project this week. While it's going to distribution, I've got a couple of weeks of vacation. So, anytime works for me."

This conversation still had the flavor the dad had heard in so many counseling sessions. He didn't want to press the point, but there was still an important issue that had to be revealed one way or the other. "Great, Bud! Sounds like you deserve a day on the slant. Tell me what you have in mind…the whole idea."

After another embarrassed chuckle Bruce admitted, "You always have known when I've got something on my mind." There was another pause as Bruce tried to shape the words just right. "No, I don't need a loan or anything like that. The truth is, I think Annie and I have a problem. Our relationship seemed to be going pretty well, when all of a sudden she seemed to start backing away. She says she still loves me and wants the future we're hoping for, but there's something working against her that I can't seem to understand, and she won't share. I was thinking that if she could come along with us on *Dreamer*, maybe you could help us find out what it is."

"Wow, I'm sorry to hear about your trouble. Does Annie like to sail? Does she even want to come along?" Suddenly there were a number of other questions tumbling around in the father's mind.

"I thought I'd check with you first, just to see if it is possible. I can tell her then that you are willing to help us work this out. And besides, if she doesn't know how to sail, I can't think of anyone who could teach her better than you, since you did a great job with me." He was using his best diplomacy.

"Well sure, I want to do whatever I can to help you, and I'd be very happy to have a whole day to get to know Annie. A leisurely passage to Anacortes will work fine. If she's available, let's do it next Friday, or Saturday if that works better." Little did Norman O'Banyon know that they were each to be on a journey of discovery and spiritual growth.

As the dad hung up the phone, he reflected upon his own past. They had been a model couple. Norman and Mary had met in college, and married just before graduation. He went on to seminary, which allowed her to complete a Master's degree in marketing. When schooling was finally finished, they had two children, two careers, and a home in the suburbs and a cottage in the mountains. He stayed at home tending the family and the parish while she traveled to more and more distant clients. There was really nothing wrong with their marriage, yet after twenty-three years, even their commitment to holy vows wasn't enough to hold them together. They were separated for three more years before a weary divorce. She found a better job in a larger city. He left the local church to become a conflict resolution counselor. It was a sad story far too common in our society, and one he had told himself until he almost believed it.

As he watched Bruce and Annie walk down the ramp into the marina, Norm smiled to himself. The fact that they were holding hands was a good sign. At least they still looked like young lovers. They were wearing shorts and deck shoes, even though the cloudy morning also deserved sweatshirts. They were trim, athletic, and obviously happy. Annie's shoulder length chestnut hair bobbed with soft curls as she walked along the dock. Her green eyes, and heart shaped face were the very essence of vitality. Norman did wonder a bit at the luggage they were carrying. It seemed excessive for a day of sailing. As soon as they were within shouting distance he greeted them with a happy wave, and a bellowing, "Welcome aboard!"

As she approached the big sailboat, her smile masked the anxious questions she asked herself, "Could this really work? Could Bruce's dad really help her get past it, and tell him the truth?" Others had tried often, and unsuccessfully. She had just about accepted the fact that she would live forever with the knowledge of what she had done.

There were hugs and small talk on the dock. "Yes this is a pretty new marina, with all the amenities a boater might need." Sorry, her boating experience was limited, and her nautical vocabulary needed some work. "But I am eager to learn." Bruce had told her that she would be with a marvelous teacher, who never shouted. Well, hardly shouted. They were directed to put their bags in the forward compartments. "We'll cast off as soon as the diesel is warmed."

"Wow," Annie smiled, "This is nicer than my condo! I love the warm wood, and this roll top desk." She was getting a quick tour, accompanied by the low rumble of the engine. Of special interest was the small bathroom, which Bruce called a "head." There were careful instructions on its operation.

"This layout is my favorite," Norm sounded almost like a boat broker, "with two staterooms forward and the master aft…I mean in the back." They all grinned at his attempt to keep the conversation light and friendly.

"Dad, is there any hurry to get underway? Maybe we could have a time to chat for awhile before we shove off." Bruce seemed pretty direct about his agenda.

"Well Bud, we are about halfway through an ebbing tide. This is pretty much the right time. It is fairly necessary for us to leave soon, or we'll be fighting the tide all the way."

Annie asked, as any good student might, "Does the tide make that much difference, if we have a motor?"

"Yeah, it really does," Norm smiled, knowing that his teaching role was beginning. "Here in Puget Sound there are two high tides and two lows each day, with about a twelve foot difference between them. That's a lot of water flowing in and out. Whether on the engine or under sail, the boat will go about eight knots, that's eight nautical miles an hour. If we have to go against a three or four knot tide, we really struggle to get anywhere. On the other hand, if we ride an outgoing stream that increases our speed by 50 percent, we can be pretty efficient."

"I vote for efficient, if I have a vote," she said with a smile. Both of her listeners noticed the happy way she wrinkled her nose. "Just tell me what to do, or where to stay out of the way." This was going to be an enjoyable passage.

The skipper said, "It's easy enough for me to do alone, but if you want to get the dock lines, Bruce, we'll stay comfy in the cockpit." Within moments, *Dreamer* was backed out of the slip, and with no wake, making its way toward the marina entrance.

Once in Elliott Bay the skipper called to Bruce, "O.K. Moose, if you will haul the main, we'll get this old girl on a slant." The halyard had been attached to the sail, and was hoisted most of the way up the mast before he needed to take a couple of turns around the winch. Powered taut to the masthead, the sail took on a smooth wing shape that trembled as it slid through the fresh breeze. From the cockpit the skipper warned that he was setting the jib on the starboard side. All the while that quirky smile remained on Annie's face. "Are you guys speaking the same language I do?"

The skipper freed a small furling line that controlled the triangular jib sail at the bow of the boat. With one strong tug on the jib sheet, the sail unfurled like a giant window shade. Annie giggled, "That's impressive," while the skipper continued to crank in the sheet until it too was taut and smooth.

"It does sound sort of foreign, now that you mention it," the skipper finally answered. "Many of the terms come from the early days of sailing. The halyards are the ropes that 'haul the yards' of sail. Sheets are the ropes that trim, that is tighten, or ease, which is to loosen, the sails. We'll keep it understandable, unless you like the sailor talk. One job we all have is to watch out for submerged logs or deadheads. If you see anything in front of us that looks like something we shouldn't bump, tell me for sure."

Annie nodded her understanding. "I'm thinking that words are the only tools we have for making instructions clear, and every discipline has its specialized words. And wouldn't it be great if we all had a team of folks watching out for the bumps in life?"

As the morning breeze filled the sails, *Dreamer* heeled slightly as it picked up momentum. The skipper was about to tell her that in fact we do have such a team if we have a working faith. But before the words came out, Annie gasped a strangled yelp, as she grabbed the lifeline stanchion. "Gads, I thought we were going to tip over! Is it supposed to tilt like this?" The color was beginning to return to her cheeks.

"This is perfectly normal. I'm sorry I didn't warn you. When the wind blows against the sails it applies pressure. The heavy keel under the boat then balances the load. It is that tension, and the shape of the sails, that will make us go when we turn off the engine." Even as he spoke, the skipper was taking the engine out of gear and pressing the cut-off switch. "Think of a cork with a nail in the bottom of it. It might bob and rock, but it simply cannot tip over." A peaceful calm filled the cockpit. Bruce finished his task of coiling the halyard, and joined them.

Annie was far from understanding the process, but she was at least confident enough to ease her tight grip. "Will it stay like this?"

Bruce answered, eager to be a part of the conversation, "Until we change course, or change the sails, we'll be on the slant." His hand mirrored the angle at which the boat was heeling. "It's fun to pour a cup of coffee when it looks like it's coming out of the spout on an angle." His happy grin eased her fears even more. She released the stanchion all together. "And you need to think about the slant when you visit the potty." They all laughed. Yup, this just might be a great day.

Dreamer rounded the green channel marker, keeping it well to starboard. Both the main and jib sheets were eased to accommodate a new course a bit more northerly. The skipper broke into a sea chantey. "Oh, a sailor's life's for me, upon the rolling sea, the sun and the breeze, my sunburned knees, another kubra libra, if you please. A sailor's life's for me." His humor was corny, and appreciated.

There was small talk about Seattle's skyline, the great restaurants there. The distant peaks of the Cascades and Olympics still had some snow, so the conversation of skiing, and favorite vacations flowed comfortably. Annie shared that she had grown up in Portland. Her dad worked for Metro transit, and her mom was a librarian. She had a younger sister still at home, but since she was the first one in the family to go to college, she didn't have much contact any more.

It is said that sailing is hours of boredom punctuated by moments of panic. In this leisurely leg of their journey there was ample time for sharing rambling memories. As the fuel tanks near the Edmonds dock were off their beam, the skipper said, "Bruce, I picked up some sandwiches and sodas. If you'd like to bring up the sack from the galley, we can ease this nagging craving for food."

"I was wondering if you were going to work us to

death, or starve us," he said with a giggle as he headed below. "I am sorry I didn't think about offering to bring some stuff along to eat. I guess I've always counted on your hospitality." Moments later he was back with a tray of sandwiches, crackers, cheese and sodas.

Annie added, "I wondered how long we would be out. I think I assumed we could stop at a fast food drive through." Everyone laughed at the prospects of taking *Dreamer* through a McDonalds.

By the time the tray was cleaned off, the skipper said, "Up ahead is Possession Point, the south end of Whidbey Island. We're at low slack tide, so we should soon be getting a boost from a flood tide."

He paused to consider how best to open the subject they had been avoiding. "It seems to me that we have been talking about a lot of things, except what you two came on board to address this morning. Now, I will keep the chatter going, if that's what you want. But I think there is something more important we could talk about."

A deep quiet filled the cockpit. The wash of waves from the bow, and a distant seagull's call were the only sounds for several seconds.

They both began at the same time. Bruce said, "Well...I sort of hoped that we..." Annie was more focused. With a relieved smile she said, "Bruce told me you would help us. He also said that you would be as direct as I wanted." Her chin trembled slightly showing an emotion that lay hidden by all the small talk. With a deep breath she began a difficult task.

"Bruce has been a breath of fresh air in my life. He is so positive, so up-beat, he is fun to be around." She paused, thinking how to continue without saying too much. "We have both had some bumpy times in the past. But it seems like he is able to shake his off without being messed up. We were doing real well, planning for the future, even hinting about something more, making plans for a new place of our own. But then, little things started to get in the way. I think we have both sabotaged those plans a bit. It's like we want to but don't." She looked at Bruce with a level affectionate focus.

The skipper noticed that she wore no jewelry, no ring at all.

"I think reality set in when we started talking about coming to church with you. Bruce said you really like U Pres, and thought we might too." She gave her head a tiny shake. "I'm just not ready or willing to add God to the confusion of my days. Going to some new big church full of folks who ask questions is not something I want to do. Does that make sense to you?" Her question was directed toward Bruce, but meant for them all. The stillness was again nearly tangible.

The skipper asked, "Is it the size of a large church, or would any congregation be too much?"

"It's any church," she answered with a sad sort of smile. Bruce nodded in agreement. "I just don't want any condemnation or judgment in my life right now. I see Bruce's positive cheerfulness, and I can't stand the thoughts of some critical damnation teaching, or super righteousness forced on me." A pink flush around her neck suggested that a lot of emotion was being held in check.

Patches of blue sky were beginning to show through the early afternoon haze. The skipper asked, "Did you attend church much as a little girl? Do your folks go?"

"No, I guess they call us 'C and E' people. We only attended on Christmas and Easter, usually because Grandma asked us to go with her." Annie was grateful that both of these men seemed comfortable with her conversation. There was an easy acceptance here. "I guess I always felt bad enough about myself anyway, without needing someone to tell me what a sinner I've been."

Well, the skipper had invited a serious discussion. Now he paused to think about the best way to address the issues before them. "Remember a little while ago, when we talked about specialized words? It seems real important to me to check the words and terms we use when talking about ourselves, and those things that are important to us. If the tone and flavor is positive, we can usually find a positive diagnosis. If we believe that there is a positive solution to our problems, we are lots more eager to find it." It was another way of asking, "Is the glass half-full or half-empty?"

"I agree," Annie said with that half smile. "In school

and business, in fact in almost all of my life, I think that is true. But when it comes to dealing with what has been done, with the sins of the past, there is no positive way to change that."

"How about if you could change how you felt about the past? Would that change it?" Bruce asked the question to be part of the conversation, but also because he was feeling a bit anxious about some of his own memories that were beginning to resurface.

Annie thought for a moment, watching the lighthouse at Mukilteo slide past *Dreamer's* beam. "I suppose if you can't change the facts of the past, there is something to changing the way we feel about it."

"That's exactly why the church is so important to me," the skipper said with a confident nod. "It is a gathering of believers who practice Grace instead of judgment. They know there is more to love and affection than criticism. It's a community of affirmation rather than rejection." It was a faith statement he truly held.

Annie looked into the skipper's eyes for a long moment, as though she was weighing the risk of her next question. "If that is the case, why are you no longer a pastor?" Her voice was soft with both respect, and regret.

"Well, I.... Wow...Hmm," he stammered, at a loss for the right response. "I guess you are close to the truth. My divorce became very problematic to a few people, who held the pastor to the highest standard of conduct, perhaps more idealistic than realistic. Once the sentiment of doubt began, it spread through the leadership. Before long I felt it would be easier, maybe wiser, and I thought kinder, of me to leave than to stay and hurt even more folks."

Bruce interjected, "That was the same time Sydney and I broke up. When she moved out I couldn't think of much else. I'm sorry I wasn't more supportive of you then, or of mom." Once again a long silence filled *Dreamer's* cockpit.

"Wow," Annie said with a much brighter voice, even though tears had filled her eyes. She straightened her shoulders. "Let's invite Annie along and get everyone bummed out. She's as much fun as a root canal." She was intimidated by the direction of this conversation. Bruce had never talked to her about Sydney.

"Oh no, sweetie," the skipper comforted her, cuddling her in a gentle one arm hug. "No, you mustn't feel badly for reminding us of some old wounds. In fact, the question was very perceptive, and good questions always bring the best answers." His smile was so genuine it returned one to her face as well.

Bruce also wanted to be part of a calming moment. "I've always thought Mr. Clinton's advice to 'don't ask, and don't tell,' was the safest way to deal with things you can't change."

The skipper shook his head slightly, and said with a smile, "For way too many things in our life, that's like trying to get rid of a splinter by pushing it in deeper. At least it's out of sight." He paused, as if thinking about the absurdity of his analogy. "A relationship that begins with denial and deception is bound for a lot of pain."

"Let's go back to the discussion about specialized words, because I think we were close to a good thought there. Think about the difference between our understanding of 'sin,' 'law,' 'guilt,' and 'shame.' If sin is anything that separates us from God, it would be possible to sin but not break a law. Yet the opposite is not the case. We probably can't break a law without endangering or hurting ourselves, or others, which would be a sin." Both Bruce and Annie had puzzled expressions, wondering how this might work out.

"Stick with this for a just a second," the skipper asked. "We are accustomed to people paying the price for breaking the law. You do the crime and pay the time. Crime is therefore an unnatural condition, which we try to avoid, or at least avoid getting caught. And," he paused to emphasize, "we feel the same way about sin. Especially the sixth and seventh commandment, killing and adultery, we see as punishable sins, like any crime. Perjury, that is false witness, is another punishable offence, but we don't get very excited about coveting our neighbor's new BMW."

"What I'm trying to say, and not getting it out very well, is that most of us think of both sin and breaking the law as the same thing. We think of punishment as necessary. But in God's eyes there is a huge difference.

Crime may need punishment and restitution. But sin needs forgiveness!"

"Here's the deal! We think of forgiveness in the wrong way, when we think about it as a justice issue, where cause, responsibility, guilt, or accountability are involved. Someone hurts us, and we assume they are guilty until they ask our forgiveness, which we either grant or withhold. It's like 'Let's Make a Deal,' with our emotions. The truth is that forgiveness is a spiritual issue that has much less to do with the offending party than with your inner thoughts. It has to do with how we internalize the hurts we receive, and how we relate to the offending party. I've heard that withholding forgiveness is like drinking poison and hoping that the other person will die; whereas forgiveness is an antitoxin that cleanses the poison of resentment out of our spirit. It is really something that you do for yourself! The vocabulary we use generally indicates how we are going to get to that forgiveness."

" Sure, we all need forgiveness, because we are forever doing what we don't want to do, and not doing the very thing we want to, as Paul said. We can agree that sin is a natural, but redeemable condition for humans. 'We all sin, and fall short of the glory of God.' And we can also agree that in the regular life we live, there are going to be moments when others hurt us, either out of their ignorance, or intentionally. So, guilt and pain may be a natural process of our conscience as it tries to help us back onto the right track. A healthy conscience is what keeps us from being pathologic in our behavior. But shame is the excess of guilt, and hatred is the excess of pain, carried to a destructive or counterproductive level."

A deep frown furrowed Bruce's brow. "You're not saying that sin and pain are O.K., are you? It sounds like you said they are just part of who we are."

"No, not O.K. at all", the skipper continued. "However, they are part of who we are. Our appetites and fears can separate us from God, one way or another." He turned to ease the mainsheet and jib sheet to catch a breeze that seemed to be swinging more from the south. "But always, God desires to forgive rather than punish us. That's the positive language that leads to a hopeful prognosis."

"Saint Augustine was one of the early Church fathers, and the premier theologian of all time. In his classic book *Confessions,* he told of a youthful prank of stealing pears from a neighbor's tree. He said that late one night a group of them went to 'shake down fruit and carry it away.' They took lots of it, not to eat it themselves, but to simply throw it to the pigs. He went on to berate himself for the depth of sin it revealed."

Bruce gave a snort of mock contempt. "If that was the depth of his sin, he was lucky."

"Yeah, it sounds pretty plain," the skipper agreed. "But his conclusion was a lot more important. He said, 'The fruit gathered, I threw away, devoured in it only iniquity. There was no other reason, but foul was the evil, and I loved it.' And remember, that was after his own admission of taking a mistress, fathering a child out of wedlock, and indulging in every fleshly passion. Augustine saw in the pear incident his true nature, and the nature of all humankind. 'Foul was the evil, and I loved it.' In each of us there is sin."

Annie had been watching Gedney Island slide behind *Dreamer*. Their speed was being helped by the incoming tide. "I wish pears were my problem." Then after another quiet pause; "What if a person has never felt close to God? How can sin separate us when we have never been together?" Her wistful look had a bit of longing to it.

"Remember those words that bring a positive diagnosis?" the skipper asked. "Whether we feel close to God or not, God feels close to us. And it has little to do with our feelings, but everything to do with the nature of God. God is Love and desires us to be kind. God is Joy and desires us to celebrate life. God is peace and asks us to be harmonious in a troubled world, to harm no one. God is Good and desires our best rather than an inventory of our mistakes."

Bruce's frown had not gone away. "It still sounds like you are overlooking sin and its consequences."

The skipper looked at this young man with the obvious pride of a dad. "No sir, we must never overlook it. I think it was Carl Menninger who reminded us that sin is spelled with a capital "I" in the middle. But the point of remembering our sin is to restore a relationship with a Loving God, rather than extracting a penalty or punishment. We must learn to be peacemakers…with ourselves, as well as the people we have offended."

"You see," he was about to make a point that would open the journey for them all, "it doesn't seem to be an issue of sin or punishment, which are external activities, but a matter of Grace, which is internal. I think forgiveness is a verb, but not something we do, or God does, but rather something that we are. It is a state of being."

"Oh wow," Bruce responded, "I've never heard you say something like that before. Where does that come from?"

"I'm not sure, but the more I think about it, the more sense it makes to me. In the Old Testament the word 'forgive' meant to cover, or send away, or wipe away. It was the root of the idea of atonement. It was so central to the people's idea of getting right with God that once a year two goats were brought into the temple. One was sacrificed so the blood could be sprinkled on the people."

Annie, who had been listening quietly, grimaced and said, "That's gross! It sounds like some primitive cult ritual."

The skipper smiled, "Primitive, but essential to the faith of the founders. The second goat received the sins of the nation by means of a ritual laying on of hands, and was driven out of the city gates into the wilderness, taking with it the sense of separation from God."

Again Annie responded before Bruce could speak, "Is that where we get the term 'scapegoat'?" Her gaze was fixed on the skipper as though she was about to grasp a truth.

"It is the very source of that 'pass the buck' idea. But in the New Testament the term 'forgive' has to do with the idea of covering, or loosening our sin, and there is a gracious stress on God's generosity."

Annie asked, "But what about God's wrath and justice? How does that fit into forgiveness?" Bruce nodded his head as though that might be the very question he was about to ask.

"Well guys, forgiveness has very little if anything to do with justice. It has to do with the inner dialogue we have with ourselves and with God. Think about it. Jesus told us to forgive others as God forgives us. Now we know that God's love is neither partial nor conditional. God loves us when we are in the far country or in the very act of sin. The more we become aware of that loving condition for ourselves, the more we can see it in those who hurt or abuse us. That might be called learning to live in the forgiveness dimension, or the mercy factor."

This time Bruce beat Annie to the response, "I like the idea of living in a forgiveness factor!" There was a fresh brightness to his smile. "I'd just like to know how to get there." The trio had been so caught in the discussion they little noticed the scenery sliding past.

The skipper thought for a few moments and finally

responded, "I'm sort of clear on how we get there, because I can see what happens to folks who make it. They seem to generate mercy out of their quiet souls while those who are not in the factor generate malice out of their troubles. Does that make sense?"

Without waiting for them to answer he continued. "Bruce, your cousin Brenda loves country and western music." A small grimace suggested that his music choice might be something else. "Now if you were to join her at a concert, she might be having a wonderful experience, while you might be aching inside. It would be a totally different experience for you each, based on your internal preference."

Bruce nodded his understanding, not quite sure where this was about to take him.

The skipper pondered, "So if something happens to you that is unpleasant, you may have options of how you might interpret the experience, based on your preference or point of view. If you get whacked in a football game, it may knock the wind out of you, but it's just part of the game, right? And if you were coming out of work, and some fellow employee whacked you that hard because he was jealous of your promotion, it would create a much different interpretation."

"You bet! I'd put him down!" Bruce's gesture of a fist left no need for further description.

"So, the same action would bring a far different re-action, depending on our understanding or interpretation of it, don't you agree? In one case it's just a game, and we shake it off. In the other it is assault, which must be dealt with properly." The skipper made a fist to echo Bruce's anger.

"I think I see where you are heading now." Bruce nodded.

"I know I am oversimplifying this," the skipper smiled, especially at Annie. "But if we are more and more aware of God's love for us and others, we will live more and more with a merciful response to whatever might happen to us. If we are not living in the forgiveness factor, we generate malice. We find ourselves angry, at war, or frightened and frustrated by the events around us."

Annie had not taken her eyes off the skipper. "Do you actually believe it can be that black and white? You make it sound too easy."

The skipper smiled at her and said, "Bruce will tell you that I believe in shades of gray rather than pure black and white. But it brings up another good model. Jesus told us that he is the Light of the World. He also told us that we are the light of the world. So, if we are living in the factor, we are more and more light. Without it, we are more and more darkness. I think there is some light in the worst of folks, and some shadows in even the best of us. It has to do with that inner dialogue about God's love."

"I don't want to interrupt this discussion, but what is that fort thing we are passing?" She pointed to a large piling wall.

Bruce was quick to answer, "Isn't that the breakwater at Langley?"

"It is, in fact," the skipper replied. "And there is a neat story to it. Langley didn't have anything in the way of a harbor, but they wanted to attract the boaters to stop into their waterfront shops, which are very interesting. So, they took charge of their own destiny by creating a very secure marina, building a breakwater and dredging out a boat basin. They sort of took a positive idea to its most fruitful conclusion. It is a model many people would like to copy in their lives."

"Are you saying that if a life is lacking something desirable, the person should just create it? Isn't that sort of dishonest?" Again Bruce was asking a question with a furrowed brow.

"Yeah, it could be. If a person lacked a good education, or job history, it would be very dishonest to create a phony resume that suggested accomplishments. But that is off the point here. I am saying that anyone who feels that their life is unsatisfying, or unproductive, can build a breakwater and dredge a safe harbor. It can be done with the proper inner dialogue. They have a choice."

Annie asked, "If that could happen for everyone, why do you suppose so many people continue to live the shallow lives they do? Why don't people change?"

"That's been a puzzle to me too," the skipper smiled, aware again of this gentle young woman's vulnerability. "I suspect that it has to do with unwillingness to do the work required, or procrastination, which may be the same thing, or maybe they lack a belief system that would even make an effort, and maybe they just don't think they are in need of it."

The skipper had been watching the decreasing wind, and consequent drop in boat speed. He said to Bruce, "We may need to roll up these sails and diesel to LaConner if we want to get there by supper."

With a bit of a wry chuckle, Annie continued as if she had not heard a mention of changing the sails. "It always seems to come back to that doesn't it?"

Still looking up at the mainsail, the skipper asked, "Hmm, to what?"

"To faith, isn't that what you meant when you said they lack a belief system? Isn't that the same thing as faith? They just don't believe it is possible."

Realizing that this young lady was fairly focused on the subject at hand, the skipper returned his attention fully to her. "Our faith shapes us, molds us into a continually changing person. You bet it always comes back to faith, because faith is the foundation to everything else."

"That's just my problem! I've got too many questions. I just don't know what to believe." Her chin trembled slightly, warning them that she was struggling with this conversation.

Touching her shoulder the skipper assured her, "It's a really big task. Does it feel overwhelming to you?"

She nodded. "I just don't know how or where to start. It feels like I need too much."

"If it is any comfort, I can tell you that from time to time we all feel like that. It's natural. People work on their faith their entire lifetime. And there is always some new wrinkle for us to work on. Buddha said, 'All that we are is the result of what we have thought. The mind is everything.'" Then pausing for a moment to emphasize the final part of the quote, " 'what we think, we become.' It is the same message as from Proverbs, 'as a man thinks in his heart, so is he.' My favorite one from a new source is from Robert Bolton, 'A belief is not merely an idea that the mind possesses; it is an idea that possesses the mind.' We really are shaped and molded by our thoughts."

After a few seconds of thinking about it, Annie said, "The best quote I can recall is from my psych professor. I think he is an atheist. He said, 'I'd believe in reincarnation if I could come back as something easier to be than human.'" She wiped the stray tear from her cheek.

The skipper studied the shape of the mainsail, which was bagging under less wind. "I'm going to need the diesel pretty soon, but there are a couple more thoughts buzzing around in my head. Let's get back to thinking about guilt and pain. A positive life outlook would say that there are no mistakes, only lessons to be learned, and the lesson is repeated until it is learned. If you don't learn the easy lessons, they become more challenging, and are frequently painful. Pain is one way the universe gets your attention. But finally, you'll know a lesson is learned when your behavior or feelings change. Does that make sense?"

Both Bruce and Annie nodded, but less than enthusiastically. They both seemed to hold big reservations.

"O.K. the second gigantic generality is this, we only have the present, this very day, to do our work. The past is over, and is out of reach. And since the future hasn't happened, we misuse the present day by spending precious energy needlessly. We primarily think about the past defensively or feel guilty, maybe even ashamed about it. Our way of dealing with the future is to fear it and worry, or get excited about it with eager anticipation. In either of these ways we violate the present by trying to bring what does not exist into it."

He then asked them an unexpected and somewhat silly question. "Are there any arrest wants or warrants out for you? Are you on any 'most wanted' list?" The question seemed absurdly out of context with anything they had been talking about.

Both Annie and Bruce shook their heads, although he made a comical face to indicate some suspicion.

"Good," the skipper said, "me neither! We have just declared that at least on some level, in this present moment, we are innocent. How do you feel about that?"

"O.K. I suppose," Bruce replied. "But it is really not front page news." His smile assured the skipper there was no malice meant.

"How would you feel if that same condition could exist at all levels of your life? If every level was worry free: work, play, your personal, political, ethical life?" He looked into their eyes individually, taking the leisure of the situation to finally ask, "your spiritual life?"

Before Bruce could answer in his usual humorous way, Annie whispered, "I'd love it. It would be like heaven!"

"What a perfect word to describe it." The skipper's smile was warm and tender. "Can you believe that it really is possible to realize that? Wouldn't that be the ultimate sense of contentment? I think it would be the perfect form of peacemaking… to our very core. It would be living, mercifully, in the forgiveness factor!"

"Hey, Mr. Muscles," the skipper said to Bruce, "if you'll get a grip on that furling line, I'll take us back into the wind. Let's roll 'em up." Even as he was saying it, the nose of *Dreamer* began to turn back into the breeze, powered by the diesel engine. Bruce pulled for a few easy wraps, then wound the line around the port winch and cranked in the rest, the self-furler becoming a neat roll of sail. The main halyard was released, allowing the big sail to lower into the lazy-jack cradle. Within less than two minutes, the sailboat was back on their original course, leaving a clean wake on the afternoon surface.

"That's Strawberry Point off our port bow. As soon as we get around it, we'll be able to see the entrance marker to the Swinomish channel. We may even be a bit early for dinner, at this rate. I have a couple of Bible stories to share with our discussion. Bruce, if you'll get that J.B. Phillips New Testament out of the nav station, you can be the reader."

Moments later Bruce asked, "Which story would you like me to read?"

"Turn to Luke 15, and read the second half of the chapter."

A quiet moment was followed by another. "O.K, O.K. Luke comes after…Matthew,…Mark,…here it is."

"'Once there was a certain man who had two sons.' Is this the part you'd like?" When the skipper nodded, he continued. "'The younger one said to his father, 'Father, give me my share of the property that will come to me.' So he divided up his property between the two of them. Before very long, the younger son collected all his belongings and went off to a foreign land, where he squandered his wealth in the wildest extravagance. And when he had run through all his money, a terrible famine arose in that country, and he began to be in want. Then he went and hired himself out to one of the citizens of that country who sent him into the fields to feed the pigs. He got to the point of longing to stuff himself with the food the pigs were eating, and not a soul gave him anything. Then he came to his senses and cried aloud, 'Why, dozens of my father's hired men have got more food than they can eat and here am I dying of hunger! I will get up and go back to my father, and I will say to him, 'Father, I have done wrong in the sight of heaven and in your eyes. I don't deserve to be called your son any more. Please take me on as one of your hired men.' So he got up and went to his father. But as he was still some distance off, his father saw him and his heart went out to him, and he ran and fell on his neck and kissed him. But his son said, 'Father, I have done wrong in the sight of Heaven and in your eyes. I don't deserve to be called your son any more...' 'Hurry!' called out his father to the servants, 'fetch the best clothes and put them on him! Put a ring on his finger and shoes on his feet, and get that calf we've fattened and kill it, and we will have a feast and celebration! For this is my son – I thought he was dead, and he's alive again. I thought I had lost him, and he is found!' And they began to get the festivities going.'"

Bruce paused to ask, "Should I finish the chapter?"

Annie nodded quickly. The skipper said, "This is sometimes called the most perfect short story ever told. Yeah, go on to the end."

Finding his place again, Bruce read on. "But his elder son was out in the fields, and as he came near the house, he heard music and dancing. So he called one of the servants across to him and inquired what was the meaning of it all. 'Your brother has arrived, and your father has killed the calf we fattened because he got himself home again safe and sound' was the reply. 'But he was furious and refused to go inside the house. So his father came outside and called him. Then he burst out, 'Look, how many years have I slaved for you and never disobeyed a single order of yours, and yet you have never given me so much as a young goat, so that I could give my friends a dinner? But when that son of yours arrives, who has spent all your money on prostitutes, for him you kill the calf we've fattened!' But the father replied, 'My dear son, you have been with me all the time and everything I have is yours. But we had to celebrate and show our joy. For this is your brother; I thought he was dead – and he's alive. I thought he was lost – and he is found!'"

"I love that story!" Bruce concluded with enthusiasm.

"It was the first text I used for a sermon when I was a student pastor," the skipper replied. "But all the way through seminary, I learned that the parable was so much more complex than I imagined. The younger son is willful, disrespectful, insulting, and ignorant. Yet he is, at the conclusion, in the house where the party is going on, while his righteous older brother, who is the only one to talk about the conditions of his brother's sins, and is fuming in the dark. The story is left unfinished for us to come to our own conclusions. If, as we hear it we identify with the younger brother, who has received grace, we may be in recovery from some inner brokenness. If on the other hand, we feel like the older self-righteous brother, who by the way, represented organized religion that was in opposition to Jesus, we may be stuck in our rules and condemnations."

"The power of the story," the skipper continued, "is in the point of view we take as we listen to it. Do you remember the three most important things in real estate sales?"

Annie and Bruce smiled at each other and answered together. "Location, location, location."

"In the same way there are three most important parts of understanding the stories that Jesus told." He paused for a moment to allow them to consider an answer. Then he continued, "Perception, perception, perception! It means that the perception we have of God is primary, but also the perception we have of ourselves, and the perception we have of the Church, or formal religion. Those perceptions, or images, tell us what sort of person we are, whether we will have mercy or malice."

Bruce raised his eyebrows in understanding. "You mean like the Calvin Klein image of who we want to look like, or the Tom Cruise GQ kind of guy?"

"No," the skipper answered, "It's a lot deeper than that. Some years ago a psychiatrist named William Glasser told about an ingenious experiment with anorexic young women. They were shown a series of pictures depicting their own faces superimposed on a series of bodies ranging from athletic to average all the way to a scary skeletal. They were asked which of the images they preferred. To the researcher's surprise all the women said none of the pictures were thin enough. What they were saying was that they wanted to be thinner than whatever they saw in the mirror. To achieve this irrational degree of thinness, they had no choice but to starve themselves. They were dying, out of the inner image they carried."

"Here is the important point I'm trying to make," the skipper said softly. "Our self image and our conduct go hand in hand. If we change one, we will automatically change the other!"

"Do you mean, dad, that if we conduct ourselves in a new way, we will develop a whole new self image?" Bruce was struggling to grasp the concept his father was offering.

"If you really believe in that new way of conduct, there will be a change, yes. If you think about this, it explains why some people start out in a new direction, but fall back into the same old habits. They didn't believe in the truth of their conduct. There is a Tomlinson quote that says, 'the world is what we truly think it is. If we can change our thoughts, we can change the world.'"

"In the story that Jesus told, the younger brother changed his thinking about his home and his father. The image that Jesus gave us in the father was of a God who is not primarily interested in the wastefulness or foolishness or sinfulness of his son. He was simply and finally glad to have his son back. The clothes and shoes, and ring are symbols of the son's restored status, and the fatted calf, which was being prepared for a temple sacrifice, was a symbol of pure celebration. Does any of this make sense?"

They both nodded, and Bruce was quick to answer,

"I'm not sure I understand that connection between conduct and self-image yet, but if I'd have had more of these conversations during that New Testament class, I'll bet I'd have had a better grade."

Annie added, "If I knew it could make this much sense, I'd have read the whole book a long time ago. This is a new way of talking about forgiveness, isn't it?"

"Yes, that's exactly what we're talking about. In the Bible there are many stories of forgiveness, most of which detail some sort of healing. It's as if Jesus was trying to show the folks that a change in their perception could bring a change in their physical condition. If they could enter a new feeling, and use a positive vocabulary, their future could become the same."

Annie's eyes were still brimming with tears. "Do you think that everything that causes hurt can be forgiven?"

"I believe that forgiveness is a personal, private, inner matter. It relates to our feelings about relationships. A storm may cause hurt, yet we don't think about the need of forgiveness there. A lightning spark may start a fire that burns down the neighbor's business. How can we seek forgiveness for the cloud that generated the flash? But in personal matters, yes, I believe there is nothing beyond the bounds of forgiveness."

"Hmm," Annie mused, "I think that's where my faith falters. There are some things too dark to think about a positive conclusion."

"Well, let's test that thought. If I'm not sounding too

much like a Sunday sermon, let's listen to another account from scripture. Bruce, how about turning to John 8, and read the first 11 verses, they may be a footnote in some Bibles. It's a familiar but really painful story."

It only took a couple of moments for him to find the place, and begin reading. "Early next morning, Jesus returned to the temple and the entire crowd came to him. So he sat down and began to teach them. But the scribes and Pharisees brought in to him a woman who had been caught in adultery. They made her stand in front, and then they said to him, 'Now, Master, this woman has been caught in adultery, in the very act. According to the Law, Moses commanded us to stone such women to death. Now, what do you say about her?"

"They said this to test him, so that they might have some good grounds for an accusation. But Jesus stooped down and began to write with his finger in the dust on the ground. But as they persisted in their questioning, he straightened himself up and said to them, "Let the one among you who has never sinned throw the first stone at her.' Then he stooped down again and continued writing with his finger on the ground. And when they heard what he said, they were convicted by their own consciences and went out, one by one, beginning with the eldest until they were all gone.'

'Jesus was left alone, with the woman still standing where they had put her. So he stood up and said to her, 'Where are they all – did no one condemn you?'

'And she said, "No one, sir.

'Neither do I condemn you,' said Jesus to her. 'Go home and do not sin again.'"

When Bruce had finished reading there was a deep quiet in the cockpit, only the rumble of the engine throbbed across the smooth water.

Finally the skipper said, "Aren't those striking images? You can see the hard looks on the faces of the men who were cruel enough to bring a naked woman into a crowded assembly. That's why John wrote that she was caught in the very act. There was no question about her guilt. And you can also see a gentle, or compassionate Jesus, who would rather write in the dust than stare at her shame. The picture for us is of a God who does not look at our sin, but sends us into the future with the merciful intention not to sin again. That is the power and the purpose of forgiving Grace."

Annie asked with a voice thick with emotion, "I don't understand then why they said their Law insisted that the woman should be killed."

"It was another image Jesus tried to get across to the people who would listen." The skipper nodded his understanding of the importance of the answer. "Their Law of Moses was the Ten Commandments, along with their interpretation that had accumulated through the years. It kept them in a justice mode, with a lot of malice for some in their world. But Jesus wanted them to know that there was a higher law, which was to love God completely, and to love our neighbor sincerely, which would promote mercy. That was a spiritual mode, an image the people found strangely difficult to accept. You see, it depends on our positive, or negative perception."

Annie thought for another long moment before she asked, "You seem to talk a lot about choice. Do you think people always have choices?"

"I sure do! In fact, I think that is pretty much the secret that makes life rich. We have a dazzling number of choices, always." The skipper's smile was a warm emphasis to his belief.

She shifted her posture to stretch out a tight muscle in her back. "This sounds like I'm trying to argue with you, and I'm really not. But what about people who make bad choices, do you think they still get more?" Annie thought that this question just might be the reason she came along today. She held her breath in anticipation of the answer.

"Well of course they do. Sure, some choices are so bad they limit the future. The consequences of some choices are fatal, like the biker who thought he could crowd out the truck on the freeway. Each year there are a tragic number of highway fatalities about graduation time. Young lives that are full of promise are cut short by some awful choices. People think that they will never get cancer so they choose to smoke or abuse their bodies. Some choices cut life short. Then the choices are drastically limited."

The rumble of the engine was the only sound in the cockpit for several heartbeats, then in a voice so small it was barely audible, Annie whispered, "I made an awful choice once that has haunted me, and I think drastically limited my future." Her eyes filled with tears that soon flowed freely down her cheeks. Looking at Bruce she went on, "I think I want to tell you about it…maybe I need to tell you about it." She caught a ragged breath.

"When I went to college I was a pretty naive person, and was very innocent. At a freshman party, I met a guy who seemed really nice. We dated for a few weeks and things started getting a little steamy. Then one night at a dance I had a couple of glasses of punch with some alcohol in it and afterwards, we stopped by the lake. I didn't plan for things to get out of control, but we had sex anyway. I told him I wasn't interested in going further with that sort of thing. But he was pretty demanding. Making out seemed to become his only reason for being with me. There was quite a bit of sex, until I finally missed my period. A home test showed that I was pregnant, which a trip to my doctor confirmed." A wave of sadness caused her to tremble, and another tear traced down her face.

"When I told him, he asked who the father was, which was the first of several insults. He wasn't interested in taking any sort of responsibility, until finally he just said he'd see me around, and left." A sob so deep it just shook her body interrupted her account.

"My doctor outlined my choices…adoption, or

keeping the child as a single parent," another long pause was thick with emotion, "or termination of the pregnancy. That was finally my choice. I didn't tell my folks, or roommate at school. I was just sick for a couple of days as far as anyone knew." Bruce moved across the cockpit to hold her in a strong embrace, which released more sobs and tears.

In a voice twisted by pain she finished, "I can't look at a school yard full of playing children without thinking of a little boy or girl who never had a chance to be, because of me. Every time I see some mom with a toddler in tow I wonder about what might have been." Her voice drifted into silence, without finishing the thought. Her eyes were empty of tears or feeling as she journeyed to that painful place in her heart.

The skipper tried to reach across the emptiness she was feeling to say, "I have heard that there are no hopeless situations, only people who have given up their hope. It sounds like you were in a nightmare, and you struggled alone."

Annie finally took a deep breath, and said, "You're the first to know, not even my parents. I constantly think about the small child that isn't because of my choice. I know there is nothing I can do to change the past, and I'm afraid of going into the future with all this guilt. What am I going...?" Unable to say anything more, she sobbed uncontrolled.

Both men exchanged a concerned glance. Bruce

said quietly, "I can only guess how hard that would be." Silence filled the cockpit blocking out the droning of the engine.

After a long pause to choose the right words, the skipper asked, "For just a minute, can you think of me as your pastor, instead of a friend?" He again reached over to gently touch her shoulder. When she smiled a wane agreement, he went on.

"I want to help you find mercy in this moment instead of malice for yourself. Let's see if we can find some new images to replace the hurtful ones that are so focused right now. If you will just let these ideas sink in without judgment, it might help. I want you to see yourself as victim more than victimizer. You didn't intend to become sexually active, did you?" When she shook her head, he asked, "You didn't plan on becoming pregnant?" Again her head shook vigorously. "And you certainly didn't intend to have to deal with the problem alone, did you?"

"No!" was whispered sadly. "Those were never my plans."

"So the first new image is that your intentions, your preferences, your heartfelt desires were never hurtful, right?"

"I never wanted to hurt anyone, especially a little child," Annie answered through her sorrow.

"Most people judge others on the basis of the actions they see, but there is a deeper judgment reserved for

God that sees on the basis of our intentions. You could never have foreseen the conclusion of what started out as an innocent, yet poorly grounded, school romantic relationship that turned into an abusive one, right?"

Her sad eyes looked at him in some surprise. "I'm not sure what you mean by abusive. He never hit or hurt me."

"No, he may not have hit you, but he did use you for sport, didn't he? Isn't that hurtful?" It was an honest way to express the truth. "And when he was asked to be accountable or responsible, he disappeared? Wasn't that hurtful?" The skipper was trying to be extra tender with a fragile and vulnerable moment. "Wouldn't you call that abusive?"

"I guess that's true." Annie's answer was slow and through lips drawn tight with new understanding.

"I also want you to see yourself in light of years of decent, moral, righteousness, instead of a brief crisis. There is another image of you rather than the harsh one you have been seeing. You were proud of your home and school, proud to be a good daughter and friend. You have thought of yourself as a happy, wholesome person, a pure and responsible student, and a competent employee. Don't let one negative decision outweigh a bundle of positive ones. Isn't it easier for you to define yourself by the abortion than by being on the Dean's Scholastic list?"

Annie flinched at the use of the word "abortion;" but nodded her agreement. "But this seems like a more demanding crisis than all that ordinary stuff."

"Yes it is," the skipper agreed. "But aren't we defined by the hundreds of innocent moments as well as the one of panic?"

"I guess so," she finally sighed with a hint of genuine relief.

"I have just one more question." The skipper was watching *Dreamer* close on Strawberry Point. "Do you think fear, anger, or grief are the only options you have as consequences to your problem? I think that's what you have been feeling. If they are dysfunctioning attitudes, do you think there might be some other enabling, or empowering choices that may have been overlooked?"

She took a deep breath, releasing it slowly. "I truly had never even thought it could be possible." A crooked little smile hinted at a ray of new hope.

Bruce, who had been quiet for most of the conversation, now asked, "Is that why you said we must not let the past or future abuse the present moment? If we define ourselves by anything but the present, we are abandoning our true selves." Both the skipper and Annie looked at him with admiration.

"Wow!" they said together.

"That is insightful of you, brother. I'm proud of you!" When Bruce smiled with the praise, the skipper continued. "I once heard that we are not humans learning to become spiritual beings. It's just the other way around. We are spiritual beings learning to be human. We must give ourselves permission to believe that healing or wholeness is a human, as well as a humane option," he said for emphasis. "It is always about choices. For example, your experience may be the lesson that enables you to become a fantastic counselor to young women who are making reproductive choices, or an advocate for sexual abstinence, or a spokesperson for Planned Parenthood. You may want to devote your life as a pediatrician, or a family counselor, helping other children. The choices, on the side of mercy, are available, and immense. "

Sitting more straight, and drying her eyes, Annie said, "I just never thought of it that way. It's like a door just opened. I can understand why you say everything is a matter of faith. If my heart defines the moment instead of the other way around, when what I believe is critical." She was feeling a new sense of hope, or peace or… It was great!

"This is Strawberry Point," the skipper announced as he eased the helm slightly to port. *Dreamer's* bow began a slow turn that paralleled the shore. "As soon as we get through this turning point, we will be able to see the outer marker of the Channel."

Annie smiled softly. "This might be a turning point for me, too! I can't remember feeling this good, like a burden has been lifted from me." She gave Bruce's hand a squeeze. "I want to thank you both for listening to my story, and not throwing me overboard."

Bruce returned her smile saying, "We like you, and besides, who could we get to tend the bumpers?" She poked him in the ribs.

"Hey, look!" Her finger pointed over Bruce's shoulder toward the shore. "There's a dog swimming way out there!"

Bruce identified her sighting, "Not a dog, I think that's a little harbor seal." They watched attentively until the shiny head dipped back under the surface.

The skipper brought them back to the conversation, "Telling our story, and claiming it, are important steps in the healing process," he declared. "I think it is hard to do, and it takes time. Maybe that is an advantage of a sailboat. We have lots of time here. I also think it is only part of the process. But what we said earlier still applies. With a positive vocabulary there is bound to be a positive prognosis. I may not be sure how it will turn out, but I'm still convinced that it will be good!"

"Dad, can you help us think of other parts of the process?" Bruce was alert to the direction of the conversation.

"I don't know, Bud. I suppose it would begin with the decision to open your heart to healing, and stop doing the things that have been hurtful. I think it would have to contain some sort of confession, asking forgiveness from the offended, if possible, making things right through restitution, if that were necessary. There would need to be some practice of changed behavior, you know, learning to think of ourselves in a redefined way, and building upon some spiritual laws of healing."

"Wow," Bruce grimaced, "that sounds like it would take a long time."

"Yeah, but it took a long time for us to come to see ourselves as guilty, or ashamed. So, it stands to reason that it might be difficult to get a new attitude. Don't you think it would be worth it though?" Both listeners nodded in agreement. Just a short distance ahead of them the red piling marker signaled the entrance to the Swinomish Channel.

"Would you be willing to help us work through more of this?" Bruce asked his dad. "I think we have just received a great start. But there is a lot more to do."

"Bud," the skipper said with sincerity, "I'm not sure I'm the person to talk to about this. Just a little while ago I was reminded that I still have some pretty big issues to deal with myself, like the divorce and the end of my ministerial career. Maybe you should seek some professional help, another counselor maybe."

With a shy smile the son answered, "You may not think of yourself as 'professional' or the right 'counselor,' but I can't think of you as anything less than that. Maybe we could all work on this together." Annie nodded in agreement.

"Here comes the marker," the skipper announced. "We'll be in LaConner in fifteen minutes. Let's talk more about it then. Right now I'd like Annie to watch the depth sounder." He pointed toward an instrument with lighted numbers on it. "It tells us the depth of the water under the boat. If you see it get less than fifteen feet, warn us will you?" She nodded her understanding. "And Bruce, if you will keep a sharp eye out for logs or dead-heads in the channel here, we'll try to only hit the little ones." Once again *Dreamer* swept through a graceful turn onto a new course, much like the passengers who were aboard.

After a couple of minutes of silence, Annie declared, "I don't see any town ahead of us. I only see logs and that rock cliff."

Bruce agreed with a "Yeah, me too."

"It's called 'Hole-In-the-Wall' for a good reason," the skipper replied. "This is like a life parable. There are times when the future looks blocked to us, as stubborn as that rocky cliff ahead of us. From here it really is imperceptible, but wait a bit and you'll see the opening. If we just trust in the course of the channel, an unforeseen way will appear. There is an 'S' curve that opens right into LaConner. It is one of those experiences that becomes clear only as you go through it." Smiling again at them, the skipper concluded, "This might be the most dramatic part of the whole trip."

Annie quipped, "That would be a surprise to me. I'm not sure my heart can stand much more. There has already been a lot of drama in this day." As they drew more abreast of the rock outcropping, a clear opening soon came into view, with a green marker on the near shore, and a red one on the far beach.

"Red right returning!" the skipper reminded them. "And in this case, we are still coming in from the sea, so we pass the red down our starboard side." *Dreamer* sliced to port around the first part of the turn, finding the secrets of afternoon shadows playing on the rocks and calm water. Almost immediately it reversed the curve of the turn, clearing the opening in the rocks with ease. Before them now a neat channel was clear, and the beginning of a community could be identified. With one more turn, *Dreamer* headed for the bright orange bridge that marked the center of LaConner. The first part of the passage was complete.

"Hey Bud, will you call the Lighthouse on the cell phone? You'll find the number in that cruising guide on the nav station. See if there is room on their dock or in their dining room for the three of us. This has been such a good leg of the passage; I'm ready for a longshoreman's supper. How about you guys?" Bruce was already dialing the number. He must have shared in the hunger.

Annie reached across to grasp the skipper's hand. "Thank you so much! Bruce had faith that you could help us. I can see why he is so proud of you." The tenderness of her hand and the sincerity of her voice were not lost on the skipper.

"You are most welcome, my precious friend. And I do believe I heard the faith word again. It really is about believing, isn't it?" There was absolute affection in the statement, both to the hearer and speaker.

"My faith has been given a big boost today, and has grown tremendously," Annie confessed. "I feel like an explorer who has just found an uncharted new land.

Now I want to discover more and more about it. I have a lot more questions, but they are all about a positive prognosis."

The blonde head coming up the companionway was carrying a large smile. "The dock is empty, and they are saving a table by the window for us!" Bruce's announcement sounded like a personal coup. "What can I do to get us ready to dock?"

Within the hour, they were comfortably seated in the Lighthouse Restaurant's dining room, looking out at an almost empty stretch of water. The skipper was explaining that this channel was the backdoor to Anacortes. "The folks who use it don't want to go through Deception Pass, which has a vicious tide. But boat use this time of year is pretty light. When school is out, and the days are lots longer, there will be many more through here."

"I've got to ask you guys something that may be none of my business." When both Bruce and Annie smiled at him, he went on. "What's with the luggage you brought aboard? Are you planning a weekend trip?"

They exchanged embarrassed smiles before Bruce replied, "I thought you might be suspicious. We weren't sure how today would go, and didn't know exactly how to ask. But," he paused trying to compose the rest of the sentence just right, "we hoped you might not mind a couple of stowaways for a couple of days. We don't want to mess up your plans. So, if we could just be with you until Lund, we could get a bus back to Seattle." There, it was said.

Annie quickly added, "I'll be happy to sleep in the salon on the settee."

The skipper shook his head. "Dreamer has two staterooms forward and one aft. There is plenty of room for us." He was already making the way possible for the request.

Annie tilted her head just a bit coyly, continuing her thought. "We want to be proper, and we also want to work some more on what we started today." Her eyes looked steadily into the skipper's. It was obvious that they had thought this request through carefully.

Before the skipper could answer, Bruce added, "We'll get plenty of groceries to take care of all of us, and I want to get this dinner check, O.K.?" He was trying to make it as desirable as possible to change his dad's itinerary.

Happily the skipper finally answered, "I'm just trying to think how long it has been since we shared a vacation. Several years, maybe the last time was skiing in Montana." His smile grew wider. "Just how much time are we talking about, a day or two?"

"Actually dad, we both took all of next week as vacation time. Any or all of it will be well used if you can just help us move forward with our plans." The two men looked at each other in a new personal territory, and they liked it.

"O.K., I'm happy to have you both along for a week.

Let's think about the details for a while. Maybe by the time we get on the dock at Cap Sante's tonight, we can choose some resort sites that offer plenty of showers, and shore support." The idea was beginning to really appeal to him. "We can decide who can cook and who will wash the dishes." His grin was contagious. "I like it, by golly!"

Annie looked at Bruce with a sly smile. "You better go into sales, with a pitch like that!"

"He's my dad!" Bruce said with mock shock. "What else could he say?" Then looking more seriously at his dad, he said, "I was pretty sure you would agree to this sudden change. You've always been the most considerate dad I knew. You're a great model." Then, becoming uncharacteristically serious, he asked, "Dad, do you really mean that you like it?"

The skipper's eyes rested on his son's face. "Of course I mean it! I've wanted some special time with you for a long while. That's really nice to hear that you do too. Sometimes it feels..." he paused to consider the rest of his thought. "I think it has been a pretty emotional afternoon. 'How about those Mariners'?" It was the catch phrase that meant, "Let's talk about lighter matters." So for the rest of the meal, they continued to explore their budding friendship.

Back aboard *Dreamer*, it took them less than an hour to complete the channel, call Cap Sante's Marina in Anacortes to get a visitors mooring, all the while watching a marvelous sunset bloom and slowly mute into twilight.

They learned about each other's favorite pet, video, food, car, male and female vocalist, the kind of music they preferred, and most fattening food they craved. It was the sort of information that good friends want to know.

When finally the lights were being turned out aboard *Dreamer,* they each understood that an adventure was beginning, the conclusion of which was very unclear.

The skipper opened a Hugh Prather book that he kept aboard for devotions. "Listen to this prayer. When I want someone else's words to shape my evening thoughts, this is a favorite. I think it sort of sums up where we are tonight."

"Lord of Eternity, God of Love, I put my trust in You tonight. Lead me to Your arms. Wash me in Your light. Fill me with Your quietness. Show me the irrelevancy of shadows – of discontents and desires, of resentments and idle thoughts – of everything I think I made of myself, apart from You. Hold me and talk to me until I see myself as You have seen me always, until I know myself as You have known me forever, until I find myself where I never left, bathed in Your joy, secure in Your love, at home, at rest, at one with You. Amen."

As the stillness of night finally filled the boat, each member of the crew was lost in thought. Annie was aware of an unattended tear that traced down her cheek. "Oh my goodness," she thought. "I can only imagine what tomorrow is going to bring.

CHAPTER TWO: ANACORTES

Become harmless to
yourself and others.

The skipper opened his eyes to a morning barely light. He smelled coffee, rich fresh coffee. "How could that be?" he thought. There had been no sounds from the galley, which was right next to his stateroom. He had neither heard, nor felt the movement of anyone awake on the boat. Still as he splashed water on his face, combed his curly gray hair, and pulled on a fresh sweatshirt, he was sure there was fresh coffee somewhere near.

Both Bruce and Annie were in the salon at the table. She still had a warm blanket over her feet, which were tucked up under her. Both were sipping from paper cups.

"Good morning, guys. What's this?" His attention was fixed on several sacks that looked suspiciously like take-out food.

"I played ninja this morning," Bruce boasted. "I put my shoes on only after I had sneaked over to the dock. Last night I saw that Denny's Restaurant, so I just got us a slammin' good start. How about some coffee? There are eggs, bacon, and pancakes to go along with it." Obviously this was a well-planned breakfast. "You've always said that breakfast is an important meal."

Glancing at his watch, the skipper smiled. "And as long as it's already 5:30 a.m., we might as well get to it!" He reached for the other cup, assuming it was his coffee.

Playful banter, jokes and friendly reminiscing accompanied the satisfying meal. When finally there were only empty trays left on the table, Bruce asked, "Where are we headed today?" It was the first hint that he was ready to talk about the major agenda for the day. Annie pulled her knees up to her chest still snug in her blankets.

"Well, I'll tell you what I've been thinking," the skipper began. "It is more important for us to focus on the process instead of ports of call. So my suggestion is that we stay here for the day. We're comfortable, there are plenty of nearby services, and I think we can use the time to do some preparatory work. But this is going to work as a democracy, so what do you think?"

"What kind of preparatory work?" Bruce squinted at him. "You don't think we came this far to scrub the boat do you?"

Annie giggled, trying to speak with a funny accent, "Wax on, Daniel-san. Wax off." She waved her hands in tiny circles. "If Mr. Miyagi has a plan for us, maybe we should do it."

The skipper laughed, "Nothing like that, although I will remember that you offered. I'm thinking that we should get cleaned up, and do some grocery shopping. I want to especially find some notebooks for us to use as journals for this task. There is also a bookstore in the shopping center. It might be a good idea to pick up some reading material, and get a Bible for each of you. What do you think?"

Bruce arched his eyebrows, "It sounds like this is going to be serious, like going back to school."

"I've given this some thought during the night," the skipper replied. "If it's not serious, it's only going to be another boat trip. What's the old quip? 'If you continue to do what you've been doing, you'll continue to get what you've been getting.' Probably that's something you didn't want in the first place. I'm more than a little interested in seeing some change in the stuff we talked about yesterday. But I'll bet change will never happen by itself. We need to get ourselves in position to receive it when it comes to us. We're going to get real intentional, and do the work that makes it happen. Do you think you can? Or do you have another suggestion?"

His direct gaze carried a hint of defensiveness.

Annie pulled the blanket off her lap, began cleaning up the breakfast trays, saying, "Just show me the shower and I'll be ready before either one of you." She didn't want it said that she was indecisive. Neither did she want to see conflict between a dad and son, for both of whom she was feeling more and more fondness.

It was only mid morning when they returned to the boat, their errands accomplished. It's amazing how much can be done when you begin at the dawn's early light. The driftwood gray overcast was bound to burn off by the afternoon. Still, the salon was a cozy and pleasant place for their work to begin.

"Wow," Annie began the morning's discussion with a bright observation. "I had no idea there were so many self-help books on this subject! I got two books. One is Dr. Edward Hallowell's entitled, *Dare to Forgive*. It looks like it will be fun to read, and he's from Harvard!" She tried her best at an Ivy League accent, whatever that may be. "A Jewish professor at Hebrew college in Massachusetts wrote my second one, I just liked the title: '*Wounds Not Healed by Time: The Power of Repentance and Forgiveness.*' The flyleaf says he divides the process of forgiveness into four phases. The first is uncovering the problem. The second is the decision phase, in which forgiveness is considered as an option." She had marked the place in the introduction that helped her sound pretty informed. "The third is the work phase, in which pain is accepted and compassion offered. The fourth is what he calls the deepening phase; I think that is going to be most interesting. I just skimmed a few of the pages and he says, 'One benefit of completing this difficult journey of forgiveness is the self knowledge you will acquire that you can overcome powerful negative emotions, and are capable of great self-restraint'." She smiled a beaming grin of satisfaction, like a schoolgirl who had completed a difficult task.

Bruce craned his neck to look at the book's cover. "Who is the author?"

"Solomon Schimmel." Again her answer was offered with knowing satisfaction.

Bruce nodded. "He sounds like a German instead of a Jewish writer." Both Annie and the skipper looked at him questioningly.

"You know, 'Schindler's List.' Oh, forget I said anything about it." His jaw clamped with an uncharacteristic grimace. After a moment he relaxed with obvious effort, and said, "I found a book entitled '*Forgive for Good*,' by Dr. Fred Luskin. His method is summed up in the acronym, HEAL, which stands for 'hope,' 'educate,' 'affirm,' and 'long-term commitment.' But I'm not too sure about any of the content of those steps." He looked at the skipper, as though he wanted to quickly pass the conversation along.

"Well," the skipper picked up his cue, "I'm also interested

in a Jewish author. I found Charles Klien's book, '*How to Forgive When You Can't Forget.*' I don't think he offers a step by step method, or acronym that sums up his approach, but he does say on the cover, 'You can forgive even when you can't forget. And only you can answer the age-old question, 'If not now, when?' I too was really surprised at the number of books from which we had to choose."

After a moment's thought, he continued, "I'll bet we could spend a lot of the day reading these books and reporting our progress. That just doesn't seem like the way to spend our morning. Don't you think we're going to need to make it personal?"

Annie smiled brightly again, indicating that she was game for any challenge. Bruce, on the other hand, seemed guarded and less than enthusiastic.

The skipper went on with the beginning of their morning. "When I was in the Navy," he reflected, "we had an interesting procedure. It was called 'degaussing.' I guess the man who designed the concept was named Gaus. I don't know. The idea was to run our minesweeper over a number of instruments that were located on the bay bottom to determine our magnetic field. By adjusting electrical current through a number of wire coils built into the hull, we could neutralize the magnetic effects of the engine and equipment, which made us safer in our task of finding and destroying mines." Both Bruce and Annie pondered his words without fully understanding the significance of the explanation.

He went on, "I think it will make sense when I suggest to you that all three of us have emotional mines planted under the surface. We look fine, ordinary, unperturbed, but there are these big explosive charges that can catch us. We can benefit from some time spent examining or 'degaussing' ourselves, so we will be less likely to trigger one of those bad boys."

"Think with me about the problems that are hidden in you. If I can identify some of mine, it may cause you to think about some of yours. Let's write down the ones we want to focus in on." Annie nodded her eager understanding. Bruce nodded also, but with some hesitation.

The skipper asked him, "Does that sound like something you are uneasy about?"

"No, not at all," Bruce was quick to reply. "But I'm just not sure I can think of anything that is hidden in me. I feel like Annie and I have talked about everything."

Her look was filled with affection and warmth. The words she spoke, however, went to the core of the morning, "Everything, except Sydney." The boat was so quiet the tiny squeaking of the mooring lines was a soft rhythmic sigh.

"Boom," the skipper said softly. "Bruce, were you aware of that mine?"

The quiet young man shook his head. "No, I didn't think that what happened a long time before we met could have any bearing on us today." His expression toward Annie was pleading for understanding.

Before she could say anything, the skipper went on, "Of course our histories have a great deal to do with us today. Think about it! There are the obvious factors of courting disasters, immature concepts of dating and relating, initial sexual experiences, STD's, there could be lasting hurts from any number of painful lessons or intimate disasters. There could be lingering ghosts of fantasies, or aching grief that has never been dealt with. There could be staggering debt, or lingering personal responsibilities, any number of factors that have formed us, and our partner, into the person they are today. There are important reasons we should, without violating their privacy, know about our mate's values and commitments."

"But before we get really involved with that conversation, let me make a generalization. Anything from your past that still contains pain is probably a mine waiting to get you. It is a moment of your life waiting to be healed." After thinking about it for just a moment, he went on, "If you will let me make this thought, it is a moment waiting to either forgive, or to be forgiven."

Annie shrugged. "There are gobs of little moments of pain as we grew up, times of embarrassment, awkwardness, social blunders that are still sensitive. But how could forgiveness work after so long?"

"Here's the point," the skipper said softly. "There are bound to be a multitude of tiny wounds we accumulated as lessons as we grew up. Those were just lessons we got over. But if some of those points of pain are more than little lessons, and are left unhealed, they continue to limit us forever. You have heard that time heals all wounds. But that is true only for physical injuries. The deeper ones, emotional or spiritual, never go away by themselves. Forgiveness is the only way they are turned into scars, which by the way, do not hurt anymore."

"I can't imagine telling her all the jerky things I've done, or all the stupid mistakes I've made," Bruce said with a sheepish grin. "I've worked too hard at trying to convince her that I'm a genuinely nice guy."

"I agree," the skipper nodded. "There's no call for a litany of errors that are significant only to us, if there is no pain involved. That can only be entertaining information. But as we hear the points of pain in another's life, we are responsible for dealing with that information. Isn't it odd that we want to know more about a car's history, if we're buying it, than the history of a person with whom we want to spend the rest of our life?"

Annie wrinkled her nose and asked, "Aren't those two different things?"

"Of course they are," the skipper agreed. "You'll probably buy a lot of cars during your driving career, but choosing a spouse is the single most important decision you will ever make. But for the sake of making a point, we are saying that honest information about our past is useful to our partner in building a closer relationship, and helpful to us, ourselves, by getting rid of the obstacles that prevent our happiness. And the opposite is also important. If we withhold information because we think they might love us less, or be critical of us, or we think we can simply live with impeding obstacles, we are saying that our comfort is more important than a stable base to our relationship."

"Dad, do you really believe that or are you giving us a theory?" A frown deepened on Bruce's forehead. Not waiting for an answer to his question, he went on, "I'm not so sure how I feel about that. I still don't see how telling all our faults can build a better friendship." He got up and poured another cup of tea in the galley. "I think that is more an invasion of privacy than a building block." His listeners were unaware of the depth of his feelings.

After a moment's reflection, the skipper went on, "I think we may have too many topics going on here. The point we may need to focus on is less relationship building, as important as that may be, and more repair of our inner self. We need to identify our hurts so that they may be healed. Then we can get about the business of building a world-class relationship."

Annie said, "I don't think you are asking for specific events are you? Maybe you mean the general things that get us. Is that it?"

The skipper nodded in agreement. "I think it was Carl Jung who said that the thing that bothers us most about other people can lead us to an understanding of ourselves. It might be helpful if we think about the traits in others that give us problems." After a moment's reflection he continued, "For example, I am irritated by people who criticize others, especially their loved ones. Maybe I should be aware of how critical I am, occasionally of course, and only on superficial matters." His effort at humor brought only a smile to Annie. Bruce seemed lost in thought.

"Whiners!" Annie grimaced. "I have very little patience for the women I know who whine about everything. They are either too busy, or they are lonely, too fat or too flat, overworked, or overlooked, forever seeking a better job. They just never seem to be happy with what they have. Does that say something about me?" Her question was almost too bright to be taken seriously.

"Yeah," the skipper responded in a two-sided conversation. "It makes me think of grumpy folks the same way. We've all been in enough motivation sessions and worship services to have a positive unbreakable attitude. Still, we wrestle all the time with keeping a shiny side up." The skipper was studying the rigid posture of Bruce who remained with his back to them both. "Are you O.K. Bud?"

"Yeah, of course I am." The words were correct but the tone and tension in his voice told them that he was not completely truthful. "I'm still stuck on the notion of spilling everything from my past to Annie. I would rather just let sleeping dogs lie, thank you."

"If that works for you," the skipper replied. "But it seems to me that you two are having trouble making future plans because of those sleeping dogs." A lengthy silence followed when each of them were thinking of what to say next.

Bruce finally continued, "I just would rather not talk to either of you about a couple of pieces of baggage I'm carrying." He turned away from the galley to reveal tears in his eyes.

"But Bruce," his dad was brave enough to speak to the moment, "we're not the one who is hurting. Your baggage has nothing to do with us, except it is preventing you from a process of growth. Can you see it is a problem for you, and not for us?"

"O.K. I see that! But if I tell you about …" he took a heavy breath, "things…then it will become a problem for you, too. I would rather not do that."

Annie and the skipper exchanged a glance, not fully understanding where this conversation was taking them.

"No, I don't want to get in the way of our task here," Bruce tried to brighten his composure, "I think I am a better listener than a talker." He moved back into the salon to sit next to Annie. The stillness in the boat was heavy enough for them to hear the soft squeak of the bumpers rubbing against the dock.

"I tell you what," the skipper began with a fresh breath, "I've been thinking about a chore that might help us here. The path at the top of the dock circles around the marina all the way around to Padilla Bay Park. A trail winds up the rocky point above the marina, to a lookout that is pretty enjoyable, even on a cloudy day. I'm going to suggest that we hike up to the point with our new books, our notebooks, and spend some quiet time alone. How about writing three letters while we're up there? First, write one to God, giving thanks for all of the ways you are blessed. Secondly, write a letter to yourself, listing at least three things you would like to change. You must be specific. For years I've said I want to lose some weight, but I've never been serious about it. In your letter to yourself, be serious. Thirdly, write a letter to someone you have injured. If you are sorry for it, tell them. If you are not, ask them to help you see your actions from their point of view."

Looking at his watch, the skipper concluded, "If we take a couple of hours for the task, we can be back here for a late lunch. So there is no hurry. Remember, the vocabulary you use will probably indicate the success we will have on our trip."

Annie, who seemed extra alert for the exercise, offered, "How about me fixing some sandwiches that we could take with us? Then we would be able to spend as much time as we need up there." Her nod and quick smile gave emphasis to a good idea. "Let's go!"

No other mention was made of Bruce's noncompliance.

A few minutes later they were making their way around the marina, chatting like visitors enjoying a boat gallery. "Hey, there's one from Alaska! I wonder if they sailed it down the passage or trucked it here." "Look at that old classic! I'll bet she has sea stories to tell." "Oh, wow! If I had a beauty like that one, I'd be out sailing every possible weekend!" As they made their way, attention was shifted to each new cadre, some common and others unique.

Annie observed, "I had no idea there were so many boats, and so many different kinds! Do they all work like *Dreamer*?"

The skipper replied with a smile, "There are as many different kinds of boats as sailors. Of course in this modern age, there are some major manufacturing companies that turn out pretty similar products. But still, budgets, use, appreciation are all reflected individually." He added, "I've always wanted to have a book published. I think the easiest would be one of boat pictures, especially graphics and boat names." The conversation was not at all important, just a helpful way to get them up onto the lookout point, and the afternoon's task.

When finally the marina sidewalk turned into a path that entered a grove of Madrona trees flanking the hill, they began a single file ascent. The marina took on a different perspective from this angle, and they could see the distant shopping center.

Bruce was beginning to pant a bit, but still wanted to

chuckle, "If I'd known this was so cool, I'd have made the hike a long time ago.

"I can see *Dreamer* way over there!" Annie pointed across the docks.

When they were finally at the top each of them had a private moment of splendor as their eyes took in the 360° vista. "Wow," the skipper sighed, "I could spend all day just watching from up here! But we have jobs to do, O.K?" They agreed on different quadrants of the point, and began an afternoon of discovery.

Annie's work:

Write three letters: one to God, to someone I have hurt, and to myself. Write in my journal notebook.

Dear God, thank you for the beginning of understanding! I'm not sure where this will lead, but for the first time in a long, long time, I have a glimmer of hope. In my mind, I know there is a way out of the pit I put myself into, but my heart has not been able to believe it. Yesterday, I heard for the first time since the operation, (which is what she had always called the abortion,) that you don't hate me, that you are as sad as I am. If I can acquire a sense of surety of that, I know I can do something terrific for kids, or you, or even me. When I look out at all this beauty before me, I must come to the conclusion that your hand is at work here. And if you are working here, maybe even in me, there is a new sense of hope I can hold onto. Even though I don't understand, I know I want to, so this is a really happy day. Thank you, again for it. Love, Annie.

("Let's see. He said list three things I'd like to change about myself. But the theme for this afternoon is "stop hurting yourself." Can I think of three ways I'm hurting myself?" Hmm.)

Dear Annie. Even in such a perfect place as this, you still carry the memory, don't you? But today I have good news! I can change my story. So, change #1 is I am not going to choose to weep one more tear for that horrible decision! If I'm not in trouble with the law, or God, or my best friends, I'm choosing not to be in trouble with me anymore! There is no gain for me to pack around all this grief and guilt. I choose to be free from it!

Change #2: I think I'll take the skipper's advise and start volunteering at the children's hospital. I can turn this grief into something really positive. I'll bet there is some sick child who I can play with, or read to, or just hold. The idea makes me tremble just to say it. I will do it as soon as we get back!!

Change #3: When I think of how excited I got talking to Bruce's dad, I know I can find a counselor who will continue what we have started here. I need help in putting my future together. I won't ask Bruce to come with me right away. I know that he is in all of my plans.

But I have been pretending to be in control of my own destiny, and in fact, I can only free fall most of the time. If I can find a professional who will help me with the steps, I know I can do it! I don't want to hurry; I want to be well with myself! Yours confidently, Annie.

("Now, to someone I have hurt." Her mind wandered from the distant past, childhood, her home, Bruce…)

Dear Baby, I don't even know if you were going to be a boy or a girl. I do know that I loved you. Even though I never had a chance to tell you, I thought it was an impossible situation. I forgot that situations are never hopeless, only people in those situations are. I didn't love the man who brought us together, yet I have always thought of you as my baby. You didn't have a chance to grow, or play, or learn, so I am going to do that for you through other children. I'm going to learn how to be a hopeful person. I'm going to become positive and excited about the future. I will carry your memory with me as long as I live, but today I want to say, "Goodbye!" There will be no more shame, or guilt or anger for us. I love you forever. Your mom.

Annie put her face in her hands and wept, but for the first time, not from guilt.

Bruce's work:

05.14.05: write three letters in the journal (doodles)

Good morning God, I'm thinking of words to prayers and hymns. I think I must not trust my own words to tell you what needs to be told. I am grateful for a family that cares for me and is so willing to help when I ask. I'm grateful for the love of a woman who sticks with me, even in the quiet times. I'm grateful for a job, a great education, patriotic urges, and an end to the basketball season. I just threw that in to prove to you that I'm not going to be real serious about this. But I do seriously want to love Annie, and I do want us to be happy together.

If this was my job, I'd call a systems analyst to trouble shoot the problem, and work out some design changes. Maybe that's just what I'm doing with dad. Hope he can work out our problem. Thanks for this time for us to do it, and oh yeah, "How 'bout those Mariners?" Forever, Bruce

Bruce looked around at the other two working on the lookout. They both seemed very engaged in their writing. He watched a ferry making its way over to Guemes Island. "The tide must be coming in," he mused, " because the boat seemed to be steering a diagonal course toward the landing." He watched until it was securely tied to the dock.

To his right he could see a few fishing boats anchored off the south side of Saddlebag Island, probably crabbing in a hot spot. It was an ideal day to just watch the hours passing by. O.K. now back to the assigned task.

Three things I would change about myself:

First, I would really like to get in shape. I need to get back into the gym and work out, play some basketball, maybe lose a few pounds. I'm not too far from where I was in college. That would be a good target, to get back to 170, and fit into a 34-inch waist.

Second, I'm way too work-oriented. I think I should try to develop some new interests, like a cycle club, or a hiking/skiing club. There must be a lot of information on the net about special interest groups. I'd really like to get a sports car, but that may be a little too much right now. I'd love a classic Corvette, or Mustang. I think I need a hobby.

Third, I will work at a better relationship with mom and Amy. It's been a couple of years since I've seen my sister and almost that long since I went over to mom's. There isn't any problem, just no good reason to go. Maybe we could plan something before the holidays.

Satisfied with his work, Bruce closed his eyes and dosed for a while. When he awoke, he rewrote number three.

Third, I really want to change the way Annie and I are getting along. I think the problem has to do with me, and my fear of being absolutely honest with her. I think if I just start, maybe it will begin a trend of better sharing.

He reread his work, and nodded. "Much better," he thought. "If we show this to one another, I'll be glad for that change." Now, there was just one more thing to do to finish his assignment.

A letter to someone I have hurt. It took several minutes for him to decide the next sentence.

Dear Kurt. We were really close buddies in high school. I'm pretty sure I know why we haven't spoken for a long time. Do you remember Emma Kline? You better, she invited you to the Tolo Dance. I had such a crush on her, and you didn't seem to care, and you didn't even like her. You went anyway, and I think I was as mad as a junkyard dog. Your car was in our driveway when I keyed it pretty badly. I remember scratching the side so deeply it even made a long dent. I denied knowing anything about it. I think finally you assumed it happened in the school parking lot. I've been ashamed of that ever since. If I could go back and not do such an immature thing, I surely would. If I could go back and pay for the repair, I'd do that too. I'd really like to get together to rebuild a valuable friendship. Maybe we can get tickets to the Seahawks. I'll give you a call, or find your email address. I really want to see you again. Your pal, Bruce

"There, that wasn't so tough!" he thought with a satisfied smile. Bruce pulled his sweatshirt a bit higher around his neck, and lay back, dreamily watching the boats making way toward the marina.

Norm's work:

Gracious God, you who provide for our every need, I give you thanks for all that is before us today, this outstanding world, beauty beyond compare. I thank you for this opportunity to share time with people who are foundational to my life. Thank you for this time of discovery. I am convinced that all of my high hopes for this son will be satisfied on this journey. Your love surrounds us, guides us, and protects us. Lord, grant us eyes to see the opportunity, hearts true enough to risk the challenge, and lives focused on the acceptance of love's miracle at work within us. I am convinced that you are at work here. Help me get out of the way that you might accomplish great things within this precious couple. Thank you from my very core.

Yours in the Spirit, Norm O'Banyon.

"Maybe that was more of a prayer than a letter," he thought. "But then, what is prayer if not a personal communication, like a letter?" He spent several moments pondering the question, and then decided it was just a matter of semantics, and not worth more time.

He found himself replaying the question his son had asked twice: "Do you really believe that, or is it just theory?" It was a haunting probe into his deepest convictions.

After several troubling minutes, he shifted his attention to the task of their afternoon:

Three things about myself I would change:

<u>Vocationally</u>, I would like to return to the local church as pastor. I think that might mean finding a nondenominational congregation, or going through the process of accreditation in some other denomination than United Methodist. Given the troubled history with the bishop, I doubt if I would ever be welcomed or comfortable in that church body. I no longer have visions, or desire, for a large congregation, and the responsibilities or prestige that goes with it. There must be a small congregation somewhere in need of a well trained, seasoned and loving pastor.

<u>Professionally</u>, I would like to return to school. The DMin has never felt like a real advanced degree. It would only take a couple of years to finish a doctorate in a church related field. I could use that same time to affiliate with a denomination. If that meant re-ordination, I think there would be merit in a new beginning.

<u>Personally</u>, I need to find some worthwhile volunteer work. Too many of my hours are empty of personal contact. I'm sure I could volunteer some time at the jail, or a senior center. It is hard to tell the difference between private and lonely. I know that I am a private person. There is a better than average chance that I am also lonely. I think I need some quality interpersonal contacts.

Once again that question reappeared in his thought process: "Do you really believe that or is it just theory?"

Leaving the assignment completely, he chose to create a testing device of his own:

Forgiveness Factor: a tool for testing openness to forgiveness:

In this evaluation, assign a score of one to ten for each question, (one being non-agreement, ten being complete agreement.) Add the subtotal for each section, and then add both for an indicator of forgiveness factor.

Belief:

I believe forgiveness is more than
motivation or positive thinking.   _____

I believe in the New Testament Gospel.   _____

I believe the spiritual side of me is as
significant as the intellectual or emotional. _____

I believe God loves me.   _____

I believe God still gives spiritual gifts.   _____

                                    Subtotal   _____

Desire:

I want to be free from the anxiety
of past mistakes.   _____

I want to describe myself with "faith,
hope, and love," rather than "greed,
lust, or anger."   _____

I want "no more secrets."   _____

I want to have no anxiety in the presence
of God, or with people from my past.   _____

I want to be less fearful.   _____

                            Subtotal   _____
                Forgiveness Factor Total   _____

Or, it could be graphed with vertical scoring representing "belief," and horizontal representing "desire." That way, you could see if a person felt motivated with desire, but frustrated with a lack of belief. The other expression might be someone who had the faith system with belief, but lacked the personal engagement of desire. It's a concept to be continued.

The skipper failed to acknowledge that he had changed the assignment for the afternoon, substituting this attempt at clinical work for the more revealing admonition.

Satisfied with his work, the skipper collected his papers and books. He looked across the viewpoint to Bruce, who seemed to be napping. Annie saw him stand, and waved cheerily as he headed back down the hill toward the marina.

"We'll be down in a little while," she whispered, just loudly enough to be heard. "I think we're going to enjoy the view for a bit more." The sun had never completely burned through the clouds, but had warmed the hilltop cozily.

Nearly an hour later, the skipper watched the young couple walking slowly around the marina. Annie's hand was cuddled around Bruce's arm in a warm embrace. The impression was pure affection. A cheery greeting was exchanged with waves.

The young couple continued the conversation that had started on the top of the bluff. Annie had asked about the relationship between Bruce's mom and dad. "Is it really as cordial as he says?" she asked dubiously.

Bruce took several steps before answering her with carefully selected words. He didn't want to offend her, nor show disrespect for his dad. "No, he says that to impress people, I think. He doesn't want them to know the truth." He took several more steps before he carefully said, "Dad hates conflict, and mom used that against him. I remember her picking a lot of fights, probably to work out some weary battles they never resolved. She wanted to duke it out, so she finally got a wicked lawyer. Instead of standing up for himself, dad became the victim, and passively allowed her to take the house with all their stuff, both good cars and most of his retirement account. She also left him with all the debts. He had to sell the cabin in Suncadia, and lived on *Dreamer* for several months. The place on Queen Anne is a rental." They were almost at the bottom of the hill before he came to a stop to look directly at her. "Dad feels like a victim, pure and simple, and I think it eats at him. Sometimes he is really negative about family stuff because it is so painful to him."

Annie didn't know what to say in response. The information seemed incongruous with the topic they had been sharing, so she was silent until Bruce guided them back toward the marina. They walked, lost in quiet thoughts.

When they were aboard, the skipper told them, "There's hot water on the stove, if you'd like some tea." Annie said that sounded perfect. Bruce thought a cold Pepsi might satisfy his thirst.

"I thought that was a pretty good task. Did you guys?" The skipper was ready to engage the conversation. "Remember, we said you needn't share anything that may feel private, or sensitive."

The other two nodded. Bruce was the first to say, "Yeah, that was a neat exercise. It helped me think of some good stuff I can do." Looking at Annie, he asked, "How about you? Or did you spend the whole time napping?" She had finally had to awaken him before they returned to the boat.

"Oh sure, I'm not the one who was snoring at the seagulls." She giggled to make sure he took no offense at her humor. "Really, it was a marvelous experience for me. I think the word is 'epiphany!' There was some neat bright insight that I have never had, and I'm grateful for it." Her smile was joyous.

The skipper was happy that this first step had gone well for them. "Well, fantastic," he said with affirmation, "me too! I had an old testing trait come to the surface, and made a device to show our forgiveness factor. I even like that term." He had his model out of the stack of papers he had brought from the viewpoint. "Take a look and see how this works for you."

Both Annie and Bruce scanned the test outline.

"Can we try it?" Annie asked with enthusiasm. "I think I'm in agreement with most of those things, on first glance." They both took paper and pencil and gave their full attention to answers.

After a few minutes of quiet work, the skipper looked at his watch and interrupted, "I didn't intend us to take a lot of time with this. It's almost suppertime. Do you want to talk about this, or something else?"

Bruce was tilting his head to see Annie's score more clearly. He checked his own again and said. "I think this is pretty good. We both scored nearly ninety!"

Annie was also comparing the results. "It looks like I had all tens on the 'desire' part. Looks like I was a little hesitant on the 'belief' part. I'm not sure what the 'New Testament Gospel' is, and I am a bit unsure about the 'significance' of my spiritual side." She brightened as she pointed out, "Hey Brucer, you were light on that one too, huh?"

His smile may have been more uneasy than happy. "Yeah, I didn't agree with 'no more secrets,' because I think there has to be plenty of privacy for people, and like we said before, the past is past, and should be left alone! I don't think we have to share every stinkin' thing we've done!" His voice had risen in both pitch and volume.

Aware suddenly that there were still a host of hidden emotions at work in Bruce, the skipper tried to deflect the conversation. "Maybe I need to rethink those questions. It seems like most of them are pretty obvious. A good testing tool has us in the bell curve, not on the high side of it. But I think the concept is good." Looking at both of their faces, each mirroring a different response, he added, "Let's go over to that Skipper's place and get some fish and chips. We can talk more about this after supper, or anything else you might like to do." He pondered how he might help Bruce get into this subject without confrontation.

Dinner was predictable, and affordably enjoyable. Platters of fish fillets and fries had been accompanied by lemony ice tea. Now, on the way back to the marina, they each were trying to finish ice cream cones before they made a melting mess.

"I'm still wondering," Annie began the subject that would focus the evening. "If forgiveness is so essential, and so easy, why isn't it common to everyone? Why is it so difficult to even talk about?" There was not a shadow of suggestion that this was anything other than an innocent question.

The skipper licked some of the melted treat from his fingers. "I've been thinking about that," he said, "as a matter of fact. I think there are two kinds of people." After another big taste, he offered, "There are people who are moving toward forgiveness, and those who are not." When Bruce gave a snort of disbelief "Duh!" the skipper added, "Yeah, I know that seems way simplified. But think about it. The ones who are traveling toward the goal of forgiveness, for whatever reason, and at any variety of speeds, are at least going toward it. And those who are not, may know they are not for a lot of different reasons. Others don't even know about it, but are still going in the wrong direction." Little did the skipper realize that he had just described the two men of the crew.

"Come on," Bruce continued to be suspicious, "Why wouldn't someone want forgiveness for past mistakes?" They were almost around the marina, nearing the visitor's dock.

"I'll bet there are as many reasons as there are people. Some are in denial, thinking they simply have no need. Others are in denial, thinking the misdeed has been taken care of by time. You know, out of sight, out of mind. They have pushed their need so deep, they can simply overlook it." Bruce nodded. The skipper went on, "Some people have a bent sense of Grace, thinking that the whole subject is unapproachable."

Annie paused to admire the hint of pink clouds in the quiet evening. "I think I changed lanes today," she said with a happy smile. "I may be one who is going slow, although it doesn't feel like it right now, but I am definitely one of those first folks. I'm moving toward it!" She gave a wiggle and a kick for a fun emphasis.

The subject changed as they approached their dock, noticing several new boats that had arrived during the afternoon. They checked *Dreamer's* lines and bumpers before going below.

With cups of hot tea all around, Bruce introduced the subject that would refocus the evening. "Annie and I have been talking about communication. It seems easy to talk with you, dad. Maybe you could give us some tips on improving our ability to talk to each other." He seemed almost relieved to have a new topic.

"Sure," the skipper replied with a grin. "I can remember most of the stuff I've talked to couples about in premarital sessions. But remember," the grin broadened, "Your mom's number one complaint about me was that I didn't talk to her." There was a bit of sadness to the smile, and considerable bitterness beneath it. "Maybe what we preach takes practice, huh?" They all smiled at his humor.

"O.K.", he began, trying to set aside his momentary distraction. "There are several different levels of communication. Have you heard that only 7% of communication is verbal? Think about this, it's important. Most of what you say to each other will be by tone of voice, volume, body language, and facial expression. Golly, there are a ton of factors that affect the words."

"So when I ask Bruce to remember what he said to me, I should also ask him to tell me how he said it too?" Annie was delighted to be a part of this conversation, and wanted both of these men to know that she understood.

"Absolutely," the skipper replied. "Most folks just want to parrot back the words, and often put their own interpretation to all the rest that defines them." After a second or two, he added, "There is verbal communication, physical communication, spiritual communication, and the whole psychological communication of power manipulation. That may be a lot more than we want to talk about here." Bruce was nodding a strong agreement.

"Here's a safe or gentle way to begin the subject. Think of rating the communication, between the two of you, from one, which represents pretty awful, to ten, which is fan-can't be improved-tastic! Go ahead, and write down a number, and yes, it will be very subjective." They both took their notebooks and wrote a number.

"Now, write a number representing your willingness to communicate, using the same scale." He repeated the question while they wrote again. "Now give another rating for your other's willingness. Bruce, how willing is Annie to communicate? Annie, how about Bruce?" Again they bent to the notebooks with answers.

"So, if you compare those three numbers, you might see how well you are doing, and who is trying harder, or who is being helped in the communication area."

As Bruce and Annie compared these numbers, he was surprised by the conclusion. "She thinks we communicate better than I have us, and I think I want to communicate more than she does. I'd better study this for awhile." Annie had a sparkle in her eyes that seemed to grow brighter.

"Then," the skipper continued, as though they were just getting started, "There is a difference in how we communicate good stuff, like compliments, praise or appreciation, and how we share complaints, objections, or even anger. Keep using that same scale. How would you rate yourself at sharing the positive stuff, you know the praise, compliments, and accolades?" They both thought for just a moment before jotting down their answers. "And how would you rate your other?" This time the pause was longer before answers were recorded. "Ready to go on?" the skipper asked. "Now rate your willingness to express problems, or to surface hostility. Wait, that's too strong, and a very biased word. How would you rate your ability to be a constructive critic?" Both pencils were still as they gave careful thought to the question.

The gathering twilight had captured the corners of the salon in shadows. The skipper got up to turn on the brass lamps on the teak bulkheads. As he returned to his place on the settee, he added, "You know we could make a big list of subjects to get this rating treatment." When Annie frowned in lack of understanding, he went on, "Well, how would you rate yourself in understanding and sharing your personal history." He said that knowing that Annie had made a very large advancement in both understanding, and being willing to share her personal history. He did not know that he was nearing a painful moment for Bruce.

He was prepared to continue with a lengthy list of possible topics, usually important issues with premarital folks. "You can rate your willingness to talk about money, sex, children, work, vaca…"

Bruce interrupted with a voice that sounded strangely tense. "What if we don't even understand that history? How can I share when I don't know why, or even what I did?" His face was dark with inner tension. Annie thought he was about to cry. The boat was so still the tiny waves lapping against the hull were the only whisper in the pool of silence.

"I suppose you just begin with what you do know, and work from there. Can you tell us how it began? Was it a long time ago?" The skipper was putting on his counselor's skills, knowing that another breakthrough could be beginning.

"Yeah, my first year in college." Bruce looked like he was in physical discomfort, his words coming with pain. "I had been a jock in high school. You remember. I thought it would just get better. I didn't have time to try out for football, and I didn't have the skill for the wrestling team. But at some dances there was a bit of pushing and shoving. I was pretty good at it. I hit an upper classman one night. I suppose that's where my 'tough-guy' reputation started."

When the skipper asked if he had been in a fight, Bruce just waved off the question. "No, not a fight, just some poking around. But I always wanted to poke harder, and poke last. I thought I was just playing around. One night I punched Lisa in the arm and knocked her into a coffee table. She stumbled; it wasn't my fault. But she said she would never go out with a tough guy again. I had some trouble getting any date after that. Everyone thought I was some kind of bully. The funny thing was that I sort of liked the role. I wanted people to be a little afraid of me. I guess the reputation just got a little out of hand."

He was so quiet the skipper tried to help him continue. "Did you get into any trouble?"

"No, not with the law, if that's what you mean. My advisor at the university suggested I get some anger management. But I sure did get into trouble with Syd." He gave a sigh that sort of shuddered. "We had a lot of arguments. Some of them were even sort of fun, shouting and raving when we weren't that upset." There was another painful pause, "I'm not sure you guys want to hear this, or if I should even say any more." His stillness lasted several moments.

Annie finally broke the tension, "If I could tell you about my life and death mistake, I hope you can trust me enough to tell about your fight." It was all she needed to say.

"I think we both knew that our deal wasn't going to lead to marriage, even though we had talked about it. One night she said she'd had enough, and was moving out. I said, 'Don't bother! I've wanted to be gone for a long time!' She started grabbing stuff to take, and I grabbed her arm. She sort of swung around at me, and called me a 'punk' among other things. I meant to cuff her on the top of the head. Instead, I hit her on the jaw, and she sort of collapsed." A ragged sob erupted from Bruce. "I knocked her out! We were both pretty shook. When she could stand, she told me she wouldn't call the police if I never touched her again, if I would allow her to leave immediately. I felt like something the dog left in the yard. I never spoke to her again." He covered his face with his hands.

As the skipper moved to his side, Annie slid her hand under his arm and held him to her. "You've been carrying that awful night for a long time, haven't you bud?" The skipper's voice was soft, and full of love.

"I am not an abuser," Bruce sobbed. "I'm not that kind of guy! I didn't mean to hurt her, I swear to God. I am not an abuser." His face was contorted by grief. With all the pent up emotions from the past thirty-six hours, he felt a rush of release. "I don't know why I did it!" Looking into the eyes of his dad, he choked, "You never hit or hurt me. Why did I become what I hate?" Looking deeply into Annie's eyes, he groaned, "I wouldn't hurt you for the world. But that's what they all say!" He rose quickly, going to the refrigerator to find a cold drink.

The skipper continued the discussion as though Bruce hadn't walked away. "You didn't become anything other than a young man trying to find himself in a confusing world."

"Oh please," Bruce said from the galley. "Not every young man smacks his best friends around." His voice was dark with self-contempt. "Not every young man loses complete control, embarrasses himself in front of the people who mean the most to him." Bruce started to return to the settee, then turned to the companionway that led up into the cockpit. "I need to take a walk!"

Annie started to get up, saying, "I'll go with you." Then seeing the pained look on Bruce's face, she stopped. "Maybe I'll stay here, and we can talk a little more about stuff."

"Thanks. Just let me settle down a bit. I'll just go up to the marina office and be right back. O.K?" He was already in the cockpit, making his way toward the dock.

As they listened to his footsteps fade down the dock, the skipper said, "Wow! I had no idea about any of that. Did you?"

Annie shook her head, "No. I've never seen any sort of anger from him, or any violence." After a moment of reflection, she continued, "But that sort of explains why he was so quiet last night. I think he has been carrying a lot of garbage too."

"It takes a lot more effort to hide those sort of feelings from his family and friends than if he could just deal with them honestly." The skipper wondered if there might be a lot more to be revealed. When they could no longer hear footsteps from the dock, they both sat in a maze of silence.

Finally, Annie spoke, "Do you think I should go out and be with Bruce? I don't know if he wants company right now, but I feel awkward just doing nothing about it." Another tense moment passed. "I just don't know what to do."

The skipper eased some of the tension. "I suppose we honor his request if he wants to be left alone." After a moment of speculation, he continued, "When he comes back, we can finally talk about the issues that have been nagging you two, but for sure you should not respond in a supportive way to his reaction. He will be able to use these moments as an important discovery."

Annie's worried expression gave way to a weak smile. "I'm glad to hear you say 'When he comes back.' It scared me to see him leave so upset." The frown returned to her brow. "But I'm a little confused. You sound like this is a good thing, an 'important discovery,' you called it. How can Bruce's anger or pain be good?" She looked closely into the soft eyes of the skipper.

"I didn't say his pain is good. But you're right. Now that the issue is in the open, we can start to deal with it. And that is a good thing." They both massaged their thoughts. "I've been thinking a lot about this today. And it seems to me that the issue is one of assault." He seemed inwardly satisfied with the thought, even though it caused another frown to trace across Annie's face.

"Whether the pain is caused in you by someone else," he continued, "or you cause the pain in them, or whether the pain is caused in you by yourself, it is all assault. It is all pain inflicted, first- degree injury. Then, as if that were not bad enough, the more we dwell on the pain or injury, the worse we make it. We compound it by fretting, stewing, worrying, feeling guilty, you know, everything we do with a shameful guilty conscience."

"Do you mean that whether someone hurts me, or I hurt myself, it's the same?" Annie was struggling to catch the scope of the idea. "And, how I think about the whole thing can even make it worse?"

"Sure! Suppose someone says to me, 'Golly, are you putting on some weight? You're looking pretty heavy these days.'" The skipper smiled because his weight was a constant challenge. "Now that might have been a rude thing for someone to say, and would hurt my feelings, a little. But if I stew about the remark, twist it around to see it as an attack on my whole appearance, I allow it to wound my pride and cause an even deeper hurt. I call that second-degree assault, and I do it to myself."

Annie was still trying to get the full measure of understanding. She asked, "Well, what if they didn't intend for the remark to injure you? What if they were just trying to say that they were aware of any change in you, which might have even been meant as a compliment? Maybe they didn't mean to hurt you at all." It was a reflection of her nature, not to hurt.

The skipper nodded in agreement. "I'm sure that most of the injury that happens to us in a given day is accidental. It happens because people are thoughtless, or careless, too hurried, or not equipped to say what they really mean. We would be way ahead if we could see all of that as less harmful to us, and more a commentary on them. But there is going to be plenty of hurt anyway."

"You mean that it's not always about me?" Annie smiled. "I always think it's about me." She found again the perky smile that had warmed the salon all evening. "It's a challenge to be objective when the power of words is so subjective."

"O.K." the skipper smiled. "Here might be the perfect starting place for us in this big process we are facing! Let's practice learning to *respond* to an assault, rather than *react* to it." He emphasized the importance of each word. "When we respond to an event, we think about and choose our action. When we react, we are sometimes, even often, out of control. You know, we react out of fear, or anger, or panic; we get defensive, or puffed up with pride." He waved his hand in an effort to show the futility of the reaction.

"I sure like the thought of being able to take the sting out of an assault." Annie continued to warm the conversation. "It makes me feel like I can do something positive when just the opposite happens to me. At least I can keep from making it worse. Is that what you're saying?"

"Yeah." The skipper was writing in the notebook he had used for notes. "*We must first become harmless, to ourselves or to others, before we can begin the process of finding inner peace!*" He spoke the words as he wrote them. "I think this is an important…"

Annie's hand interrupted the thought as she turned her head to listen to approaching footsteps on the dock. "I think Brucie's back!" There was a happy relief in her voice. Her smile broadened as the hatch cover slid open and Bruce stepped into the light of the salon.

"You guys miss me?" His crooked grin belied any fears that the evening might be marred.

"Yes we did," she said emphatically. Patting the settee cushion beside her, indicating where she wanted her wonderful friend to sit, she continued, "Your dad has just helped me with a big idea. He said we could…I could…" there might have been a nervous blush with the correction, "I could learn to respond to the things that hurt me or others, rather than react. In the first, I'm in control, and in the second, I'm not." Looking at the skipper for assurance, she asked, "Is that sort of what we were talking about?"

Looking at his notebook, the skipper smiled, "I think you got more out of that than I did. That's exactly what we've been trying to deal with, and it's a very big task."

Bruce retrieved the cold drink he had left on the galley counter. As he took his place beside Annie, he said, "Thanks for the break. I still feel kind of shaky, but I'm glad to finally get that out in the open." He took a sip of soda, looking from one face to the other. A moment of gentle quiet held the three. "Right now it feels too large to deal with. It was hard enough just to tell you." Their solitude rocked gently against the dock lines. Moments of quiet reflection gave Bruce time to frame his next thought.

"I just don't know how to get a handle on this. It feels way more than just changing the way I think about it. It's way bigger than an attitude shift. Words aren't enough to lift this off me." His face remained gentle, even though the admission was harsh.

Finally, the skipper said, "I know I promised not to preach during this trip, but I just remembered a sermon from Good Friday a couple years ago. It was entitled 'From Malice, to Mercy.' I think it might be appropriate. You need to go anywhere for a few minutes?" It was his way of asking permission for an extended reflection. When they both shook their heads compliantly, he shared an important understanding.

"Every one of the world's great religions has something to offer. Only a closed mind would hold that we have in Christianity the only truth. But saying that, I do feel that only Christianity offers us a personal relationship with a Lord who empowers us to respond to the injuries…I think we called them assaults…instead of reacting to them. His teaching and his conduct were consistent with a harmless person. He taught his disciples to forgive those who offend them seven times seventy times, which is to say perpetually. Their custom held that anyone who could forgive three times was a righteous man, and could not be expected to take it any further than that. He taught to turn the other cheek, go the second mile, loan money without expecting to be repaid. He ate with outcasts, and ministered to those who were considered hopeless."

"All of that is marvelous teaching, and if our world could only follow that example, it would be a wonderful place to live. But that teaching flew in the face of the rigid faith of the religious leaders of his day. His popularity and wisdom was an affront to them, so they plotted his removal. The more they tried to silence him logically, the more he demonstrated the incompleteness of their system. Finally his death was the only option they could see. They plotted his arrest, even with the betrayal by one of his disciples. His trial was a mockery to justice. He was whipped savagely, humiliated, forced to carry his own means of execution as long as he was physically able, taken to a place of death and nailed to a cross, and lifted naked to die in excruciating pain. I can't even imagine the scope of such an assault! But what is most fascinating to me is that he did not attempt to defend himself or fight back, or somehow resist his adversaries. Whether you believe in the divine ability to call down angels, or the loyalty of his disciples to mount some sort of armed resistance, he responded in amazing mercy. He allowed himself to be trapped, betrayed, mocked, tried and convicted, brutalized and crucified without any form of physical resistance! He took the malice upon himself."

"But he not only did not fight back, he even brought mercy into the arena, by praying for his executioners. Imagine him saying from his cross of hatred, 'Father, forgive them. They know not what they are doing.' Imagine in the last hours of his life, he comforted the thief who was sharing the moment of death by promising, 'Today, you will be with me in paradise.' Whether you believe in the divine nature of Jesus, whether you believe that he was the incarnate Son of God, you must admit that something extraordinary happened on that barren hilltop. Theologians have argued since that very day about the depth of meaning in Jesus' death. Remember, the Roman Centurion who was at the scene, said, 'Certainly, this is the Son of God.' The nature of Jesus is a matter of personal faith. But the fact that he did something that eternally affects humankind is not! He could have resisted, but did not. He broke the chain of natural reaction to assault, by transforming malice into mercy. He responded in love!"

The skipper paused to let the impact of the moment be fully realized. "Christians often say that Jesus died to save us. That has always been problematic to me on several levels. But on this one it makes absolute sense. Jesus died in mercy, breaking forever, for us all, the natural reaction of malice that needs retaliation, or violent retribution, or revenge. We know that routine acts of malice, followed by other aggravations of malice, keep a tide of meanness flowing freely in our world. But when someone interrupts that sweep of pain by absorbing the malice without resistance, or retaliation, the tides are forever changed."

"And Jesus said to his disciples that they were going

to do even greater things than he had done. Suddenly we think about a Mahatma Gandhi, or Martin Luther King Jr. or any number of selfless humanitarians who face malice, armed only with mercy. In a secular, psychological sense, we see people doing what Jesus first did, resisting the natural reaction to return hurt with hurt, blame with blame, and hate with hate because somewhere, sometime on a lonely cross someone broke forever the chain, and promised that we would have the power to do even greater mercies."

"Wow! Does that make sense to you guys?" The skipper looked into both faces and saw the focus of understanding. "I'm seeing this much clearer this evening. However we might feel about church teachings, does this seem helpful to you?" Bruce had a thoughtful smile, and Annie was nodding her head in affirmation. Moments of heavy contemplative silence filled the boat.

Annie was the first to answer. "It feels like a fog has been lifted for me. I feel like you just explained the secret of scripture. I also feel a true desire to read it now." Her eyes were dancing with the reflection of the brass lamps.

"Me too," Bruce offered. "Although, I feel a little like that Pogo cartoon where he said, 'I met the enemy and he is us!' I'm not sure how to digest all this when I feel like the assault is coming from within me! To tell the truth, I'm struggling with the idea of theology having anything to do with how weak and shaken I feel right now" His smile faded to a concerned frown. "I just don't see how

Bible study is going to apply to these terrible memories. I'm still stuck on the idea of what I've done." He shook his head slightly as though trying to clear cobwebs.

"Buddy, that's why we are here tonight," the skipper answered softly. "This isn't Bible study, or theology, although they may become useful tools in our process. This is sound psychology! We must become harmless to others, and to ourselves as well. If we are going to get any headway on this discussion, we need to know, without even a tiny cloud of doubt, that the chain of reaction has been broken, allowing us to choose a merciful response instead. It is not a matter of us doing something for ourselves, other than acknowledging that we have the gift to be free from it." He paused for just a moment, wondering if he was beginning to sound like an evangelic calling for a crisis decision, a most uncomfortable notion. "How would it feel to truly believe that the past is past, that old feelings can be put away forever?" Looking at Annie he finished the question, "How would it feel to only have positive feelings about little children?"

So quiet it could almost have been mistaken for a sigh, Annie replied, "Wonderful." The three sat embraced in the possibility of fresh mercy.

The skipper sensed that they were in an important moment. He said quietly, "Nothing significant is going to happen unless we realize that we have been carrying a wounded heart. We've learned to hide it, and ignore it, even pretend that we don't know it's there. It is like a bitter chunk of malice, frozen in our chest, keeping us from realizing the really good stuff in our lives. And, it's predictable that until we make a decision to change, it will stay there forever. I'd like to get rid of it, and become harmless to myself, and others. Wouldn't you?" He looked at their faces in the soft light of the cabin lamps.

"You make it sound easy." Bruce interjected. "Do you really think it can be that simple?"

"I'm not sure we can think of it as easy. But simple has some possibilities in that we make a decision, and then find the next step, and the one after that. I have no idea how many steps might be in the journey, but I promise that we can make it together."

Annie's smile grew even brighter. "I feel like I've already started. It's like I'm in a new place to discover, a new era of growth." She looked at Bruce, who returned her smile, with a bit less vigor. Once again the boat was silent.

Finally, the skipper picked up his notebook, then, looking at his watch he said, "It's getting pretty late. How about let's finish the task we were talking about earlier, the communication tool." He was offering them all a way to break the tension of fresh insight. "Recall the scoring on these comparison questions, one is low, ten is high. We were asking, how willing are you to express negatively charged subjects?" After just a brief pause, "And how would you score your other's willingness? And," he didn't allow time for another anxious explanation, "What subject would you like to discuss if you knew it was safe to share?" Making sure that they both understood the question, he went on. "There will be lots of time tomorrow to talk about this. For tonight, make a list of the topics you would like to explore together."

"And finally," taking a big breath, he was genuinely glad to reach this point in the evening, "take your notebook. Write the word 'malice' on the first page, as large as you feel it." He gave them a moment to finish the task. "Now circle it, and draw a diagonal slash through it. No malice allowed here! Underneath that, write, 'I choose to live by mercy!' Write it as large as you feel it." There was chuckling from Annie as her letters spilled over onto the opposing page.

With a sigh, the skipper said, "I don't know about you guys, but I'm pretty darned weary from all this. Let's call it a day by sharing a prayer from William Barclay's Prayer Book." He read, "O Great and Gracious God, from whom every perfect gift flows freely, Help us to find this night, wisdom to know what is right, and the strength to do what is right. Enlighten our minds with your truth; warm our hearts with your love; fill our lives with your power that we may go out to live for you: through Jesus Christ our Lord. Amen"

Before the skipper could get up from the settee, Annie asked, "Maybe you could help me understand those printed prayers. I've never quite known how to feel, using someone else's words when I pray to God. Do you suppose God hears that as spiritual plagiarism or something?"

Bruce answered before the skipper could, "Sweetie, the evening is finished. Should we let him get some rest? Personally, I feel like I've been over a bumpy road, and have more than I ever expected to think about."

"Yeah," she was twinkling with enthusiasm, "But I'm kind of wound up right now. You want to take a walk up to the shower house?" How long had it been since she felt this good, this alive?

Oh, good the night!

Notebooks:

Annie wrote: "I'm happy and sad at the same time. I'm happy that Bruce has finally shared a dark secret with us. It was really hard for him to let the story be heard. I'm sad that he sees himself in terms of that mistake. I wonder if he has listened to the lessons the skipper has given me. Think about the big picture. There is more gentle kindness in him than anger or violence. In spite of the tears, I'm happy that we can work on this now. I wonder what the morning will bring. Will he be different? Will we?"

Bruce wrote: "Now that it's out, I wonder why I worked so hard to keep it hidden." (Doodles of a sunrise) "I feel released, free at last, free at last…"

Norm wrote: "It is unrealistic to be both his dad and his pastor-confessor. I'll try to relate to his past as though he were any other young man in the fellowship group seeking guidance; it is only fair that he gets this worked through. It is a real challenge to trust the process."

CHAPTER THREE: DEER HARBOR
A bay full of luminaries

When Bruce opened his stateroom door to the fresh morning, he found the skipper and Annie seated at the table, a pile of paper sacks in the middle. The fragrances of coffee, pastry, and sausage blended into a very welcoming medley. "Am I late, or did you guys stay up all night cooking?" His arched eyebrows tried to be warm and teasing, but the absence of his boyish grin suggested there was still some lingering apprehension from last night.

The skipper answered, "I thought it was my turn to cook, so I quietly slipped up to the drive-in. French toast sticks to dip in maple syrup, how good does that sound?"

Bruce was quickly making his way to the table. "It sounds like a shower, or anything else I might have been planning can wait." Opening a sack, he brightened, "Hot chocolate, juice, and hash browns to go along with it! Wow! This beats what I usually have on Sunday morning!" Even out of a paper sack, they shared a morning feast.

Annie explained to the sleepyhead, "We were just talking about church. I didn't know if there might be a church nearby for us to attend. The skipper was explaining to me how the church year works." She wanted to impress both the men with her new information.

"Did you know that this is the season of Pentecost?" She looked briefly at the skipper for confirmation. "It begins fifty days after Easter. In fact, there are seven seasons throughout the year." Trying to recall them in order she said slowly, "It all gets started with advent, then Christmastime." (Christmastide, the skipper corrected.) "Oh yeah, that's the twelve days of Christmas. Then is Epiphany, which means to reveal or show, then lent, and Eastertide." (She got that one right!) After Pentecost is King…" She looked at the skipper for help.

"Kingdom tide, if you're following an old calendar form. The new ones count the Sundays after Pentecost until advent begins." The skipper finished another French toast stick.

"I can sort of remember hearing that in confirmation classes. It sounds pretty dry to me this morning." Bruce was more interested in the contents of the sacks than a calendar.

"Wait Brucie," (she loved to catch his attention with that endearment) "there's more to this. Did you know that the worship service follows a macro plan? It's a drama that we do without being aware." Her smile was that of confident fresh information. "If we begin by praising the glory of God, we will begin to know our own brokenness, which leads to confession. If we do that, we will hear a pronouncement of forgiveness, and then instructions from scripture, music, or the sermon." She gave another quick check toward the skipper to make sure her new information was correct. "The worship concludes with our response to the instructions and a blessing. Isn't that cool? I didn't know that was going on while I thumbed through the songbook." Her expression was innocent, and totally happy.

"I don't know," Bruce said trying to get in the mood, "I know a lot of folks who worship in a whole bunch of different ways. I'll bet they don't care what kind of macro they're following." There was just enough edge to his words to remind his listeners about the discussion last night. A long silence followed with each of them trying to find some kind way to end it.

Finally, Bruce found a totally different subject, one that was safe, and took the focus off of him. He asked about the charts, and a small electronic device at the end of the table. "Are we going to go somewhere today?"

"Yeah," the skipper was glad for a chance to change the tone, and share some new plans. "I think we will move out to Deer Harbor on Orcas Island. It's just west of Pole Pass, and a favorite cozy marina to duck into."

Bruce squinted a bit, as though trying to recall, "Have I been there with you? I can't remember what it looks like." Then examining the little hand held device, he asked, "Is this a new cell phone?" It looked very interesting to a computer person.

"That's a new Garmin GPS," the skipper said with a smile. "I just added it to the inventory for the vacation."

Leaning over Bruce's arm, Annie examined the small instrument. "What can such a small device do for the sailboat?" She was thinking of the large deck winches and heavy lines. This looked frail in comparison.

"GPS stands for 'Global Positioning System'," the skipper explained. "This little rascal can communicate with satellites, factoring coordinates, and calculating our latitude and longitude position so closely that it is amazing." There was an admiring sense of wonder in the skipper's explanation. "With this, we cannot lose our way. It never gets lost!" Then, showing them the small display window, he went on, "GPS technology has been around for awhile, but it was too expensive for small time sailors. Then, with the Gulf war, they became affordable and are now almost cheap." Once again he admired the device. "It calculates our course, speed, and even plots a lay line to keep us on track. There are other features that baffle me. I guess it's like learning to use any new tool."

"Very cool!" Bruce exclaimed. "May I see the

instruction book? I'd like to know more about ....did you give it a name? Maybe we should call it 'Jeeps!' You know, 'Gee,' 'P,' 'S,'" he said it slowly to try to explain his humor. "How cool would it be to never get lost?" His face was filled with the same admiration and wonder of his dad's. "Or maybe we should call it 'Jeepers I'm good!'"

"Well," the skipper said, reaching for the breakfast sacks and paper plates, "I've already programmed the way points into 'Jeepers' to take us all the way to Deer Harbor. So as soon as you guys get cleaned up and ready to go, we're out of here. I'll get the diesel warmed up." They each headed for their tasks with enthusiasm brought on by more than a new toy.

"Will it work?" wondered the skipper.
"How can I keep up this pace?" wondered Annie.
"Can I face the truth?" wondered Bruce.

Within the hour, Bruce was releasing the spring line, freeing *Dreamer* from the dock. Scrambling aboard, he declared, "All clear! We're underway." The sleek hull slid out of its marina slip, turned into the main channel and headed for open water under low heavy clouds. The crew was grateful for the protection of the dodger, which acted as a windscreen, and shelter from any rain that might come.

As soon as they passed the "No Wake" sign, the skipper eased the diesel up to hull speed. "I think we will just power across the strait this morning," he said assuring his crew. "The wind is real light, and that's a big shipping lane. The quicker we can cross it, the safer we'll be." The sheer rock headland that formed the marina park began to slide past their port side.

Looking up at the rocky face, Annie noted, "It certainly looks different from down here. Isn't that where we were yesterday?"

"It is. We had a bird's eye view. From up there we could see clear across the strait to Decatur Island. That's our first waypoint."

Annie would have asked, but Bruce beat her to it. "I don't understand what that means. I think it's a new term to me." Annie nodded, that was just what she was going to say, too.

The skipper pointed to the binnacle that held the ship's compass. "When we finish this big turn around the headland, we'll see far out in front of us a navigation piling. Beyond it, about six miles there is another island that we can just barely make out. The line between the island and us is called a lay-line to our next turning point, or waypoint one. So far so good?" They both nodded, mixed understanding.

"Here's where it gets a little sticky," the skipper smiled. "The tide is at full flood right now, which means it is coming in at top speed, about three and a half knots. If we steer by the compass, about 242°, we will be far off course because the tide will sweep us from south to north. But if we steer by 'Jeeps', we'll have a compass heading of about 225°, which will actually take us on the lay-line." Holding his hand at a slight angle, he tried to demonstrate how they could slide across the incoming tide. "See this line?" he held up the display of the GPS. "Our actual position will show up along it, or on either side, which will help us correct." Annie still had that squint that suggested she might catch on later.

Dreamer carved out into the Guemes Channel. There was not another pleasure boat in sight. "Oh a sailor's life's for me…" the skipper sang, a bit too quiet to persuade his companions.

"I think I see the navigation marker! Is that it way up to starboard?" Bruce was pointing at a distant mass of fluffy gray. "Is that fog in the strait?" His voice had a touch of dismay.

The skipper answered, "I do believe it's 'yes' to both questions. Bud, will you go below? In the nav station there is a bell. Bring it up and slide it in that bracket by the hatch." He pointed to help indicate the shiny brass base. The boat lumbered a bit as it began to feel the effects of the incoming tide.

"Are we going to be able to go through the fog?" Annie's voice was just a bit on the worried side.

"No problem, mon!" The skipper quipped his best imitation of a Jamaican accent. "We've got a good boat, with all the right equipment, plus we have the very best crew. Ya, mon! No worries." *Dreamer's* bow rose over a swell with a small lurch. "No worries!"

As they approached the marker, it became apparent the fog was growing more dense. It was no longer possible to see the far island. Bruce and Annie exchanged an anxious glance. What had begun as an easy passage was quickly becoming a challenge to their nerves.

"There might be a worry or two here," Bruce said softly.

The powerful diesel pushed them quickly past the marker. Ahead the fog now appeared to be a solid mass. "No worries," the skipper assured them. "We all have a simple job to do. I'll keep us on track. Bruce, watch and listen for any other boats. Tell me if you even think there is somebody out there with us. Annie, you can have two jobs. Ring the bell three times every minute or so, and watch that depth sounder. It's set on a sixty fathom scale, and we'll be in deeper water than that. So, if you see it in less than a hundred feet, tell me. O.K.?" They both understood their tasks, but neither of them believed there were "No worries!" They slid into the gray fog, losing sight of everything!

The skipper slowed the diesel a bit. He said they were making about six knots. It seemed frighteningly quiet. There was no conversation in the cockpit. Ding, Ding, Ding. Annie was doing her part. Another minute drug past. Ding, Ding, Ding.

"This is amazing!" the skipper spoke excitedly, yet

softly as though the fog could hear them. "I'm steering ten degrees south of our course, but the tide is pushing us just as true as can be. It's compensating us right along our lay line! It's fantastic!"

Ding, Ding, Ding.

"Dad, I can't see a thing out here." Bruce wanted to ask if they should turn back until they could see more clearly.

"Good, Bud, keep watching. As long as there is nothing out here to see, there is nothing to worry about. Right?"

"Yeah, right!" came the murmured response.

Ding, Ding, Ding. Yet another minute crept past. Ding, Ding, Ding.

Bruce turned again to his dad. "I feel dizzy trying to look for some object when I can't see a horizon or anything. There is just no point of reference. I can't even tell what's up or down!" His voice was tinged with exasperation.

Ding, Ding, Ding.

"I know it's weird. I'm challenged to believe this little tool," the skipper replied, looking again at the GPS in his hand. "But we are right on track, and as safe as though we could see clearly."

Ding, Ding, Ding.

"It doesn't feel like it, but sound travels really well across water, even in the fog. Powerboats have horns to honk, and we sailors ring bells. Believe me, if someone else were nearby, we'd be able to hear. Rosario Strait is about six miles across here, and we are in a ferry lane, so chances are that in this hour, we'll hear a ferry horn."

Ding, Ding, ("did you say ferry?") Ding. Annie looked up, startled by this news.

"It's O.K." the skipper assured her. "Those big guys all have radar that sees through this soup. They will know that we are here. As long as we just hold our line, we'll be fine. And if we are in their way, we'll hear them toot five short times. That's a warning. But, we are not even close to being in their way. Believe me."

Annie's face looked a bit pale with anxiety. "Do I have any other options?" The smile was an effort to be brave. Ding, Ding, Ding. She thought to herself, "I only have to do this sixty times in an hour, and I've already done twelve or thirteen. Only forty-five more!" Then after a pause, "I hope that is enough!" Ding, Ding, Ding.

Aching minutes struggled across the stage of the foggy hour drama. Bruce was thinking, "This isn't a bit safe, or enjoyable. Why are we doing this?" Annie's thoughts were much the same, "This teaches me to get on a boat. I hope we get through all right." Ding, Ding, Ding. The skipper was thinking, "This is the greatest darned device I've ever had. Without other bearings, we are right on course! Amazing!" *Dreamer* slid across a glassy surface, which only reflected the gray emptiness of the fog bank. The little conversations stopped completely. Ding, Ding, Ding.

At last, the skipper said, "We're about a half mile from Thatcher Pass, so the depth should start to come up, Annie. And I think I heard a ferry horn, but it's still way around the corner." Wanting to assure his tense crew, he added, "We're exactly where we should be. Jeepers says that we are in the Pass right now. I'll bet we see the island in just another minute or so."

Ding, Ding, Ding. Three pairs of eyes searched the emptiness for any sign of land.

No solid shapes emerged from the fog, although after several minutes, Annie did announce that the depth was changing, and Bruce said he could hear the ferry horn off the port bow. His hand indicated a slight angle to their progress.

Annie said with a sudden excitement after she rang the bell, "I can hear an echo from over there!" She pointed to the starboard side of the boat. "And I think I can see blue sky up above us!"

As quickly as they had entered the fog bank, they slid out of it. To their surprise, they were about a quarter mile from a sheer rock passage, which the skipper identified as Thatcher Pass. Indeed, they were exactly where they intended, and behind them, well to port, the shape of the green and white ferry was fading back into the fog. "No worries, mates!"

Bruce declared that he was most pleased that the ordeal was over, and with permission, he would go below to relieve himself, a task that was several minutes overdue.

Annie agreed to stay in the cockpit, but declared that she was next, as soon as possible.

When finally they had negotiated the turn into Lopez sound, and each had a warm cup of tea to help put the first leg behind them, Annie asked, "Why is there such dense fog on the other side of this island and here it's clear and sunny?" Their visibility was nearly unlimited now, with islands near and far plainly in sight.

The skipper answered, "There are a couple of factors, but they are connected. Fog happens when the air around us cools to a point it can no longer maintain the humidity in it. Tiny droplets, which are condensed out of the moist air, form into clouds if it's higher in the atmosphere, or fog if it's lower. The fog in the strait is probably created by the in-coming tide, which is cold ocean water that chills the surface air. And, since we are on the windward side of the island, the air is churned by a little westerly breeze, so it doesn't reach that dew point. The good thing is that it is never very thick this time of year."

Bruce gave a snort of relief, "That was plenty thick for me. I still feel sort of disoriented from trying to see through it. I know why they call it 'pea soup!' That was yucky!" Annie agreed, adding that if she didn't hear a bell for a long time, it would be just fine with her. For several minutes they were quiet, delighted that *Dreamer* was back up to speed, headed for a new port of call.

Annie finally asked, "There are so many islands in

here, how do you remember where we're going? They all look pretty much alike."

The skipper smiled, "These are the 'San Juan Islands.' That's Lopez over there, this is Blakely, and way up there is Orcas. It's a big one." Looking down at the GPS, he added, "Our next way point is straight ahead, at the north end of Lopez."

Annie continued with her question, "I still wonder how you can find your way around. Are there signs that tell you which island is which?" Her crooked smile was very pleasant to both the other two.

"In a way, yes, they are all identified on the charts. As long as we know where we are," he held up the GPS, "we will always know how to identify them. I sort of think of it as 'reading our way through.' You know, you do chapter one, then two, until the book is finished."

"I'm not sure if I understand you. We do know where we are going, don't we?" Annie was no longer worried, now that she didn't have to ring that bell.

"Sure we do," the skipper replied. "Maybe I should have said there are steps in our journey. Step one was across the Rosario Strait; step two was through Thatcher Pass; we didn't even know we were in that one. Step three is up Lopez Sound, step four is to Pole Pass, and our last step today is into Deer Harbor. What I mean is that we can't fret about any except the one we are currently in, you know, one at a time." Checking around to make sure they were free from any other traffic, he asked, "Anyone else want to steer?"

Annie shook her head, but Bruce agreed happily. As he moved aft, he mused, "That's a bit like what we have been talking about isn't it? We have to go through the process, step by step." When Annie shook her head, indicating that she wasn't following his thought, he added, "Well, we can't talk about a serious relationship until we get passed some of the hurdles that have been in our way." It was a subject he wanted to talk about. "We can't think about serious stuff until we work out some personal details, and we can't do that until we can come to peace with some of the junk we've been carrying for too long." Looking at his dad, he asked, "Didn't you call that 'reading your way through it'?"

"Yup, I did." Turning his attention to Annie, the skipper asked, "Does that make sense now?" When she nodded, he went on. "Can you imagine the stack of text books you guys have read from *Run Spot, Run* to those technical manuals you need to do your job? Think of all those schoolbooks, in college, graduate school, what a mountain of reading! It would be discouraging to think of reading the entire pile. Yet, you did it a book, a chapter, a sentence at a time. You read your way through it. I think that's how we should understand any undertaking, just another endeavor we read our way through."

Bruce asked, "What's our chapter for today, and I don't mean Deer Harbor? And am I right in thinking that there is not enough breeze to get the sails up right now?" He was ready, if not real eager, to find out what discoveries they would make.

The skipper had finished his cup of tea, carefully placing the empty cup in a holder where it wouldn't get knocked over. "You are right about the sails. We'll just stay on the diesel for a while." Looking again at Annie, he added, "I'm thinking we might continue to look at some of the points of pain we have hidden. And by the way, let me tell you both how proud I am of the progress you have already made." He looked first into Bruce's eyes that met his with a steady gaze, then into Annie's that were wrinkled with a perpetual smile. "We've pulled up the edges of some nasty scabs, and I suspect there is still some disclosure work to be done, because we will never repair that which we won't admit is broken. You two should be pleased with the courage and honesty you have already shown." After a moment he went on. "I've thought of a couple of exercises we might do today. One has to do with your priorities, and the other is rules for a clean fight."

Bruce whooped, "Clean fight! That sounds like an oxymoron." Continuing to grin, he asked, "Don't people fight to win? It's not like football, or tennis with lines. I don't understand how a fight can be fair." Annie's smile had not faded, and her gaze remained on the skipper.

The skipper smiled too. "Tell you what, let me take over the wheel again, and you guys can get your notebooks. I think there are several other things we'll talk about before we get to the rules. I had sort of planned to do this when we get into the harbor. But now is a perfect time, and there could hardly be a more perfect place." Little Willow Island was being left behind as *Dreamer* rumbled through the morning.

When they returned to the cockpit, Annie brought her bunk blanket with her. She pulled her feet up under her, then tucked the blanket snugly around. "No one said I had to shiver to get there, did they?" Her smile was a contagious joy to both of her companions.

"Let's see," the skipper began, looking at his notes as well. "We were talking about communicating the things that might be a problem, and you were going to make your own list of subjects that deserve more conversation. How about this: Is there anything your partner does, that you find irritating enough to be a problem?" He grinned at them thinking of the infinite number of possible items on that list. "How can you convey this, so that your partner will understand your feelings and want to change?" He watched them both writing quickly to record the question. "I think that might keep you busy for a while."

Here at its greatest point, Lopez Sound seemed like a vast inland sea. He was surprised at the light traffic, even on this May Sunday. His smile grew as he thought how fantastic this whole trip was developing. It would certainly be one that he would remember.

Several minutes more passed before he went on. "Lots of folks are working on the assumption that they share the same priorities with their mates. It can be a big surprise to find out that that idea is leading to some of their problems. Here's a list of general priorities: just copy them and then rate them, number 1 for your top priority, 2, 3, and so on. Then, compare your list. It may be easy, or surprising. Write down, 'family', then below that, 'job', and below that, 'service,' and below that, 'recreation,' and then, 'Church,' and finally, 'God.' There is no particular order. The importance is the way you number them, and the comparison you have with each other."

Bruce asked, "You are saying there can be only one number one, aren't you?" It was obvious, but he just needed to make sure.

"That's right. For example if you had 'job' as number one, and Annie had 'family' as number one, it would warn you that working late, or on weekends would cut into her highest priority."

Annie waited for him to finish before she asked, "What do you mean by family? Is it the two of us, or our whole extended family?"

"You can decide what it means," the skipper replied. "It could also mean you and the children you will have together. It may even define the timeframe when that family will happen." The idea of grandchildren was a fresh one for him, but quite welcome.

"I just have two more suggestions for your tasks today.

Are you ready to move on?" When they both agreed, he said, "O.K. Write down, 'One thing I could do that I know my partner would appreciate is…' It might be a courtesy, or breaking a habit that you know irritates, or providing some thoughtful help. I think you've already thought of several that you could write down. "

"Finally, this one could take some time. But this is one of my all-time favorite exercises. Compose thirty compliments that you might honestly give your partner. Then see if you can tuck one a day into your conversations over the next month. Do it so carefully that they may not even be aware that you have just presented them with one of the thirty. This does two things. It helps you keep your conversation tone positive. In other words it improves the way you speak to each other. It also improves the way that you listen, because you will want to be able to ask,' Is that one of the thirty?' It's like a love game that builds the habit of complimenting and praise. Good stuff!"

Bruce asked, "What happens if she doesn't understand my compliment? How can I get points if she doesn't know?"

The skipper's smile grew, "Well, Bud, it's not a competition, so the winner will be each of you as you grow in the ability to compliment without sounding strange. Hopefully you will manage to do it so gracefully that she won't see it as one of the thirty. And hopefully there will be a lot more than just one a day. But make sure there is at least one."

Looking again at the GPS, he said, "We're closing on the third way point. We'll make the turn across the top of Lopez Island, and then pass the ferry docks at Shaw and Orcas. If we are on time, we should go through Pole Pass at high slack tide, which will put us right into Deer Harbor. We are definitely reading our way through this day, and I like it!"

Brad Taylor, the harbormaster was waiting for them as they slid into the guest moorage assigned for the night. "Good to have you back! It's been way too long since you were in here." Annie was amazed at the ease with which he flipped the mooring lines around the dock cleat and with only a casual second flip, had the line secured. "How long will you be here?"

"Probably just one night," the skipper replied. "It depends on how fast these folks run out their bar tab." All four of them chuckled at the humor. "Do we need reservations at the Winchester for supper?"

Looking at the marina, only sparsely dotted with pleasure boats, he quipped, "Not a very large crowd yet, but it still might be a good idea to give them a call." With a warm smile, he added, "I'm going up that way. Could I do it for you? What time to do you need to feed these deckhands?"

When the arrangements had been made, and Brad was walking back up to his office, Bruce asked, "Does he give that sort of service to all the boats that come in here? Or are you a special customer?"

"Yeah, both, I guess." The skipper then shared an interesting account. "Brad is the brother of a former church member. He was always getting into trouble in high school. Ultimately, he committed a crime, and did some prison time. There, he sort of got his agenda straightened out. When his parole hearing came up, his family asked me to speak a good word on his behalf, which may have been the first time anyone stood up for him. He felt I was a champion for him, and used me as a reference for this job. I stop in probably once or twice a year. He is an outstanding harbormaster, and loves this place. He tries to generate more business through outstanding customer service."

"Do the people know he's an ex-con?" Bruce's question had an edge of coldness to it.

Looking into Bruce's eyes, the skipper asked, "Do you think that would make any difference?"

"Well, sure I do!" he replied with a guarded conviction. "People should know when those kinds of folks are around."

Annie, who was still looking up the dock toward the harbormaster's office, mused, "I don't know. It seems to me that when your slate is clean, it's nobody's business. If he did his jail time (that seemed softer than saying 'prison') he should be given a chance for a fresh start." Looking at Bruce, she asked sincerely, "Do you really think he should be made to go public?"

Bruce squirmed a little under the closer question.

"No, I guess, not really, especially when you talk about a fresh start, and a clean slate." His boyish smile indicated his contrition.

"That's what we were talking about on the way up, wasn't it?" The skipper was about to help them make an important connection. There is such a difference between justice, which is frequently blind, and mercy that frequently doesn't look at the past." Thinking a bit about how he wanted to say the rest of the idea, he went on, "Brad is a person who has learned a big lesson. And he is a great example of a man living in mercy. There was plenty of malice before; that's what caused the trial and prison. He had a tough time behind bars, too. There was malice there. But now, he has the job he loves. He's married, and they hope to start a family. He is finishing a great house up there on the hill. He is exactly where he wants to be. Isn't that mercy?"

"Yeah, it is." Bruce answered quietly. "I feel sort of foolish all of a sudden. I was quick to condemn. But when I hear you tell his story, it's just the way I want mine to be."

"Mine too." Annie added in a whisper. There was a peaceful calm around the boat. Hardly a ripple stirred on the cove.

Looking at his watch, the skipper finally brought them back to the task of the afternoon. "We were going to talk about rules to a fair fight weren't we? Let's get our notebook out and see how this works."

When they re-gathered in the cockpit, the skipper said, "The reason the words fair fight sound strange is that usually when people fight, they are trying to win something." He looked at the two faces to make sure there was agreement. "They try to get their own way, or prove that they are right, or a million other selfish reasons. Since conflict will always happen between two people, let me just tell you that it is natural, normal and neutral." They both looked up at him questioning the idea of conflict being neutral.

"Yes, it is! But how we respond to it frequently is not. Suppose you came home some Friday night, after a tough week at work, and wanted to take Annie out for some sushi." Bruce nodded, and predictably, Annie made a grimace. Sushi was not one of her favorites. "Suppose she made a counter proposal that you come over to her place and she would fix a quick vegetarian quiche." This time Annie grinned, getting the drift of the conversation, and Bruce made a face at the word, "vegetarian." "So," the skipper continued, "conflict is natural, in that you each have food preferences. It's normal in that you have learned to like those certain foods either from your family or your experience. And it is neutral in that no value statement is being made about the nutrition of either."

When Bruce shrugged, the skipper tried to make his point. "But if you, brother," looking at Bruce, "tell her that quiche is freak food, and you wouldn't feed it to your dog, you could just about count on a scrap. Couldn't you?" Bruce was grinning at the simplicity, and over-statement of the example. He nodded in agreement.

Turning to Annie, he asked, "And if you told him that only primitive barbarians eat their meat raw, you probably wouldn't have much fun at table talk, would you?" She also nodded in agreement, even though the example was pretty corny.

"At base, most conflict is about that complicated at first." The skipper smiled, "Do you know that within the first three minutes of most house fires, a cup of water is sufficient to put them out?" His two listeners were completely baffled by the remark. "Think about it. Most fights, or conflicts, if you would prefer, begin so simply that a cup of reason, or simple explanation would put them out."

"With that as an introduction," the skipper drummed his fingers as a fanfare, "the first rule is, *'the purpose of a fair fight is to gain a deeper understanding of your partner.'* Write that carefully: a deeper understanding, of your partner. Anything else is trying to prove who is bigger, or tougher, or smarter, or right. And that requires someone to lose, and someone to win, maybe. A fair fight has a mercy purpose. To use Martha Stewart's words, 'it's a good thing.'"

"The second rule is, *'Make sure the time is right.'* It takes into consideration the fact that either of you might be at an unusual low. It looks at the external effects that might be at work on either of you. If Bruce has just missed a promotion, or gotten a speeding ticket," Bruce grimaced at the thought, "it probably would not be the right time for you, Annie, to find out why he isn't taking the garbage out." Turning to Bruce, he continued, "If Annie is having a difficult period, you would be ill advised to make her go camping with you. It seems so obvious in an example, yet these are the simple ways conflict begins. Make sure the time is right."

"The third rule is just as obvious. '*Check your weapons at the door.*' Words are the most hurtful things when they are misused. You've heard 'Sticks and stones can break my bones.' Well, words can break your heart! So make sure that your words are not lethal. Most women attack masculinity, and men tend to negate the identity or existence of their opponent. Name-calling or swear words are obvious fouls. They tend to enflame the process rather than control it."

Annie interrupted with a question, "But, how about teasing? Sometimes it's just playful to call names or talk rough." She was completely engaged in the conversation.

The skipper nodded, "It's probably up to the tolerance, and comfort level of the couple. Generally, however, things said in humor will fester like an infection, coming back to the surface later in many unsuspecting ways. There is no way Bruce could call you 'chubby' or 'saggy', or tease that he might go home with that cute new engineer, without tearing into the fabric of something precious to you. Does that make sense?" When she nodded understanding, he said, "Teasing is meant to be fun, but it is like playing with fire."

"Do we need to say anything more about that, or shall we go on?" They both smiled approval to move on.

"Rule number four is as much good etiquette as it is a clean fight. '*Never display a fight in public.*' The point here is a simple one. Only honor each other when you are not in private. It goes without saying that you should honor each other in private as well, but sometimes things are said which others should never hear. And when there are children in your home, it is doubly true. This leads right into the next one."

"Rule number five is, '*Lower your voice during a fight.*' That means lower the volume, lower the pitch and lower the tempo. Most folks talk louder, their voice becomes higher in pitch and they speak faster as they become excited or angry. If possible you should sit facing one another, knees to knees, and eye to eye. That way, facial expression and inflections can be understood more clearly."

"Rule number six," he watched both of them turn the page to write down this next installment, "'*Use a positive communication style.*' That means phrases like 'I feel….' Or clarification questions like 'Do you mean?' Avoid anything that is an accusation, like 'You always…' Think of the way you would communicate in a staff meeting, attended by your boss. Your partner should get no less consideration, or accord. Does that one make sense?" It was probably the most obvious so far.

"There are only two more. Rule number seven is '*Stay with one issue until both are content.*' That implies that neither of you can stomp out angry, or jump into the car and get away. It's not fair to go into the bedroom and pout, or the garage and sulk. It suggests that some equitable resolution is reached, or at least both are ready to let it go for a while. Here is where negotiation tools are really important. I have a couple of great resources if you think they might be useful."

Without waiting to ask if they were ready to go on, the skipper said, "Rule number eight is '*put it away until both are ready to re-discuss the problem.*' That means neither can drag it out as a means of proving some future issue. 'You said this, or you did that.' When it is over, is should remain over."

"Is that something that makes sense to you guys?" They had been so busy writing in their notebooks there had been little feedback. With their ascent, he gave them one more step in the rules process. "O.K., if you are in agreement, sign your names at the bottom, and date it, just like an official document. The point is, if there is a time when Annie feels like you are using hurtful words, Bruce, she can call a foul, just like a tennis serve out of the line. Or Bruce, if you feel that Annie is ready to go hide in the bathroom, throw that foul towel, like a clipping penalty. What I'm suggesting is that in a fight, you might be able to defuse the anger by talking about the manner in which you are talking, rather than the content of it. O.K.?"

They spent several more minutes talking about some of the rules, and how they might use them. Finally, the skipper said, "I've just one more suggestion for us this afternoon. We have a couple of hours before supper, and I'd like to walk up to that little store before then. How about writing in your notebook some of the places you feel your slate IS NOT clean." He emphasized the words to make sure they understood. "You two have been marvelously honest. I think it is commendable. And I also think it makes you feel pretty relieved. Let's stay with the idea, and do a bit more house cleaning. When you think of the inner baggage, or even garbage, that you are carrying around, identify it so you can get rid of it." He thought for a moment, then said it yet another way, "In what areas of your life would you like to have a fresh start? Let's make a list."

"I've been thinking about an exercise we could do after supper." Both of his listeners were keen with attention. "If I can get some paper sacks, and some votive candles from the store, we could make some luminaries to float on the bay." Bruce's frown suggested a bit more information. "We could write our baggage list on the sacks and send them off on the tide." The skipper looked at each of them to collect their agreement.

Bruce was the first to answer. "Well O.K. but could

that be dangerous to the other boaters, you know, having candles floating around them?"

"We'll be thoughtful enough to go down to the back part of the bay, well away from everyone. I think it might be an effective way to express a sense of release."

Annie's lips pursed in a questioning pause, "Do you mean you want us to write a list of complaints, or is it more like confessions?" She was struggling with the assignment.

The skipper's assurance was evident as he replied, "In some ways those two concepts are pretty similar. Think about it. A confession is a complaint about an injury or injustice we have done to ourselves, or others. But a confession is also an acknowledgement that we are seeking a positive change in our life. When we confess a problem, we are finally honest enough to deal with it. And we won't fix what we won't admit is a problem."

"Ah, wait a second," Bruce's voice was now tinged with suspicion. "You are not going to suggest that we write down all those private things we were just talking about, are you? It was one thing to think about them. But writing them down, you know, making them public, is going too far." He shook his head in a semi-serious frown.

"Bud, confession is just between you and God. It is for your eyes only, as private as you need it to be. But pretty clearly, it is also needed if you are going to deal with a problem. If there is a problem between you and another person, it is only going to be dealt with if you bring it out into the open. What you refuse to recognize in yourself, you are bound to continue."

Annie was nodding in agreement with Bruce's hesitance. "I'm not so sure about this either. I mean, I can write it in my journal, I suppose. But that is not making it public."

Now the skipper's smile broke into a full grin. "Wait guys, you don't need to make anything public. I'm not suggesting that you spill any gory detail or painful memory. I am suggesting that you identify any painful part of the past that you do want out of your life! Let's just keep this simple and easy. It's not therapy, just an exercise in freeing some of the tension we are carrying."

"I remember a seminary friend who said, 'we can't confess anything that God doesn't already know. But, until we do confess it, our pain is the abyss that separates us. When we confess, it becomes the bridge.' That's a poetic and profound truth."

"It seems to me that what you are suggesting requires an element of trust," Bruce said with a look of growing understanding.

Annie was quick to pick up on the idea. "I'm not sure what I can trust when it comes to sharing my secrets. I surely can agree that none of it is news to God. But it might not be too well received by anyone else."

The skipper had one of those insightful moments. "Let me make this comparison. This morning we were in the fog, and it was a bit confusing, a bit frightening, and a bit uncomfortable. Right?" He sought their agreement. "Yeah, maybe more than a little of all of that." Their faces had wrinkled into frowns of reflection.

"But through the fog we had one reliable thing that we could trust, didn't we? We had the GPS! It knew where we were, and where we were going. It could show us how to reach our destination without bumping into any rocks or reefs. Right?" Both listeners nodded in understanding. "We didn't question whether we should accept the GPS, or whether we should look for any other guidance devise. Isn't this a pretty clear analogy of how we can relate to God?" As the nodding heads continued to show agreement, he finished the thought. "We believe that God's intent for us is only loving, not condemning. We believe that we are never lost from divine favor, nor forgotten in our journey. We believe that God's destination for us is more wonderful than any we could plan for ourselves. So," he paused to let the question settle in, "why would we not trust sharing our pain with such a gracious God?" A tear traced down Annie's cheek.

Bruce held a long gaze with his dad. "Dad, do you really believe that, or is it theory?" There was that disturbing question again!

A deep silence held the boat for a moment. "I do believe that, Bud, with all my heart." Then taking a long breath, he said firmly, "So, I'm going to go up to the store and see about some things for us to work on this evening." He needed a brief break himself. "You guys can work on your notebooks, or play a game of cribbage, or…" his voice trailed away playfully.

Both Bruce and Annie smiled. "Or?"

Before the dinner hour, the notebooks of each member of the crew had fresh entries:

Annie wrote: If I could build a bridge to God using my painful memories, I would begin with the obvious. I confess my irresponsible behavior as a girl who looked for love in the wrong way with the wrong person. I confess being weak to his desire, and weak in my morality, even weak in my value of myself. My greatest pain would never have happened if those prior choices hadn't been made. I confess not thinking in terms of consequences, but more in terms of momentary conditions.

I confess a lack of interest in my family before I left for college. I could have been more supportive of mom, and more thoughtful to dad. I confess a kind of greed that wanted nicer things than my sister, and a willingness to flaunt those things in front of my friends. I confess not being a part of a happy family, when the chance was mine. I confess feeling anger at them rather than myself.

I confess laziness about the big problems of the world around me. I would rather not think about poverty, the violence of war, political issues and elections. All of it is too confusing and complicated for me. I confess that ignorance is my choice.

Annie's page had several erasure smudges. She had labored with her response.

Bruce's notebook read:

There has always been some 'pain' in my life. I didn't make the little league team. Several of my friends did. I didn't make the track team in middle school, and didn't even try for baseball. The success I had at football was because of my size rather than talent. I tried at debate, choir, and the school play, but quit when I didn't have much there either. Dances and proms were not much fun without an actual girlfriend. I guess the abyss before me is the fear of failing, because I have done it so often.

I'm sorry about the lies I've told to mom and dad. I'm sorry for the things I did that I needed to hide, stealing Jerry's letterman jacket, setting fire to the recycle paper collector, breaking the neighbor's garage window. I'm sorry for being a bully, for terrorizing freshmen, pantsing them before an assembly. I'm sorry for insulting people who hold a different point of view than I do, for being a racist, probably a bigot. I'm really sorry for the violence I have felt in my life toward people who did not deserve to be hurt. (I wonder if anyone ever really deserves violence.)

Most of Bruce's page was empty.

Norm's notebook said:

I am aware of the pain in my life caused by my actions, and my inactions, by the things I have done, and left undone, by the things I have said and left unsaid, by my efforts and lack of efforts. My years of service have been punctuated by seasons of disservice and carelessness. If I listen to my own words, I should list each and every sin. I should name each and every person that I have hurt so that I may go back and ask them all for their forgiveness. My list would be extensive! I wonder if it is even possible to go back to apologize to everyone I have neglected. Perhaps reminding them that they are ignorable would only deepen the hurt. (A heavy ink line was drawn through that last sentence, indicating some frustration with the response.)

The more I think on the subject, the longer my list grows. Are there any sins I haven't committed? I suppose I haven't whittled any graven image; but pride, lust, laziness, deceit, gluttony, and profane behavior are all mine. I have been shamefully weak in my convictions, and vague in my stand. I have abused my body and neglected my family. What sin can I not confess? I suppose the one that still has the most sting in it for me is that I had a high and holy responsibility that I let slide into obscurity. I disdained that which I was called into, trained for, and ordained to do.

O God, of Infinite Compassion, I come to you tonight to say that I am sorry for the abyss I have created between us through action or inaction.

For the work that I did carelessly;

For the work that I have left half-finished;

For the work that I haven't even begun, forgive me Lord,
And help me build a bridge!

For the people I have hurt, disappointed, or ignored;
For the people I have failed when they needed me most,
Forgive me Lord, and help me build a bridge!

For the friends to whom I have been disloyal;
For the loved ones to whom I have been untrue;
For the promises I have broken and the vows I have
    forgotten,
Forgive me Lord, and help me build a bridge!

For the way I have been disloyal to you;
For the way in which I have grieved you;
For my failure to love you as you have always loved me,
Forgive me Lord, and help me build a bridge! Amen

"Should I use a pen or the felt marker?" Annie's
question was seeking instructions for their task. "I know
no one else will see it, and you did say it was just for me
to do. Is there a right way?" Her frustration grew out of a
desire to do the task well.

They had shared a fine dinner at the Winchester
restaurant, which commanded a marvelous vista of the
marina and surrounding bay. They watched the towering
clouds to the west begin to reflect the hues of sunset,
pink and purple.

The plan for the evening was finally clear. Upon some brown paper lunch sacks, they had agreed to write down any situation in their life they felt might be described as an abyss, separating them from God. With a small amount of sand in the bottom of the sack, and a small votive candle lighted inside it, their "confession" could be floated into the ebbing tide. The skipper had found enough candles for them to each have eight.

"I'm sort of repeating myself now. Do you think I just don't have enough to confess?" His nervous laugh told the others that Bruce was still working on the process.

"If it's the right one, Bud, you can say it as often as you need to. Once is enough, if you believe it is really gone." The skipper had finished his sacks, and watched Annie ponder just the right words to write on hers. "It's going to be pretty dark soon. Let's remember to take along the flashlights, and plenty of matches." Seeing that she was finished, he added, "Better bring along a warm jacket too."

From the marina parking lot, they found the country road that circled the bay. After a couple of blocks, walking in silence, they came to an old boat yard at an intersection. "I think if we turn here, we'll get to that point we could see from the boat. A long time ago there must have been a house there. Some sort of apple tree is still there." They trudged on in the gathering twilight.

"This is so cool!" Bruce's enthusiasm was genuine. "The reflecting lights from the boats and the marina are gorgeous!"

"This has been a very different day," Annie mused. "This has got to be the beautiful part of it!"

"O.K. guys, if you'll put a couple of handfuls of sand in your sacks, you can then put a lighted candle in. Be careful not to burn yourself." The skipper watched them begin the process. "Tip the sack just a little," he said to Annie, "but not enough to catch the paper on fire. That's it, right in the middle." When it seemed they were well filled, he added, "Now give the top of the sack a little crimp to close it, and see if it'll float."

Bruce was the first to set his sack on the water. It tipped slightly, but rested on the water's surface. "Hey, it really works!" He reached for another.

One by one the luminaries bobbed on the smooth bay. There was the barest breath of wind easing them from the shore's edge. The three stood pensive as they watched their tiny fleet add to the reflected lights of the bay. Several minutes passed in silence.

"Do we need a prayer, asking God to heal our hurts and forgive our brokenness?" the skipper asked quietly.

Annie's voice was as soft as a sigh. "I've been doing that since I lit the first candle." Bruce whispered behind her, "Me too." They continued to watch the slow progress of their offerings, now blended into a loose blanket of light twenty or thirty meters offshore.

Suddenly, one of the paper sacks ignited from the heat of the candle. The flame ate away at the paper bag until there was no buoyancy left to float the sand. As suddenly as it had flared, it sank from sight, a tiny wisp of steam marking its demise.

"Oh dear," Annie gasped. "Is that supposed to happen?"

As the skipper started to explain that the crimp at the top of the sack was supposed to hold in the heat until that very thing could happen, another sack flared into a bright flame, then as quickly, disappeared.

"Annie, do you believe it is gone?" The skipper's question was not about the paper sack, but about the words she had written on her sack. "Do you believe it is finally gone?"

A voice, tiny with emotion, and laced with tears answered, "I do now." Another sack flared into flame, and then two more. For nearly an hour they stood by the old apple tree on the point looking out into a dark bay as one by one the paper sacks flared and sank. The remaining three that did not ignite, reached a choppy part of the bay where they tipped over, lost their buoyancy and sank quietly into the night. The three made their way back to the boat, holding onto the silence as though it were a mantle of grace. The work of mercy was underway!

Annie's notebook: I believe it, I really do! I believe that the nasty thoughts I've had about the past, my mistakes, my desperation, depression, anger, the whole thing, is over! I don't have to think about myself as evil anymore! Tonight, I feel a deep sense of relief. There is a holy stillness in me and around me that I have never known!

Maybe the darkness was necessary for me to have this light. Maybe the ugly was necessary to find such beauty. I don't know. I am so much happier tonight than I ever dreamed possible. Thank you, thank you, thank you God!

Bruce's notebook:

Norm's notebook:

When the things we plan, turn out so much better than we could have hoped, there must be a higher power at work. When we are taken further than we ever thought about going, a higher guide must be at work. Tonight I am thrilled that my son is using me to build a bridge for their future. I am exonerated from some of the feelings of abandonment or neglect that he has received in the past. If the subject is second chances, I feel like I have found a wonderful reason to be glad. Tonight, I am a happy man!

These feelings remind me of the thrill I knew early in my ministry, when satisfaction and wonder were not ever far away. Being so involved with the development of these two precious people has ignited a distant flame, and reawakened a melody I remember. Tonight, I am a very happy man.

The page was concluded with a rude sketch of a sunrise peeking over a wooded hillside.

There was an additional entry in Norm's notebook before the lights of *Dreamer* were extinguished for the night:

Gracious Lord, I feel a deep sense of your peace tonight. I think we all do. I ask that you help us now move into living in that peace. Help us rid ourselves of the bitter and angry spirit as you have washed us in your peace. We can control our temper and our tongue. We can nourish no grudge within our hearts, and no memory of injury within our minds. Grant that true brotherly and sisterly love may banish any resentment.

Lord, give us this night, the peace that passes understanding. Take from us the worries that distract us and help us trust more. Take from us the doubts, which disturb us, and help us feel sure of what we believe. Take from us the wrong desires from which our temptations come, and help us become truly pure in heart. Take from us the false ambitions, which drive us, help us find a fresh contentment in serving you where we are, and as we are. Tonight, we have no sense of the estranging abyss, just a peaceful bridge. You have forgiven us! Thank you. Amen. Amen. Amen!

Bruce carefully slid the hatch cover open, finding, to his surprise, the skipper already enjoying a glass of iced tea. He whispered, "Wow, I thought I'd be the first one up this morning." Looking out at the mirror-smooth bay he added, "There's not a ripple on the water. I slept as solid as a rock. How about you?"

"Like a baby. But I did spend some time thinking about that beautiful scene last night. I've never seen anything quite so memorable."

Bruce was nodding in agreement. "Did you know they were going to burst into flames like that? It was really dramatic."

"No, I had no idea how it was going to work. Annie jumped when the first one caught fire." He smiled as he remembered the moment. "I did feel like it was definite that something special happened though. How about you?"

"Dad," Bruce chose his words carefully, "I can't remember a time when everything seemed to fit together so well. I feel like we've been to church, or to church camp, or... I don't know. I just feel like a new person this morning. And it is for sure more than just a good night's rest!"

"Yeah, me too." The skipper's warm smile was only a reflection of the affection he felt for his son. "Is Annie up? I don't want to make a bunch of noise if she's still under the covers."

"I haven't heard anything from her yet. She was pretty moved last night. I think she wrote in her notebook for a while." Looking up the dock, he went on. "I'm thinking I'd like to go for a short run, work off some of this excess energy. Want to go along?" A wide smile demonstrated his sincerity. "Do you good!"

"You enjoy a run, and I'll finish this chapter. I've got to stay a page or two ahead of you guys if I'm going to be any sort of a teacher today." He laughed, suggesting that there was little possibility in staying ahead of them.

Bruce was already on the dock, quietly making his way toward the marina office. He crossed the parking lot, paused to stretch, and turned left, following last night's path. Little did he know that he was headed for the next chapter in his healing process. He set out at a brisk jog.

Approaching the intersection that led down to the point, he heard loud voices, angry voices. "Git the hell off my porch, you hippie sons-a-bitches!" Bruce turned toward the voices. They were coming from the old boatyard on the far corner. "This ain't a Go'dammed bus stop! Now go on, beat it you bums!" Bruce hurried across the gravel parking lot toward a run-down building with a big porch, and several milling people.

"We've been waiting for the bus here for years. We're not doin' anything to hurt you, old man," one of the surly young men growled.

"This ain't no public bus stop for you punks! It's my house! Now beat it, or I'll call the sheriff! Git the hell out of here!" It was obvious this could be ugly in just a second.

Bruce kept running right up to the porch, stopping only when he was between the cluster of youth and the angry man, who stood defiantly in bib overalls, with no shirt or shoes.

"Hey, hold on a second," he said, surprised at how calm his voice sounded when his heart was beating so fast. "Hey, wait a minute. Can I help you guys settle this a little?" He was just trying to keep the confrontation from turning violent. He noticed that the old man had a large club in his hand, ready to wage havoc on the unwanted kids. "Let's talk about this, what do you say?" He moved a bit closer to the man on the porch.

"Go' damn um!" the tirade continued. "They make noise with their boxes, and leave a pile of trash for me to clean up. I've put up with it for years! I'm sick and damned tired of them here every morning." At least he was talking about the kids, rather than shouting at them.

One of the youths, dressed in jeans and a blue and green jacket with a sports logo on it, answered angrily. "We've been waiting here for the bus as long as I've been going to high school. There isn't any other place to get out of the rain." His defiance was mirrored in the glares coming from the other youth gathered nearby.

For just a heartbeat, Bruce wondered why he was even getting involved in this argument. No one had asked him to mediate the problem. But since he was already this far into it…. He turned toward the group of high schoolers, "It's not raining this morning. Maybe you all could wait out by the corner, until the bus comes, and he can chill a bit. O.K.?" It was the suggestion of an action plan that allowed both parties to move away from the confrontation. "Let me talk to him for a second, O.K.?" The youth at the back of the group began to ease away, toward the corner, grateful for an escape route.

Bruce stepped up on the porch, beside the old man. Putting his hand on the bare back, he suggested, "How about us going inside? I'll bet you're cold out here with no shoes. It's pretty chilly this morning." He was applying just a gentle nudge to get the old fellow headed for the open door. With only a glance at the troublemakers who were nearly out to the corner, the old man went into his warm kitchen. There in just a few minutes he shared a story of loneliness and emptiness that had robbed him of the dreams he had when he and the boatyard had been young.

His name was J. J. Johnson he told Bruce. He had been assigned as a U.S. Navy yeoman to be an information liaison to the Australian navy. On his way home he had enough leave time to spend a week in Fiji, where he met a lovely young woman, and with her family had discovered a joy of tropical simplicity. The memory of glorious clear blue water, sandy beaches, towering sunsets, and a myriad of colorful fish, exotic food and fruit, held him spellbound. He wasn't sure if he wanted to marry her, but his heart was aching when he had to continue his journey back to the U.S. He vowed that he would return to Fiji, and her. Then, after he was discharged, he had found this boatyard, had promised himself that he would just get himself financially established before he went back. That had been almost fifty years ago. He had never been married, never gone back to the South Pacific, never really established the boatyard. It was a sad tale of a disillusioned life. Bruce listened carefully, as the story unfolded.

"I need to go out and talk to the kids, if they are still waiting," he told the man who now seemed soft and weary. "But I'll be back in, if that's O.K." He hurried out to the cluster of youth, still standing beside the road.

As Bruce approached them, there was a guarded wariness. "Hey guys, I'm sorry for all that swearing." He was looking at the young man who had been the object of the tirade. "I'm on a sailboat at the dock, and we're about to leave. Could I get your mailing address? I'd like to share the story he just told me. I think it would be pretty easy for you guys to help him allow you to wait for the bus…on his porch. We just don't have enough time this morning. O.K?" He thought he could make out the sound of the approaching bus.

"Yeah, I guess. I don't want any more trouble, though. What an old…." He was pulling a piece of notebook paper from his backpack. He scribbled, "Matt Evans, 449 Saratoga Rd. Orcas Is, WA 98280." Then he added, "I've got email if you want. That could be easier. Mattdog449@msn.com." As he gave the paper to Bruce he said, "Thanks for the save. I really thought the old geezer was going to come after us this morning. Usually he just yells from inside." The bus rounded the corner and with flashing lights, opened its doors for the students. "Thanks, you did good!" and they climbed aboard. The episode had lasted less time than a modest jog around the point. But for Bruce it had epic meaning. He went back to the house where he told the man that they were sorry for causing him any distress, and had apologized. He said that he would write a note to them all, just to stay in touch. As he left, Bruce grinned, "Who knows maybe I'll send you a Christmas card."

"That'd be nice," the wrinkled old face grinned back. "Don't think I have got one of those for a long time." He gave Bruce a wave and closed the door.

Bruce decided to finish the run that he had started, even though several minutes had gone by in the interlude. He picked up his pace all the way out to the apple tree point, paused just long enough to admire the tranquil morning, the reflections that still wanted to spin and dance on the water's surface like children in a playground. Then with purpose, he sprinted back toward the marina. He had an adventure to share with Annie…and his dad.

"I couldn't believe how calm I felt!" Bruce had given a full account of the episode. "It was as if I were just with some friends who were messing around. I didn't feel any panic, or danger, or anger. In fact, I felt more worried for the students than anything. I really thought that old guy might whack them with that club. It was amazing." He was still warm from the brisk run, as well as the encounter.

Bruce asked the skipper, "Are we planning to leave soon? I've got a letter chore that I'd like to do before we push off."

Looking at his watch, the skipper quipped, "What time is it now? Oh yeah, it's Monday." Annie giggled. "I think we have as much time as you need. Remember we are now on island time, which is a bit more laid back than standard." Then after just a moment he added, "I've had a shower, but Annie said she'd like breakfast before she goes up. You know," he arched his eyebrows, "with hair drying and all." He paused to get back onto the subject. "She did go up to the store for some killer cinnamon rolls, though. They might get us through the major hunger." The day was underway with purpose and discovery, and they hadn't even left the dock!

Bruce asked, "Did you say we were going to be in Roche Harbor tonight?" When his dad nodded, he asked further, "What does that take, a couple of hours?"

"If we have a favorable tide, no longer than that. It's only seven or eight miles. I think we can stay on the diesel if we get into heavy tide in the channel." The skipper was looking at the chart book. "It is almost low slack, so we have quite a bit of leisure this morning."

With a grateful sigh, Bruce replied, "I don't want to hold us up, but I really would like to scribble a couple of notes that I can mail at the store. I think it would be good for them to get the letters as soon as possible. Also, I feel really motivated this morning, and I don't want to lose this opportunity." He was headed below toward his notebook, and breakfast.

The two letters were hurriedly written:

"Dear Matt,

Hey, it was great to meet you. I had a chance to talk to Mr. Johnson, the boat yard owner. I think you might like to get to know him too, when he doesn't have that stick in his hand. He's a pretty lonely old guy, with no family around, never had kids. I don't think he's as grouchy as he was scared. He was in the Navy, and really would love to see those old days again.

If I could make a suggestion to you guys, I think there is a way that you could ingratiate yourselves pretty easy. If you would stop by after school some day, you could tell him you are sorry for bothering him. You could make a deal with him. You guys could clean up the porch area, maybe rake the gravel, and make it look neat. I'll bet he would be happy to have you wait on the porch for the bus.

I'd like to see you again, and really get to know you. I hope the future is more pleasant than this morning. I'm sure there is a happy conclusion to this story, if we just look at it in a new way. I'll be thinking positive thoughts for you. Best wishes to you all.

Bruce O'Banyon"

"Dear Mr. Johnson,

Thank you for the cup of tea in your cozy kitchen. I'm glad we had a chance to talk about those school kids. I've taken the liberty to write them, and suggest that they come by the boat yard to apologize to you. They might even have a suggestion or two about how they could earn the privilege of waiting for the bus out of the rain. But that, of course, is up to you.

I'd like to stay in touch with you, even though I don't know when I'll have a chance to be back on Orcas Island. I sure like it here. I'll be keeping you in my prayers. I know the future can hold some great things. Yours cordially, Bruce O'Banyon"

When Bruce dropped the letters in the mail drop at the store, he had an abiding sense of well-being. He felt more at peace than he had for a long time.

(*Addendum one:* subsequent communication with Matt Evans:)

Email 05/22/05: "Good morning Matt. We just got back to Seattle. Wow, was that a good trip! I'm glad we had a chance to meet, and hope that everything is O.K. with the boat yard. Did you ever go back to talk to Mr. Johnson? Tell me, what's a Mattdog? Hope to hear from you. Bruce O'"

Reply 5/22/05: "Dear Mr. O'Banyon. Great to hear from you, too! You're not going to believe all the stuff that has happened in just a week! It is so cool! I took your advice and went over right after school, told him I was real sorry, asked him if I could make it up by cleaning up, getting rid of the trash and stuff. My mom said that would be the right thing to do, too. He acted pretty mean, but you were right, he really isn't. I told my dad about him and I think there are some parents going over to the yard next Sat. They're going to do a work party or something. Bottom line is, we get to wait on the porch, and he's even kind of nice to us. Thanks for all your help. You really did good! I'll keep you hooked up with the news. See ya'

p.s. "Mattdog" is a name I got in computer lab at school. My teacher gave it to me, said when it came to a problem, I'm like a dog with a bone. I just won't give up until it's worked out. I like it.

Mattdog Evans."

Email 5/31/05: Mr. O'Banyon, you are going to be so pleased! Tons of stuff happened this weekend at the boat yard. Several parents went over there last Saturday for a work party. They said it was to clean and paint the front porch, so we could use it for a bus stop. I think it was bigger than that. At least that's how it turned out.

My dad has been out of work since the ferry started selling round trip tickets from Anacortes. He worked the ticket booth here on the island. When his job went away there just wasn't much else for him to do. He tried to work at a couple restaurants, serving. Anyway, when he went over to the yard he talked to Mr. Johnson for a long time. Then yesterday some of the dads went back. It was a holiday. Dad took an old T.V. and a VCR and a bunch of videos from the South Pacific for him to watch. The dads are cleaning up the boatyard. I think they're going to reopen it as a launch and a haul-out for bigger boats. I'll keep you posted. You were right! Things are working out better than I ever supposed they could. You sure did good!!! Your friend, Matt Evans"

Email 6/16/05: "Hi Matt. How's it going on the island? I thought you might be interested in a program we have here at Microsoft. Promising high school students are invited to shadow several of our people here. It's a great way to learn what's available in the way of career paths. It is also a step up in the career development program we offer for college scholarships. If you're interested, I'd be happy to be your sponsor. We could spend the day together. I'll show you around. It doesn't happen until September. But applications are coming in now, and space is limited. Let me know soon if I can save a spot for you. How's Mr. Johnson? I'm still thinking about you all. Bruce O'"

Reply 6/17/05: "Wow, that is great! Of course I would love to visit Microsoft! That's like the mother lode, the source. Didn't all life start there? What do I need to do?

The other great news is that dad is working with Mr. Johnson. I think they are partners in the boatyard. I don't know exactly how, but dad is going to own it someday. He said it was like working shares, or cropping, something. Anyway it's really cool. The place is looking really neat, and there is more business than anyone expected. Dad is really proud, and happy. It is so good to see! Do you think you could come up to the island for a visit? It would be awesome!

Your friend, Matt E"

The three sat in the cockpit, fresh cups of tea still steaming. The diesel rumbled below the deck plate, a sure sign they were about to get underway.

"I think last night was what Dr. Schimmel called the 'uncover stage.' It is the moment we acknowledge that we have hurt or been hurt by another." Annie seemed content in her new understanding of last night's luminaries. "I've always had the wrong idea about confession. I thought it had to do with finally saying that I was sorry for some action. I thought I had to tell someone, maybe a priest, probably God. Now, I know I had to tell myself where and why the hurt was, so that God could help me get past it, or beyond it." A warm smile had been on her face all morning.

"I'm sure some preacher somewhere has said, 'If you will name it, you can tame it.'" The skipper's humor was an effort to add understanding to the conversation. "We just won't give any effort to something we don't see as a problem. But once we identify the rascal, we are free to do something about it."

Bruce was quick to say, "I'm just glad we didn't have to use one of those tiny rooms and a priest behind a screen."

"Bud, there is a host of folks who believe that form of confession is the most direct way to the bridge. The priest is their guide." Looking at Annie, he added, "There are also a lot of folks who find it an obstacle to their bridges. What we did last night was the important first step. We identified our injuries, and we did something positive about them."

Annie's voice was soft and warm. "We turned them into lights." It was still a beautiful memory, and a lovely concept: injuries into heavenly lights.

The skipper tried to sum up their experience. "I think what we did last night was consider the possibility that we had other options, or alternatives, rather than simply dragging those painful memories with us, wherever we go. We can be free from them finally!"

Since the boatyard incident, Bruce's attitude had been very positive. Now, however, he asked a question that sounded like the day-before-yesterday-Bruce. "How can I know that anything really changed with those candles?" His smile was not completely gone.

"Bud, the only way I can answer that is you can never 'know.' You can be convinced by a change in your behavior, however. You can feel a forgiven attitude toward yourself or others. And I think I've seen that this morning. I think you can develop a strong faith that acts forgiven. When you think about it, that's a lot to expect!"

"Do you mean if I act forgiven, I am, and if I don't I'm not?" Bruce was puzzled, but the smile was still there.

"We are all in a learning place," the skipper replied, "but I am sure of this. As long as the wound in your spirit is untreated, it will stay raw, and feel as sensitive as a fresh wound, forever. When it is healed, you will have a sure clue in that there will be no more pain or discomfort there." He looked at Annie. "Does that make sense?"

"Yes, it does," she beamed. "And when you say, 'treated' do you mean we grieve it?"

"I think Kubler-Ross's steps have become classic to us. We deny, then bargain, then become angry, depressed, and finally arrive at acceptance, which is a state of recovery. Do you see those steps in the way you have treated your hurts?" The skipper wondered where he might be on that scale.

Annie seemed to have taken the lead in the conversation. "I do, or did, right up until last night. I think something happened out there on the bay that was larger than my efforts. I'm comfortable to say this morning that I became part of a holy process last night. I received something pretty special." Her head nodded vigorously as though she wanted to place an exclamation point on the sentence.

Bruce asked, "Would you think that this morning's encounter at the boatyard would qualify as different behavior for me?" He was pretty sure of the answer, just wanted them to confirm it for him.

"Brucie," Annie loved to call him that, "I think you were super this morning, maybe even heroic." When he shook his head at the compliment, she added, "How else would you describe moving into the middle of a squabble to be a peacemaker! That also sounds like really changed behavior to me. I'm so proud of you." Now he actually blushed. "Then, you really kept the contact going by writing letters to both of them. I think that is changed behavior."

The skipper reached over to ruffle his son's hair. "Yeah, me too," he said with a lot of affection. "I'm very proud of what you did this morning."

Looking out toward the open end of the bay, he continued, "We're well beyond low slack tide. I think this would be the right time to push off for Roche, if we're going to make it before supper."

Annie smiled wistfully, "I'm a little sorry to leave. This feels like a special place to me, now. I'll carry the memory of last night's candlelight for a long time."

Bruce nodded, "Me too. Maybe we can come back on the ferry, and spend some time at a campground, or a nearby bed and breakfast." He was making plans for the future.

"Anybody need anything else from the store?" the

skipper asked, bringing their conversation to an end temporarily. "Any last potty break for a couple of hours?" When both heads shook, indicating they were content for the time being, he said to Bruce, "Bud, if you'll take care of the bowline, I'll unhook us back here, and we'll be on our way. Let's make sure to wave to Brad on our way out." In just a moment or two, *Dreamer* was easing back, out of their slip, swinging around to face the open water at the front of the bay. It was a beautiful morning.

CHAPTER FOUR:
ROCHE HARBOR,
SAN JUAN ISLAND:
Identify the process of optimism

It was great to be underway again! The journey seemed more focused as they eased past Steep Point, the southwest tip of Orcas Island. Their course took them near Jones Island, out into the San Juan Channel, and directly toward Spieden Island, with its uncharacteristic dry brown slopes. The islands, which surround it, were lush green with spring growth.

"I'm not sure why it's so brown," the skipper explained. "Maybe it has little soil to nourish the grass, or maybe the island is too rocky for the rain to soak in. I just know that it is the easiest way to fix our location when we are passing through these islands. It always looks sort of barren." *Dreamer* was making great progress on the incoming tide under sail, with the crew sitting on the high side of the cockpit. Even Annie seemed comfortable with the morning ride.

"Maybe," Bruce quipped, "it is being punished for having a bad attitude." His big smile seemed more available since his boatyard adventure. "You know, they say you turn dry and wither up if you are grumpy for too long." His chuckle was another warm part of the morning.

"If that's the case," the skipper responded with delight, "we'd better have another round of tea with those oatmeal cookies! Nothing fixes my grumpiness quicker than those yummy things." It was a marvelous morning.

"I've been wondering," Annie smiled, knowing that she was changing the subject, hoping to continue the serious work they had started yesterday. "We spoke about some communication rules. I'm wondering if there are more. What other details should we be writing in our 'to do' books?" It was always fun for her to see how ready these two men were to join in a task.

The skipper's smile suggested that, indeed, there was considerably more to talk about. "Goodness, yes! We've just touched the surface of the exchange of information with words. Good communication happens in a variety of ways, verbal just being the most obvious. There is also the communication through your resources, you know, what you do with your checkbook. There is physical communication, touch, tenderness, or intimacy." Both Annie and Bruce exchanged a delighted wink. "There is, I guess," he went on, "a soul communication, as you two come to a decision about your spiritual life together."

Annie seemed to be the one interested in guiding the conversation. "I know we have a lot of work to do with our budget. But that seems pretty straightforward. I think that will take care of itself." Bruce nodded his head in agreement.

"I wish you were right," the skipper replied. "The truth of the matter is that there are more difficulties over a couple's money than you can imagine. More people split up over money problems than any other subject. They may think they are fighting about in-laws, kids, sex, or the color to paint the dining room. But it is really money problems that are the root of their worries." When he noted their frowns, he added, "Truly! Money in a marriage is power, and who controls the power is a struggle for most couples. You might want to put off the subject for a while, but make sure you spend some quality time coming to grips with all aspects of it. Really." He wasn't sure that either of them was hearing the importance he wanted to share.

"Well," Annie's smile suggested that the topic was about to change, "how about physical communication? Can you help us talk about that?" A playful smile radiated from them both.

"Sure I like to talk about sex!" The skipper wanted to join in their fun. "But I suspect that my son questions my ability to know much about the topic." When Bruce snorted his agreement, he continued. "Most folks have trouble thinking about their family members having intimacy, mothers, dads, daughters, or sons. We'd rather not think about it at all. Having put that aside, let me remind you there is a whole bunch more to physical communication than sex. Do you have your notebooks?" Annie pulled hers out from her jacket. Bruce went below for his.

Moments later the next step in their healing process began. "Remember, in a wholesome understanding of our physical communication, the underlying questions must always be, 'How can I honor my spouse?'" He watched as both wrote the sentence in their notebooks. "It's the same concept as a fair fight. If you are thinking about physical communication as a way of controlling the other, or prurient interest, lewd opportunity, even simply being entertained yourself, it's a misuse of the most precious gift you'll ever have."

"Think of the ways you can honor the other by taking maximum care of yourself, first. What can you do to improve your physical self?" The skipper paused to collect the next questions. "For example, can you get more regular exercise? Write it down if you think you can. How about a better, or a balanced diet, what would that take? How about drinking more water? I don't want to sound like a nag, but how about alcohol, how much is too much? Do you get the right amount of rest, at the right time? Are there any harmful habits?" The skipper was watching them write busily. "How can you take better care of yourself?"

"The next item is, Do you appreciate your own body? Is there anything that you would like to change, hair color or style, facial hair?" Annie grinned hugely. "Then," he paused to make sure they were ready, "Do you appreciate your partner's body. Anything you would suggest changing?"

The steady breeze out of the south was moving them briskly along their track. Ahead was the point that marked Spieden Channel. They were making great progress.

The skipper's smile was an attempt to put them at ease, as well as himself. "I am not implying anything by this next question. It's one I ask all premarital couples. Will you rate yourself, from one to ten on your sexual relationship? How pleased are you with the touching, tenderness, excitement of your relationship? If you will compare numbers, it will give you a sense of your comfort zone, and the area of agreement or difference in your perceptions. How would you rate your ability to talk about sex, including hang-ups, desires or fantasies? How about your taboos, can you talk about fears?"

"There are a couple more items I can think of, if you want to go on." Annie's curls bobbed as she nodded quickly. "O.K. From one to ten, rate your comfort in knowing details about your partner's sexual history." They both looked up, a little startled. "I know those details may feel very private, or very past. The question is how comfortable are you in not knowing?"

Dreamer had stayed on one steady course since they cleared Jones Island on the east side of the San Juan Channel. The wind and tide remained steady.

"This last one may seem automatic. It is vital to share, however. Rate yourself from one to ten on your acceptance of the principle of absolute fidelity in your sexual relationship as an underlying basis for a maximum relationship. What constitutes an infidelity? If you have close friends, what are the acceptable limits of physical contact, or emotional involvement?"

When Bruce looked up with a questioning look, suggesting that the matter needed some clarification, the skipper added, "How much interaction with another person constitutes infidelity? Office contacts may grow into romances; touches, or hugs between friends become more welcome, more intimate. It doesn't take intercourse to commit infidelity. Remember, Jesus said if a person only looks with lust at another, that's adultery. Where is the line, in your view?"

Looking nervously at Annie, Bruce was the first to speak. "Wow. That seems pretty strict. I'm not sure that anyone could get through without breaking that rule." Annie was nodding in understanding, but not agreement.

"That's right," the skipper continued. "The question is one of degree. Where is the line? Some cultures require women to cover themselves from head to toe, so that no improper conduct occurs. The other extreme is the clothing optional beaches of Europe that suggest a far more relaxed standard."

"You are saying, "Annie had a look of confident understanding, "it is a point we need to talk about and reach a clear agreement, not that there is any specific rule." Once again her curls bobbed in emphasis.

"That's what we've been looking at for the past hour: how well you can communicate in a variety of ways." The skipper was peering ahead. Coming into view at the far end of the island was a distinctive landmark.

"Do you see that battleship ahead of us?" he asked with a smile. Both Bruce and Annie spun to stare along their course.

After a moment, Bruce answered, "I remember! There's a big rock just outside of Roche Harbor that looks like a ship." Pointing a couple degrees off the port bow, he asked, "Is that it?" Annie squinted to see more clearly.

"Do you mean that we are already at Roche Harbor?" Annie asked with surprise. "I thought it'd be hours before we got in."

"Time flies when we're havin' fun," Bruce quipped. Looking at his dad, he asked, "Should I be doing anything to get us ready? Are we going to anchor, or dock?" He wanted to show that indeed he was a willing crewman.

The skipper answered, "It's been a while since you've been here. Where we used to anchor is now filled with a long dock, and dozens of moorings slips. I'm positive there will be room for us on the dock. As long as this breeze holds, and we're still riding the flood, we'll keep the sails up for another ten or fifteen minutes." He eased the wheel to bring *Dreamer* more onto the south side of the channel, out of the light tidal chop. "You can check the mooring lines, and bumpers. Let's set up for a portside tie-up. That way we have a 50% chance of being right." As Bruce moved forward to the task, the skipper called out, "I'll get the stern line back here. Just make sure we have the long line on the bow." It was definitely more fun to sail with a crew!

By the time they were in the inner harbor there was only a breath of wind on the glassy-smooth water, and the bright sun was warm on their skin. The sails were snugly secure, and they could also see that only about a quarter of the dock space was filled. Lots of room!

"Oh wow! I've forgotten how picturesque this place is!" Bruce declared with appreciation. The De Haro Hotel stood at the top of the docks, like a weathered sailor, in from the sea. Beside it the green and white restaurant, adorned with deck tables and umbrellas, was more than a little inviting. A bit further, along a narrow path from the hotel, a small white chapel with a stately steeple stood in the afternoon shadows. "This looks like a beautiful painting!"

Annie giggled. "Do you think a painting is better than the real thing?" They each appreciated the beauty of the port of call.

When they were securely tied up, with lines all ship-shape, Annie asked a question that would lead to a whole afternoon of conversation. "It seems to me," she looked at the skipper, "that you try to have a very optimistic attitude all the time. You've been up all the time I've been with you. How does that work? I think I have up days, but just about as many challenging ones."

"Great question, Annie." The skipper looked up the dock. "I've been thinking about a cheeseburger at the De Haro Hotel deck. I'll buy, this time. Maybe we can talk about it there, O.K.?" Bruce was already reaching for his jacket, obviously in agreement.

The burgers were served with frosty mugs of Redhook ale. Annie had iced tea. There were only two other tables in use. They had plenty of time to explore the question Annie had raised.

The skipper began by pointing out that almost everything is a choice. When we are born, our culture, family, ethnic roots may be determined, but almost everything else is a matter of choice. "I was in seminary with a professor who stated that he chose to be a pessimist, and who prided himself that he was frequently disappointed by people around him. When I considered his statement I realized that this is a faith-based issue. It takes about the same effort, and the same strategy to be either an optimist or a pessimist, neither is automatic to a certain status, or station in life. The difference is that one is based on a belief in something, and the other is not." He studied his listeners to make sure they were with him. "Pessimists may sound tough-minded and hard, but when life deals them a harsh blow, as it almost always does, they crumple and fold because there is nothing to support them. Optimists are sometimes called Pollyanna, but my experience is they are also very aware they live in an imperfect world in which love ends, innocent people are cheated and sick people die. But, because they have a strong interior belief system at work, when setbacks or disasters happen, tough–minded optimists call them just that: setbacks, disasters or tragedies. They don't try to hide from them or explain them away. They deal with the challenge."

"Winston Churchill is a perfect example of what I'm trying to say. A year into the last century, when he was just 26 years old, he spoke in the House of Commons, making his inaugural address. He was too young to have the respect of seasoned politicians, too skilled not to receive envious criticism from the younger ones. They called him the 'Blenheim Rat'. But 38 years later, when Great Britain was on the verge of defeat, King George VI asked Churchill to form a new government. The oldest head of state in Europe answered that he had nothing to offer but 'blood, toil, tears and sweat'."

Bruce acknowledged, "Blood, sweat, and tears! I've

heard of them!" A crooked smile wrinkled his face. Annie nudged him in the ribs, "Funny! Now listen!"

"O.K. so not everybody gets asked to be the head of state." The skipper continued. "But tough demanding times do come to us, everyone. How we choose to meet them is up to us." When his listeners just looked back at him, he said, "The optimist thinks of himself in terms of a problem solver; the pessimist sees himself as a victim. The optimist looks for multiple options; the pessimist sees none. The optimist anticipates problems; they surprise the pessimist. The optimist talks freely about negative feelings and then finds healthy ways to manage them. The pessimist only denies having those feelings. The optimist looks for the good in bad situations, while the pessimist is only confirmed that bad situations are happening. Optimists avoid phony pep talks. Pessimists avoid pep talks all together. Looking at those six characteristics, both styles require about the same effort, and the same, albeit opposite, strategies."

Bruce had been waiting for a chance to ask, "What do you mean by an optimist is a problem solver? Don't they just look beyond problems?"

"Not on your life, Bud. I read an article that said good managers are not failure oriented; they rely on synonyms like, 'glitch' or 'bungle' or 'error', or 'hard lesson,' rather than talk about failure. If they were optimistic managers, they would rather try 20 deals with a success rate of 75% than 10 deals with a 90% success rate. Think about it, the greater failure rate produces half again what the lesser rate does. But they don't focus on the failure. Rather, they see productivity. That's tough minded optimism."

"I don't know, dad. That starts to get a little fuzzy when you say that a higher failure rate can be more productive. I hate to fail! It makes me feel depressed." Bruce's levity was put aside as he shared a moment of vulnerability.

"You're right Bud. No one likes to fail, I imagine. But we all do, from time to time." The skipper was aware that the bells on the little chapel, just around the corner, were ringing the hour with a familiar hymn. "And failure hurts. Sometimes the only way out of a bad situation is through it. In other words, sometimes we simply must work through the bad situation in order to come to grips with it, and put it behind us." He silently remembered the words to the hymn: 'Oh what peace we often forfeit, oh what needless pain we bear...' He paused, listening to the melody. "The healthiest optimism does not come by blocking out our emotions. Rather, it comes by fully processing that suffering, by working our way through it. Sometimes depression is caused by swallowing some other emotion – the most common is grief or anger."

Annie nodded her understanding. "I've always thought of depression as major sadness."

"I don't think they are the same thing, Sweetie." The skipper's warm smile showed his new fondness for this delightful lady. "They look alike, and I think are often confused for one another; but, sadness and depression are really different. Depression is not so much a feeling of sadness as it is a reduction of feeling altogether."

Bruce said, "I'm not sure I follow that."

"Think about it a little. When you are depressed, you just feel empty, weak, or aimless. So the road to optimism is not to deny those negative emotions. It is first to accept them for what they are, and then to express them. Talking freely about your negative emotions is sometimes the first step toward overcoming sadness. It's a good way to get in touch with the power of optimism." The bells were just finishing the hymn.

"Is that what you meant when you said that optimists could look for the good in bad situations?" Annie asked.

"Yeah. Like most strategies, there is more than just an element of common sense in this. But when faced with a problem, many people do something of the reverse. They dwell on the negative aspect of it. They exaggerate the problem and make it appear to be even bigger than it is. The optimist knows that this is worse than useless. He doesn't deny the problem, but he turns his mind in a different direction, looking for the good in it."

Annie stayed with her question, "I'm still not sure that I follow all of that. I understand about focusing only on the negative, even making it bigger. Can you tell me about a positive focus?"

"I can remember a sermon illustration about a fire that destroyed Thomas Edison's laboratory. He was 67 years old, and had just lost $2 million worth of equipment and the records of his life's work. As he walked among the charred skeleton of so many hopes and dreams, he was anything but defeated. He said, 'There is great value in disaster. All our mistakes are burned up. Thank God, we can start anew.'" The skipper gazed at the calm harbor, his thoughts meandering toward the little chapel around the corner.

Several moments passed before Annie said, "I can see now how this connects with the topic we have been studying, you know, forgiveness. We get to start brand new. We get to move beyond the negative stuff, and really focus on what we can do with the future. Isn't that it?"

"That's it exactly." The skipper seemed almost distracted by a deeper thought. "Do you recall the words of the serenity prayer? AA uses the prayer almost like a motto. 'O God, grant us the serenity to accept what cannot be changed, the courage to change what can be changed, and the wisdom to know the difference.' We can focus on what we can do with the future. Isn't that what you asked, Annie?" The skipper wondered why he couldn't get the little chapel out of his thoughts.

Bruce wanted to be part of the conversation. He asked, "Dad, do you really believe that? It seems like you've done a fantastic job rebuilding your future. After being a pastor for so many years, I wasn't sure how you were going to be happy as anything else." Warm eyes looked at the skipper.

"I'm not so convinced about that fantastic job," the skipper replied with a bit of hesitation. He didn't know that he was about to take a major step toward recovery. "I'm also not too sure I should talk about the changes that have happened to me. I think there are some things we just shouldn't share with our family. I mean some burdens that they weren't meant to share." He looked fondly at both his young listeners.

"I've always believed in the truth of the stuff you've taught me," Bruce replied at once. "Weren't you the one who said that information is neutral? It's what we do with the information that gives it positive or negative value." Annie was nodding in agreement, although she was not completely sure that she understood.

Bruce asked the question that opened the door. "Do you still have some pain about the church?" A very long silence followed, lengthy enough for Bruce to begin rephrasing his question. "I mean, is there still..."

The skipper 's voice was as soft as a whisper. It was time to allow the truth to be spoken. "Yeah, I have considerable pain about the end of my marriage, and the end of my ministry. I've tried to cover up most of it, just pretend that everything is alright, but deep down I know that just doesn't work. In the marriage it was a lack of commitment. I was more in love with ministry than your mom. I knew that we were in trouble. I could see it disintegrating, but didn't do anything about it."

Taking a slow deep breath, he continued, "I think

my problems began when I made a commitment to the previous bishop, Bishop Taylor. He asked me to go to Issaquah, a new church start that was in trouble. The organizing pastor had begun well enough, but didn't have the vision, or strength, or leadership qualities to move the project along. I was ready for a substantial appointment after the years at Kelso."

Annie interrupted, "What's an appointment? It sounds like something more than a calendar date."

"That's a whole different conversation. Basically, when I was ordained in the United Methodist Church, I joined a regional conference, which is guided by a bishop, like a CEO. Each year, along with the cabinet of superintendents, he makes decisions about where the three hundred pastors in the area should best serve. At the annual meeting, called 'conference,' assignments, or appointments are announced where the pastors will be serving. About three quarters of them are effectively working in their assigned places, and so they remain there for another year. The other quarter, are ready to be reassigned, either because they have reached the end of their useful ability, are retirement age, or they have skills needed in some other situation. In the old days, many were transferred to new situations because they had bungled the ministry responsibilities. Does that make sense to you?"

Annie shrugged, not sure how to answer. She was about to ask another question when Bruce reached over to touch her shoulder. He didn't want to deflect the topic that had begun. "Which bishop made a deal with you?" He wanted to hear the rest of the story.

Again the skipper was still for a long pause. "Bishop Taylor asked me to go to Faith UMC in Issaquah. He said he was sure it was a place with amazing opportunities and challenge." A wry smile curled the skipper's lips. "He was surely right about that. I had the most dynamic seven years of my ministry. We did some simple changes to the original building, allowing a little more seating, and a much better worship setting. I made the stained glass windows and kneelers so it would look more like a chapel than the house it had been."

Annie looked at Bruce and mouthed "Kneeler?" He explained, "Where you kneel to receive communion." She nodded understanding, again.

"My agreement with Bishop Taylor was that I would remain there until the new facility was built and staffed. It was an exciting and very satisfying time. There was dynamic growth in the community, and it was reflected in exciting congregational growth. Ultimately we built the sanctuary with a gorgeous design for 1.6 million dollars. Bagpipers helped our expanded congregation march from the old chapel, singing all the way. It was great!"

Annie squinted her new puzzlement. "I don't understand what could be painful in that."

"No, not from that," the skipper continued, "But

from a lack of trust. The problem came in the form of some twisted thinking on my part. Because I had made an agreement with the bishop, I began to think I could make those appointment choices, at least for myself. When I asked the new bishop, who had replaced Bishop Taylor, for one last new appointment before retirement, I had the arrogance to think I could see the big picture." He had to take a deep breath to control his emotions; his chin trembled with the grief of memory. "I really thought I could be assigned to one of the two or three large churches that needed leadership. I quit relying on the Church or the Spirit." A tear traced down his cheek. "Instead, I wanted to make my own deal. The bishop had no knowledge of a promise made by his predecessor. He did know of my separated marital status. He also had some of his favorite candidates to advance." He paused again, considering how he could best tell them the rest.

"Finally, the bishop asked me to go to Walla Walla, a large old church, but one deeply divided by a racial conflict. Once again I would be going into a flawed situation. I asked him to pray about it. I was not inclined to leave family in the Seattle area, sell the boat, and rent the house. Your grandmother was there. She was 82 at the time, with failing health, and I was her only family left. I didn't want to be on the other side of the state for the next six or seven years. But most important, I failed to remember how God had been at work in all my situations, and how delighted I had been when I was simply obedient."

Bruce nodded his head in new understanding.

The skipper continued to speak in that soft voice, full of feeling. "I had said 'No' to the bishop, and worse, I had said, 'No' to my own faith. It's really pretty difficult to get more conflicted than that. By the next cabinet meeting, a new pastor had been invited to take my place at Faith, and those large churches were also assigned. There was something of a dilemma for them to place me. And, I had challenged the bishop's authority. It was a mess. In the final meeting of the year, they chose to assign me to Ocean Shores, a small mission situation, paying an entry-level salary, a third of what I had been receiving. In all that confusion, there were some folks in the church that took the opportunity to question my ethics and morality, like fighting a fire with gasoline. Many of my fellow pastors also understood the appointment as a form of punishment from the bishop." His stern face and another silence helped Bruce and Annie understand the source of his pain, if not the depth of it.

With a heavy sigh, he continued. "There is one other element. I had sold a big old sailboat to a young man. Do you remember *Rhumb Runner*?" Bruce shook his head. "It was a 62 foot masthead ketch I purchased to retire aboard. After fixing it up, I realized it was too big for me to single-hand. When I put it up for sale, the boat broker had convinced me to carry the sales contract, to collect that interest myself. It could be a nice moneymaker. For three years payments were made."

The next sentence was spoken with difficulty, his voice heavy with emotion. "The guy that bought the boat came into my office at Ocean Shores with a knife." Alarm flared on Bruce's face. "I always thought of myself as athletic, stronger than most. It took him less than five seconds to put me on the floor. My hand was still outstretched to shake his when the knife was at my throat."

Bruce growled, "Amy told me something about that, but I didn't know it was that bad."

"He really didn't want to hurt me badly, just scare me into releasing the boat contract to him. He poked and sliced my skin enough to terrify me, and threatened everyone else in the family. There wasn't anything for him to get just then, so he cut the phone wires, disabled my computer for some reason, and urinated on me. Then he fled." Tears of recollection brimmed the skipper's eyes.

Drawing in a deep breath, he finished the tale. "The good thing about Ocean Shores is there is only one road back out to Aberdeen. I suppose a smart crook would have plotted a back road exit. This guy was caught in Gray's Harbor, and plopped in jail. He did some time for aggravated assault, but he also got an attorney and said that I had started the altercation. The whole mess was very expensive. I had to be tested for hepatitis and HIV. I saw a post trauma stress counselor, and really couldn't stay in Ocean Shores. The bishop's office did not contact me once through the whole ordeal. My superintendent called once. I decided to get a real job, so I requested early retirement, and the bishop was glad to give it to me." The air on the hotel deck seemed still, and thick to breathe.

With this much of the story out, he wanted to finish the episode. "I was living on Dreamer, seeing the counselor, worrying about my finances. I needed a job. I drove a shuttle van for the Pro Club, and even tried the security graveyard shift at Microsoft. Some friends from Faith wanted to give me support. I could also help them through their transition to the new pastor, which wasn't going too smoothly. They invited me to teach a bible study on Sunday evenings, a general fellowship. For some strange reason, the new pastor took exception to our meeting, even though it was in a different community, miles away from Faith. He saw me as a threat. Before a month went by, the bishop was writing letters to the congregation, labeling my activity as 'unquestionably unethical and immoral'." A smile trembled on his lips. "If I was going to be burned at the stake, you'd think it would be for something more serious than a simple bible study group."

Bruce shook his head, "Unbelievable!" Annie just stared at the floor.

Eventually, I sold everything but *Dreamer,* paid off all my debts, got a job with Resolutions Inc. as a counselor. I listen to other people's troubles and try to write a practical solution. It feels pretty petty when I think about it. I've rented a condo on Queen Anne hill, so I am close to work and the boat. I'm O.K." The words were said without a lot of conviction.

"Dad, can't you appeal your situation to the new bishop. Wasn't there a change recently?" Bruce was trying to think of some constructive suggestion. "Isn't there a board or committee you can contact?"

"I was pretty vilified at annual conference, Bud. I think I was something folks could get righteously excited about, safely. I pretty much sunk my career with my willful decision not to be obedient. I did make an appointment with the new bishop, Bishop Calvin, to confess my willfulness or combativeness, and ask for his prayers."

"How did that go? He had to appreciate all the good years of service you had given. Didn't he?" Bruce was amazed that this entire episode had happened in his dad's life, without his knowledge.

"Well, he had read my service file, written by Bishop McCormick, his predecessor, and the one I had defied. I don't think he had much admiration invested in our conversation. He was polite, and I didn't ask for any reconsideration. I pretty much got what should be expected. If I chose the behavior, I really had to accept the consequences. My pride in thinking that I should have a larger assignment, my lack of reliance on the Holy Spirit, my disobedience in refusing the bishop's leadership, flew in the face of what it means to be a conference pastor. I blew it! I'm not saying that what I did negated the 34 years of ministry that went before it. But in some people's eyes, that's exactly what I did. When I quit, I traded a lot of honor for a load of shame, and I suppose, guilt." The skipper looked down at the deck, glad he had told them, but sorry they had to hear it.

Annie was the first one to break the silence. "But isn't that more like business than ethics? I mean, you didn't break a law, or hurt anyone else. You just didn't want to be transferred. That happens in business all the time. It's not unethical. At least it doesn't seem like it to me." She was trying to find some way to ease the tension she felt in the skipper.

"From the outside, I'd say, 'yes, you're right.' But from the inside, I betrayed my word, and the promises I made when I agreed to be a UM pastor." When Annie shook her head, not understanding what he had just said, he clarified. "When I became a United Methodist pastor, I made some holy promises, which I broke, intentionally. There were a lot of sweet friends that I let down." The more he spoke about the past situation, the more condemned he felt. "I think that is all about ethics."

The chapel bells began to chime the half-hour. They listened to the familiar hymn tune.

"Dad, I think this whole trip is about our futures." Bruce was surprised how clearly he was seeing a process before them, and how strong he felt about it. "First Annie, then me, now you, we are saying the same thing. There is something snagged in our past and we need to get beyond it. Didn't you say that we can't change the past, so we might as well learn to accept it? Isn't that what we've been doing for the past couple of days? I think it has to work for you, just like it is for us."

The chimes rang out the tune, "I once was lost but now am found. Was blind, but now I see." The words were almost too familiar. He found himself thinking about the exercise on the top of the park in Anacortes. Why had he omitted a letter to someone he had hurt? Did he really believe it, or was it just theory? Who would he identify as the recipient of his assault? A surge of sadness rippled through the skipper.

"You're kind to think along that line, Bud." The skipper's words were gentle to mask the turmoil of emotion he was feeling. "The truth is I pretty much got what I deserved, and I need to accept the fact, that part of my life is over."

"Yeah, over in that little part." When his dad looked up with what could have been the beginning of an angry response, Bruce added quickly, "I just mean that the United Methodist part is over. I'll bet there is a huge part of ministry that would welcome a guy with your talents and experience. In my world, there are headhunters eagerly trying to find guys like you that they can place in new jobs." He wanted to finish his thought. "I know you have felt huge loyalty to the United Methodist Church. I just think there is a much larger part of the church in general, one that you might not have considered as a new field of doing what you most love to do." His smile told the skipper that this young man, of whom he was completely proud, was offering ministry through a hard moment.

"That's just a very hard thought for me to get around," the skipper said slowly. "When my entire life has been founded on an exclusive truth, it's pretty tough to switch."

"Tough, yeah," Bruce continued, "But not impossible. I think of new companies all the time, even though I'm well cared for and happy where I am. I know there is a bigger picture."

"Bruce, I think you're right as rain." The skipper wanted to ease the moment. He was also aware of a growing realization. "If you guys want to go back to the boat, or take a walk up the hill, I'd like a bit of private time to visit that chapel. Do you mind?" He felt on the verge of a discovery. Some time in the chapel would be most welcome.

Bruce looked at Annie, "I don't mind taking a walk." She nodded in agreement and stood up to leave. "But dad, can you do in the chapel something that you haven't already done since the wheels fell off some time ago?" The last thing he wanted to do was sound argumentative.

"Yeah, I can!" There was a fresh strength in the skipper's voice. "I have been thinking about myself as a victim, in marriage, from the bishop, from the attacker, even from myself. I made some really bad decisions, and acted irresponsibly. That has been my focus. Didn't we just agree that an optimist is someone who has a strong inner belief system? I need to begin thinking of myself as someone who still has twenty or more years of service left to give, someone who can make, and keep commitments. It cannot be in the United Methodist Church. I do sincerely believe that bridge is burned. It might not even be in a church. But I haven't given it serious thought as a positive optimist. I'll wager there are a host of possibilities I haven't considered."

He stood up, stretching muscles that had stiffened in their long conversation. "I'll get the check, and see you back at the boat in an hour or so. O.K.?" He wasn't sure what the next few steps of the journey would hold, but the skipper was convinced that something truly important was in front of him. He found the path that led to the chapel.

A low cloud cover set in with the tide change. The evening was filled with muted shadows, and stillness. A pattern of the hotel lights was reflected on the calm water of the bay. Dinner conversation had been casual, as though they had not been through a major process during the afternoon. Annie wanted to tell about the Masonic structure they had discovered on a hiking trail, deep in the woods. Bruce reminisced about the first time they had visited Roche Harbor. He had been in the sixth grade. They were eager to hear about the skipper's afternoon, but unsure how to begin the subject.

Now, back aboard Dreamer, the teapot steaming on the stove, he began to share with them about his time alone.

"I'm not sure how old I was when I first felt the charm and warmth of the Church." He paused to capture a happy recollection.

"Was that the one you grew up attending?" Annie wanted to help him, as he had helped her remember tender moments from her past.

"There is an important distinction to make here," the skipper slipped back into his teaching mode. "The 'Church' spelled with a capital "C" refers to the whole, universal, sometimes called 'catholic' Church. It is the wonderful idea of Church that many call 'the Body of Christ.' Without the capital "C", church refers to a local parish, or a particular congregation."

Her gaze suggested that Annie might have a glimmer of his explanation, so the skipper continued. "Most of the major moments of my life took place in that sacred space. I was baptized as an infant, but I can still remember my confirmation, and my dedication as a young acolyte." When Annie looked at Bruce questioningly, he just whispered "Later." The skipper continued, "I remember the wonder of being called into ministry, ordination as a deacon, and then amidst colleagues and family, ordained elder. There was such splendor in annual conference meetings." Again Annie looked at Bruce for clarification. "Later." The skipper reminisced, "Wedding ceremonies, and services of baptism and holy communion were high and holy honors. The Church has been the singular place for major events in my life. It just seemed right for me to be there in prayer this afternoon."

Looking at each of their faces, he went on, softly. "You two have helped me focus on a process that I have been avoiding for quite a while. I was carrying a load of general guilt, and bad feelings. I felt like a victim and a villain at the same time. The only thing that could spring me free was a sense of total forgiveness. I knew that it wouldn't affect the consequences of my past, but relieve it to move ahead. I have wanted that but just didn't know how to take the step. At the same time I have been sidetracked by a sense of pride, feeling that I was above a need for spiritual healing. So I avoided the very thing that could get me off center. I needed a sense of forgiveness. Thank you both for being such good listeners, and supportive friends." His gaze embraced them both.

"What I realized this afternoon as we talked was that God loves me, has always loved me. God didn't need me perfect, adequate in every sense. In fact, God has loved me through every weakness and set-back, every foolish blunder and mistake, or should I say every painful lesson?" All three of them smiled.

"This afternoon, as we listened to the chimes ring "Amazing Grace," I realized that God has always loved me, which means I was loved before, during and after my ministerial debacle." Bruce flinched at the last word. "No, I mean it. God's love didn't stop because my ministry did.

God didn't love me less. In fact, as I was lost, there is every reason to believe the Good Shepherd cared more for me. Remember the story of the 99 sheep?" Bruce nodded his head, while Annie gave a small shrug.

"The conclusion I found on the hotel deck was that all the pieces for my forgiveness were in place... except for my honest acceptance of it. It was just up to me to believe it, and receive it. That's what I did in the chapel. I prayed that simple prayer from Jesus' parable." Again Annie shrugged and shook her head. She didn't know what parable he meant.

The skipper reached across to touch her knee in encouragement. "He said that one day two men went into the temple to pray. One was a Pharisee, a religious leader devoted and righteous, the other a tax collector." When Annie's questioning looked asked for more explanation, he added, "They were collaborators, working for the Romans, and considered 'sinners.'" She nodded her understanding so the skipper continued.

"The Pharisee stood and prayed a boastful prayer by himself, thanking God that he wasn't like other men, extortioners, adulterers, unjust, or even like this tax collector. He went on to list all his pious righteousness. The tax collector, on the other hand, would not even lift his eyes to heaven but sadly prayed, 'God be merciful to me a sinner.' Jesus said that it was that tax collector who went home justified... made right with God." The skipper had anticipated Annie's questioning look.

"For years, I have been caught up in the safety of theological discussion and the structure of the Church. I needed to be reminded that it's not that complicated. I needed to pray that simple prayer, and really mean it. 'God be merciful to me, a sinner.' Each word is like a note in a beautiful chord of music. 'God – be – merciful – to – me - a – sinner.'" Saying it slowly helped emphasize their importance. "There is my faith-base that will produce optimism in my future! " He had a wide and very believable smile.

Bruce wasn't exactly sure what to say, so he asked, "Do you think you can be back in the Church?"

The skipper shook his head in good nature. "I don't think the two are related in any way. I guess I might be open to the idea, but it doesn't matter. By accepting God's forgiveness, I have a real desire to just take the next step. I have a sense of peace, or a fresh contentment that knows that if I couldn't do anything to cause God to love me less, I don't have to do anything to make him love me more. In fact, there isn't more love than God has for us right now." A sense of stillness filled the boat.

Bruce was again the first to speak. "When you say 'take the next step,' what do you mean?"

"Golly, Bud, I'm not sure we have formulated the process, or perfected it. But it seems to me that the next step after accepting the fact that we are forgiven is starting to live like a forgiven person. As of today, I'd like to have a new attitude, wouldn't you?"

Bruce was already singing the tune to "I've got a new attitude!"

Annie finally spoke up. "Maybe that's why I've had such a happy feeling for the last couple of days. You helped me see beyond my bad feelings. I've got a new attitude, too!" Her smile was radiant.

The skipper chuckled, and continued with his thought. "I have always believed we are process people. We find structure in taking steps through a process. First we had brokenness or assault, then the pain of guilt, then the hope of healing, then the hope of forgiveness and recovery began, now I think we might talk about the idea of 'restitution.' That might be the next step in our process."

When he received two puzzled frowns, he explained. "Restitution is making some sort of repayment for the damage we have caused. It is a justice issue that tries to compensate the injured parties." When Bruce's frown deepened with a shake of his head, the skipper said, "I think we can talk about this more tomorrow. My suggestion comes from a new hymn of the church. The words are something like this." He sang in a soft baritone voice, "God forgave my sin in Jesus' name, I've been born again in Jesus' name, and in Jesus' name I come to you, to share his love as he told me to. He said, "Freely, freely, you have received, freely, freely give. Go in my name, and because you believe, others will know that I live."

It was pleasant to listen to him sing. After a moment

of reflection, Annie asked, "I'm real unclear about repayment. I wouldn't know who, or how to pay for my problem." She still had trouble speaking the word, 'abortion.' Bruce also added, "And I truly doubt if Sydney ever wants to hear from me again, let alone receive a payment for something I did." It was clear that this was a subject in need of more conversation.

The skipper added, "I'm not sure I want to cut a check to the United Methodist Church, either. I think there is a point here that we should explore. But let's save it for tomorrow." Rising to go into the galley, he asked, "Anyone else for another cup of tea?"

When both Bruce and Annie indicated they were satisfied, she asked, "Speaking of tomorrow, are we going to stay here, or move on? I sure like this place." Her emphatic head-nod punctuated her affirmation.

"We could stay right here," the skipper answered. "I'd like to see that Masonic shrine. We could do that early, and still ride the flood tide across the strait to Bedwell Harbor. That's on the Canadian side of the islands. They are called 'Gulf Islands,' and are only about eight miles from here. So we could find a late lunch in B.C., 'eh?" He tried to make his accent a bit comic.

Bruce was aware, once again, how delightfully this trip was evolving, almost as if it had been planned. "I'm up for anything. So far the trip has been much better than the Chamber of Commerce travel brochures promised." His smile was warm and especially grateful for his dad.

"If you're going to turn in, maybe we will walk back up to the hotel for a bit of hospitality. We'd love to have your company though." Annie joined in his smile.

"Thanks. I think I can use some time in my notebook, and an early bedtime. It feels like this has been an extra big day. Before you go would you like to share a prayer I found in the chapel? It's from Robert Schuller, entitled *Your Plan*. When they both settled back, earnestly welcoming the prayer, the skipper read, "I have come to you Lord, for a new lift, a new load, a new love, a new light on my life's road. I have a powerful, positive suspicion that you have a plan for my today and tomorrow, and that beautiful plan is unfolding exactly as it should! I will stop trying to understand, and instead start enjoying whatever comes my way! Amen."

The skipper concluded with a sigh, "That sort of sums up this day for me. I'll remember today for a long time, I guess even call it a milestone. Night Bruce. Night Annie."

Notebook entries were made by each member of the crew:

Annie wanted to try to find a way to emphasize the word 'accept.'

"We are asked to accept a gift that was given a long time ago for an emergency we are having today. I'm not sure how vast the gift might be, but I am sure that accepting it is a major step for me, too. I'm grateful for this chance to become the sort of woman I always hoped I could be."

A, always applaud; gratitude is the foundation to build upon.
C, change of behavior goes along with change of attitude.
C, care for those we have hurt, even, and especially, ourselves.
E, enthusiasm is the building supports.
P, prayer is the design for the new attitude
T, today is the only time to begin a new attitude future!

Bruce reflected upon the relationship he enjoyed with his dad:

"He has always been a hero to me. I have never thought about his weaknesses, just his strengths, never thought about his temptations, only his achievements. Today I saw a side of my father that shows his humanity. He has fears, and doubts just like the rest of us. He can be confused, wounded, lost, like anyone else. I'm not sure I have ever loved him more! It takes nothing away from his talents, gifts, or abilities. I think he is helping me see that I can be loved in spite of my mistakes, or lessons, as he likes to call them. This trip may have been our idea, but I think he is into it now more than I had thought possible. Wow! Who would have thought so much good could come out of a last minute, unplanned trip. I could almost believe there really is a big plan at work here."

The skipper started to write reflections of a theological nature. Once he opened his book, however, he wrote:

"Glory! Glory! Glory! Praises…. JOY, JOY, JOY! God is good! God is Joy! God is love! God is a forgiving, giving, giving, giving God! God is a joy-giving, heart-warming, life-changing, load-lifting, love-sharing God! I truly feel that there is a new attitude within me, a fresh sense of optimism, and a new faith center. GLORY, GLORY, GLORY! I have accepted God's forgiveness. Praises, Praises!"

He thumbed back through his notebook to day one, and the task assigned to the park above Cap Sante's marina, the one he had avoided. He wrote a letter to Bishop McCormick, someone he had hurt.

"Bishop Brian McCormick, good evening. Thank you for reading this much overdue letter. I am finally able to say, 'Please forgive me for causing you such a challenge.' I was seduced by the success of the Kelso church, and the beautiful accomplishment of the Faith sanctuary. I allowed myself to believe my own press reports, relying on results rather than the Spirit that produced them. Today the sadness I feel is not only the loss of conference trust and camaraderie, but also the failure to realize the plans God had for my ministry in the unfinished years."

"Your leadership was strong and singular in its

purpose to minister to the annual conference. I have confessed, and been forgiven, I believe, for my willful reliance on something less."

"I pray that you and your family are well and enjoying your retirement status. I can imagine that you are a frequent guest at Willamette's Tuesday morning chapel, walking the familiar grounds where our odyssey began. I treasure the memories that grew from such an ordinary seed.

My future is still being focused. Whether it is in a local parish or not is still unclear. I am sure that it will be realized in a revived and dynamic faithfulness, which I have come to see as a forgiven sinner.

I pray peace for your home, and for mine.

Norman O'Banyon

CHAPTER FIVE:
BEDWELL HARBOR, B.C.

Restitution is the action
of repentance

"First Officer O'Banyon" the title sounded like something from an old English sailing ship, as did the "Aye, Cap'n!" The skipper enjoyed the easy repartee' of the morning. "Hoist that main sail, and fetch the whisker pole from the bow. The wind's right for a bit of 'wing-on-wing' this morning." "Aye, Cap'n!" This time the reply came with a growling rattle like an old pirate. The large triangle of Dacron began to tremble its way up the mast.

"You guys are like a couple of little boys, playing pirates." Annie was curled into her corner of the cockpit, out of harm's way. "What's a wing and wing, and did you say whisky pole?" Her grin was light and amused, appropriate for the morning.

The crew had enjoyed a grand breakfast at the De Haro Hotel, strolled leisurely through the gardens. Even though it was too early for the roses, a few flowering baskets were valiantly offering color to the morning. A few lingering lilacs, with late tulips and daffodils still lined the walkway. They had made one last visit to the grocery store, and taken steaming cups of hot chocolate for their stroll down the dock to *Dreamer*.

Now, clear of the harbor, their course was going to take them around Stuart Island to South Pender, which was part of the British Columbia Gulf Islands. Battleship Rock was in their wake.

"It's just more boat terminology." The skipper was watching their progress as he pulled on the jib sheet, unfurling the headsail. "Wing-on-wing is the term when we set the main on one side of the centerline, and the jib on the other. We need some extra equipment to hold the jib out, so we hook a whisker (he emphasized the correct word) pole from the mast to the eye at the clew of the jib." When Annie flashed him a bewildered look, he clarified, "From the mast to the ring at the corner of the jib. That way, the jib can't flap around or collapse. Wing-on-wing is the most efficient way for us to sail down-wind without a big spinnaker. We just need to pay close attention to our course and the wind direction. It's fun to do." As he was explaining the process, the skipper was easing Dreamer's course more and more downwind. Finally, with the main out full on the starboard side, he told Bruce to hook the jib in while he pulled the port jib sheet to bring the sail to the other side. Their efforts were rewarded with a soft "thump" as the sail filled and held steady. The pole was set in the mast ring with a sharp "click."

The skipper asked, "Do you feel the drop in the wind?"

Annie was surprised to feel the calm in the cockpit. "How are we going? There isn't a bit of wind!" She held up her hand to try to find any breeze.

Bruce came back to the cockpit, having rolled up all lines and tidied up the deck. "It is relative, isn't it dad? We are going the same speed as the wind, so it feels like there is no wind."

The skipper smiled, not because the answer was correct, but because he like to hear Bruce call him "dad." "You are right as rain, Bud. The breeze is still fresh, but this is the most stable and easy direction to sail, straight downwind. We just need to mind our course, keeping that wind right into the sails." He knew he was repeating himself but the point could not be overstressed, especially if someone else was on the helm. "Anyone else want to drive?"

Annie squirmed because she thought it might be her turn. "I would if you are sure I won't get us into trouble."

Bruce was moving in to sit right beside her. "I'll help you watch. I'm glad to be your co-pilot."

"Deck officer Pearce has the helm!" the skipper called out in his old sailing ship voice. Everyone smiled. "O.K. Annie, your course is 300° on the compass, or on a straight line with the right edge of that distant island. You will need to keep a sharp watch, because we are also riding a strong flood tide." When she gave a mock alarmed look and would have stepped away from the wheel, the skipper assured her, "It means an in-coming tide. It is a stream of water coming from our port quarter (he pointed to the back left side) across to the starboard bow. If I have compensated for the tidal effect, we should slide right around the west end of Stuart Island. We'll just read our way, maybe give our course a bit more westerly. 'Oh, a sailor's life's for me, upon the rolling seas.'" The song was by now familiar, and far from tiresome. It made all three of them smile.

Even though Annie had the concept of steering down pat, her execution was a bit untrained. Twice she strayed from the course enough to allow the main to lose its effectiveness. The big sail simply went limp.

"Careful!" Bruce was immediately helping her get back on course. With a "thump" and a bit of a jolt, the main refilled with the breeze. He smiled and reassured her, "Every good helmsman is acquainted with the wind. Once I steered us into an accidental jibe." He wasn't sure she understood, but it seemed like a comforting thing to say.

"Just once?" the skipper broke in with mock surprise.

"I can remember a number of near knock-downs." When the ensuing argument seemed to be getting a bit loud, Annie simply said,

"'T won't 'appen again, sirs. I'll be a wee bit more careful, I will for sure." It was her turn to try the cockney accent.

Battleship Rock slid further and further aft as that familiar quiet held the crew. It truly was a gorgeous day.

Several minutes later, Annie broke the stillness with a question. "You said the course was 300° … right toward the edge of that island out there, didn't you?" When the skipper looked up from the pages he had been reading, she continued, "I'm steering more like 280° but I can't hold on the island. It's like I'm being pulled toward these rocks over here." Bruce and the skipper looked with a start. "I must be doing something wrong, huh?" True enough, *Dreamer* was getting dangerously close to the rocks at the west end of Stuart Island.

"Bud, if you'll go free the whisker -pole, I'll buy us a little more room." His voice was calm, but there was quick concern on his face. The skipper was moving toward the port winch. As soon as the latch was loose from the sail, he spun the jib sheet off the spool, and began retrieving the starboard sheet. The movement was smooth, but with the dispatch of urgency. "Now Annie if you will bring us to port, we'll see if we can avoid that collision." True alarm flashed over her face this time. He also took several turns on the mainsheet winch, tightening in the powerful sail. As the sheets were drawn taut, the boat began that familiar tilt, and turned away from danger.

Annie's voice was choked with panic. "Bruce, you take it, please....please!" The new course changed everything. Suddenly there was breeze, and motion, and a widening space from the rocks. Bruce reached over to the wheel without leaving his seat.

"Remember, hours of boredom, punctuated by moments of panic. We're O.K., really!" It was the best he could do to reassure her. Even though Dreamer's bow was pointed toward the center of the channel, her course was still northerly, as though they were skidding to the right.

The skipper explained, "We are feeling the effects of the tidal sweep. The in-coming tide is washing us around the end of Stuart Island."

Sure enough, as Annie watched, they eased around the threatening rocks, open water widening with each second. The crisis had lasted only moments. Yet she wondered how she had been so shaken by it. "I didn't even know I was getting us into trouble. It just happened so gradually." Her pale face was turned toward the skipper, as though in apology.

He smiled back at her, trying to comfort her anxiety. "You weren't very close to trouble. But it was good that you called our attention to it when you did. In a couple more minutes, we would have been too close to those rocks. Then we would have used the diesel to move us away."

Seeing that she still needed a bit more assurance, he continued, "We call it the 'boiling frog effect.' You know, if you toss a frog into boiling water, it will fight like fury to get out. But if you put the frog in a pan of cool water on the stove, as the water heats up, the frog adjusts or accepts the heat, until it's too late. We are creatures who adapt to the dangers around us when they happen gradually." Stuart Island was already several hundred meters behind them, safely, and Battleship Rock was already around the end of the island, out of sight.

Annie wanted to put some conversation into the moment, as a way of releasing some of her tension. "Yesterday I think I heard you say that when our life has been founded on an 'exclusive truth,' I think you said it is very hard to change." Her gaze shifted from the skipper to Bruce, and back. "I just screwed up, again. The exclusive truth I'm used to is that people usually react loudly to those mistakes. I feel really badly about it, but it seems to be super hard for me to do anything but mess up." The skipper realized that she was trying to apologize for either a steering error, or for reacting in panic because of it.

Listening to the gentle wash of the boat sliding through the tide, she finished her thought. "I'm sorry for getting too close to the rocks, and I'm puzzled why you didn't yell at me." A wane smile punctuated her apology.

"Sweetie," he looked at her caringly, understanding that the agenda of the day had just been introduced, "there are several things that come to mind, all at once. First of all you didn't make a mistake. You learned a lesson about steering in these strong tidal currents. We weren't in any danger…. more inconvenience if anything. And finally, yelling is only useful at football games. I think those folks you mentioned, who yell at mistakes, are really operating out of fear, or something like it."

"Think about it," the skipper said with a warm smile, "we had a small maneuvering problem. Let's not make it any bigger than that. If we keep our attention on solving the problem, correction is made, or order restored, or improvements are accomplished. All of which are good things. The problem gets solved. But, if we allow our attention to be people oriented, if we just think about who did what, who can we blame, we don't solve the problem and we probably aggravate the situation."

"Is that what you call an exclusive truth?" Her smile was growing, the usual perkiness returning after her scare.

The skipper thought for a moment before answering. "I suppose it is." Then trying to explain it a bit more, he added, "It's not that I don't occasionally do the lesser stuff. But I do believe that it is not likely that a negative, judgmental attitude can exist with a positive encouraging one. They just don't blend. So, in this case, I guess it is an exclusive truth. You can't be merciful and have malice at the same time."

By now, they were halfway across Haro Strait. "You know, we must be very near the boundary. Does it feel like we're in Canada, Bruce?" They were each aware of their progress.

"I'll check the chart, 'eh?" came the quip from Bruce, although he didn't leave his place at the helm.

Annie wasn't quite finished with their conversation. "I don't want to sound real dense, so let me ask it this way; how do you become a merciful person? How do I get over some of those ugly old ways of thinking about myself, or others?"

The skipper, while listening, had also been looking ahead, toward the island off their starboard bow. "Bud, do you see the opening between the Penders?" He pointed to give some direction to his question. "We'll just swing around the tip end of North Pender into Bedwell Harbor. I think there is a green marker piling." When the helmsman nodded his understanding the discussion continued.

"I don't have any more evidence on this than how I feel. But I'm pretty sure that it must be a conscious choice that we make." His eyes found Annie's looking intently. "Think about it this way. If God wants to forgive you, and whoever hurt you, all you need to do is work through the injury and accept the mercy. If God wants you to be a more loving or kind person, and offers the abilities necessary for that to happen, all you need to do is accept it, and begin living as though it were so. It must be a lot more complicated, but at least this is the start. You must decide on your own, and do it." His eyebrows arched, inquiring if she understood or agreed.

"Just do it." She repeated almost to herself. "It sounds like that Nike commercial. Just do it!" Her smile didn't fade.

The skipper nodded his agreement. "Do you know that 'Nike' is Greek for 'victory?' I like that a lot! It means that we can make ourselves a promise today, a promise to be victoriously merciful."

"I'd like that, wouldn't you Brucie?" Her smile was as warm as the morning. "Say it again, so I can write it in my notebook." She looked up quickly to make sure that her enthusiasm hadn't offended. "Please," she added.

"Promise yourself," the skipper felt as though he were dictating an important speech, "to be so spiritually well today…. that no hurtful memory can distress you," he thought for just a moment and went on slowly, "to be so strong…. that nothing can disturb your peace of mind…. to be too wise to worry…. too tolerant for anger, and too courageous for fear." He slowly concluded, "Promise yourself to be a person of mercy…. one day at a time." He watched her write hurriedly.

When she had finished the page, she remarked, "That sounds a lot like the AA folks, who say they can stay sober one day at a time."

"I can't think of much difference, actually." The skipper was quiet for a moment before finishing the thought. "They are trying to get over an alcohol addiction, and we might be breaking a malice addiction. We've been hooked on hurt, anger, guilt, or some other form of malice, maybe for a long time. But we can choose to be rid of it by living mercifully one day at a time."

Bruce wanted to be part of the conversation, so he asked, "But dad, how can we keep our minds focused on being merciful, all day long? I think there are all sorts of things that plow into our concentration." As he had been listening, he had also eased *Dreamer's* sheets, so they were once again sailing nearly directly off the wind.

"That's always a challenge for us. But suppose, for the sake of the discussion, that you two were to win an all-expense paid wedding and honeymoon, all expenses!" Both Bruce and Annie were grinning happily. "Suppose that you learned your gowns, and tuxedos, the flowers, the photographer, the rehearsal dinner, ceremony in a large church, the reception, the limousine, and a fantastic two week vacation honeymoon, in the location of your choice, would be at no expense to you." He let the thought percolate for a moment.

"I may be wrong, but I'm thinking that it would be hard for you to think about much else, working out the plans, the details, and the checklists. Nothing could burst in on those thoughts because it would be a primary, maybe even the primary focus for you."

Both Annie and Bruce understood his thought, and nodded vigorously.

"I'm pretty sure that's how it must be with mercy and malice. When we decide strong enough for mercy, make it a conscious core value or focus, we will experience malice less and less. And the more we get hooked on mercy, the easier it will be to add more and more areas of our life to it."

Annie continued her smile, "I like that! I want to be hooked on mercy." She gave Bruce a look filled with affection, and tenderly more. "I want us to be hooked on mercy forever."

Peering ahead, the skipper asked, "Have you spotted the marker piling, Bruce? It should be in pretty close to the beach." All eyes stared in the direction of the approaching island.

"Yeah, there it is!" He pointed off the starboard bow, further to the right than they had been looking. "Do you want me to go around it, on our port side?" The question suggested a clear understanding of the proper process of entering the harbor. "We'll need to ease the sheets a little more, won't we?" Again his question suggested sound seamanship.

The skipper was already moving to the winches, to pay out a bit more line. "Good read, Bud," he said with a smile. "That's about as far as we can ease without jibing over. But I think we'll be able to keep the sails up all the way into Bedwell Harbor. We'll need the diesel to put her on the customs dock. By the way, you both have I.D. with your picture, don't you?" It was a little late to ask such an important question. When they both nodded, he asked Annie, "Did we finish the conversation about mercy?"

She pulled her feet up under her, comfy in the corner

again. "I don't know what else to ask. But I love the stories you share to help me understand. I could listen to more of those all day." It was the sort of compliment that any fellow would welcome.

"The ones that come to mind are those I've used in sermons related to the teachings of Jesus. You know, going the second mile, turning the other cheek, repaying evil with good." He thought for just a moment.

"I remember the account of a tiny church woman named Mrs. Tilly, who gave us an indelible example of living in mercy. She was from Atlanta, never weighed more than a hundred pounds in her life, and looked about eight years younger than God." Annie grinned her familiar crooked smile. "She joined forces with a group of forty thousand women in the thirties and forties in what they called the Association of Southern Women for the Prevention of Lynching." Annie grimaced at the word. "She was just a little before her time, working tirelessly for mercy and peace. She was active in advocating the desegregation of public schools, which got her a lot of obscene phone calls, calling her everything but the gentle woman she was. She had an engineer friend hook her telephone to a phonograph, and remember, this was before the days of answering machines, and perhaps the genesis of its development. When someone would call her late at night the answer they heard was a mellow baritone voice singing the Lord's Prayer. The calls soon stopped. She had met malice with mercy."

From the helm, Bruce chuckled, "Cool! That gives me an idea for my answering machine." After a second's thought, he added, "But I don't have many death threats coming my way." There was good- natured chuckling in his humor, a sharp contrast from his attitude just days before. "This course is working out fine. When shall we roll up the sails?" Already, they could see inside the harbor to the first of the mooring docks.

Within a few minutes they were tied up on the customs dock, a necessary first process when entering Canada. While Bruce and Annie stayed on the boat, the skipper found the customs office closed. A note on the door directed him to use the available phone to call the Vancouver office of the Canadian Coast Guard. He gave them the required information, names, birth dates, and residence; they gave him a temporary visitation permit number that had to be displayed in a dockside boat window. It was a simple process, even after 9/11 restrictions.

The harbormaster had a wide choice of visitor slips available on the "C" dock. The crew was happy to have a selection. They chose a starboard side hook up, on the north side of the dock. They would be nose to the wind, and away from the noise of the pub at the resort, an ideal situation.

When everything was secured and tidy, Annie said, "I'm still sort of full from that great breakfast, but I'll bet you are interested in something to munch, huh?" She was happy to be able to predict Bruce's response.

The resort was attractively painted white with light blue trim. The hotel, grocery store, washroom and shower house made up the main part. A pub and enormous deck opened to the marina docks, which were protected from the east by a massive rock outcropping. The setting was both tidy and picturesque.

"We're in Canada, 'eh?" Bruce's grin was boyish and sincere. "I was thinking that a Molson and a plate of fries would be a sweet snack until we have a serious meal, maybe even some fish and chips. Sound good to you, dad? I'm buyin'!" It seemed he was ready to pick up any lunch check. Those were the affordable ones.

"Why don't you guys go ahead? I think I have a little bookwork to do. I've been thinking about another evening exercise for us. I'll catch up with you in a bit. O.K.?" The skipper also thought the two of them could use some time as a couple.

Forty-five minutes later, as he made his way up the ramp from the dock, he could see them sitting side by side, their heads together in conversation. Whatever goals they had when beginning this trip, it seemed evident that they were working. The skipper looked out at the vista of boats, trees, clouds with bright spring sunshine, with the promise of a beautiful sunset. "Yup," he thought. "Life is definitely good!"

As he joined the others, on the pub deck, basking in the afternoon warmth, Bruce looked up. "Glad to see you. I was just telling Annie about my first memory of this place. I think I was about eight years old. I was fishing from the docks right over there." He pointed toward the fuel dock. "I remember calling it the 'nursery' because I caught a bunch of small rock-cod."

"I remember that trip too, Bud. I think you were using a hand-line with mussels for bait."

"That's what I remember too! It's funny, though, I can't tell you much else about that trip. Were we here for several days?"

"I just remember a couple days. And I'm surprised you don't remember the yellow jackets. They were here a lot. You got a candy bar for every ten you caught. I think we made a trap with a plastic jug, cut some openings in the side of it so they could crawl in and not out, and baited it with some fruit juice. As I recall, you had a bunch of candy that afternoon."

Bruce grinned his boyish joy. "How can a guy not remember fun like that?"

Annie was enjoying the memories too. "Yeah, fishin', trappin', killin', and candy, what more could a boy want?"

"It sort of reminds me of an analogy of what we are trying to accomplish on this voyage. Those yellow jackets represent the stings and insults that we have experienced. We know that we can contain and eliminate them. The challenge is just knowing how." The skipper hoped that his idea wasn't too remote.

"Dad, we were just talking about yesterday. And by

the way, this trip is sensational! Each day seems bigger than the one before, which seemed huge! I want to thank you again for doing this for us." Annie nodded her appreciation as well. "Yesterday you said something about restitution as part of the forgiveness process. We were just talking about how that might work. And to be honest, we don't know how it can." Bruce was sincere as usual.

The three of them looked out at the harbor. The smooth surface of the bay was flat with only a tiny ripple from the wind. The tide had crested and was now receding, a relentless transfer of water in and out of the harbor. Finally, the skipper began the conversation. "In the Old Testament, there is the idea of an eye for an eye. I think it is called 'equal retaliation.' It really is an ancient concept of justice. Basically it means if someone does something bad to me, I get to do something bad in return. If someone damages something of mine, I get to damage back. Exodus gives a pretty clear picture of how the restitution thing works; there we get the notion of recovering the loss, replacing or restoring that which was damaged."

Bruce had been listening carefully, with a frown. "But dad, we can't see where there is a way that restitution can apply in our case. Could I repay Sydney for my bad behavior? She didn't lose anything. She didn't miss work, or have lasting injuries." He shook his head a bit to show his confusion.

Annie was quick to add, "And I can't imagine who or what I could offer restitution." She raised her eyebrows in a questioning shrug.

Eager to get beyond the literal discussion of restitution, the skipper explained his concept. "Look, it's not a legalistic thing, but rather a way for you to show yourself that you are serious about the whole process. Much of the hurt we experience is so general we can't locate a perpetrator. If it is us doing the harm, we might have trouble finding the victim." He gazed out at the picture perfect setting. "The point is, something needs to be done to demonstrate our contrition…to ourselves. We've got to prove it to ourselves." He repeated himself to make sure the point was clear.

"I think we can have really lovely sentiments about making a fresh start, of becoming finer people, but all the beautiful sentiments in the world weigh less than a simple lovely deed. I think it was Shakespeare who said that 'action is eloquent.' Restitution, then, is doing something beautiful because we did something ugly to someone, someplace at some time in the past. We want to 'make it right' if we can." He continued to look out at the marine scene. "We want to make it right …for us."

Bruce wrinkled his face in confusion. "Dad, I don't get it yet. I just don't see what I could do to fix…" His voice trailed off leaving the thought stranded like a boat on a reef. He gave his head a tiny shake.

"O.K. Bud, let's see if we can make a personal example.

Let's say that you have promised Annie that you will help her move to a new apartment next Saturday. You want to score some big points, and show her how strong you are." They both grinned.

"But," he paused for dramatic effect, "you forgot that you have Mariner tickets, and really want to see all their home games. So you jack up a phony story about work, and go to the game in spite of your promise. She discovers your lie, and has her feelings hurt." Annie pursed her lips as though she had actually experienced the hurt. "So you invite her out to a very nice dinner where you apologize, and promise never to fib to her again. It really is a repeated scenario between lovers." Both Annie and Bruce nodded to affirm the truth of it.

"Now do you think you are buying her forgiveness?" He asked the rhetorical question. "I hope not. That is a dangerous sickness that can infect a relationship until things take on an unrealistic importance. I think, rather, you are trying, by an eloquent action, to show her you are truly repentant, sorry for your misdeed. And you are showing yourself, with sincere commitment, that you have grown to a new level of relationship. That, I believe is the nature of restitution."

Bruce asked, "Are you saying that restitution is as much for me as it is for the person I injured?" His direct gazed showed a deep interest.

"Actually Bud, I'm suggesting that it is more for you than anyone else." Then, giving the discussion just a moment to develop, he added, "If restitution corrects an injustice, or repairs a previous wrong, it has accomplished a good thing. If it guides you onto a higher plain of living, it has achieved its purpose. That is a great thing! As you said, it may be difficult, even impossible, to do anything with or for Sydney. Hopefully she has put the episode behind her satisfactorily. So, the challenge is for you to do the same thing. Maybe you already have. "

The three sat quietly looking at the calm scene before them, and further, into the possibilities of their conversation.

Finally, the skipper broke the silence by saying, "I'm going to sound like a drill sergeant, and I don't mean to push too hard. However, I have a plan for the rest of the afternoon. It will take about four hours. So, if we want to do it before supper we'll need to start pretty soon. Want to hear it?" His smile was an eager attempt to reassure them.

Annie spoke immediately. "I'm game. I have been in a constant state of pleasant surprise since we began. I'm betting this is going to be more of the same good stuff." Looking at Bruce, she asked, "How about you, big guy? Are you in for some more adventure, or do you just want to sit here and eat more fries?"

"Can I have another Molson with it?" The smile on his face assured her that he was willing to follow the plan for the full afternoon. "You bet I am in. I can't remember having more fun!"

"O.K." the skipper checked his watch. "It's a quarter to two. There is a path behind the pool that works over to that beach park by the anchorage. It looks pretty empty over there so let's use it like we did the lookout at Anacortes." He offered them each four folded pieces of paper, each numbered and bearing the time they should be opened and read. "Let's go potty, grab a bottle of water each, and make our way over to the beach. The idea is to separate ourselves a little distance from each other, and follow the instructions on your papers. Read only one at a time, and do what it suggests. O.K.?"

Bruce grinned, "Sounds like a scavenger hunt."

Annie was quick to add, "Sounds like a treasure hunt."

The skipper concluded, "Sounds like we're ready to go."

The trio made their way along a needle covered dirt trail, their footsteps muffled by the softness of the forest. The trees overhead were mostly Hemlock and Cedar. Here and there a Madronna stood out accented by its smooth red trunk. The spring afternoon was warm and still, like an overture to a concert of discovery. As their pathway found the access to the shoreline the first to stop was Bruce. He found a large log as a lounge chair. Annie continued on for fifty or sixty meters before a smooth rock invited her to stop. The skipper traveled on down the beach until he found a dry sandy mound that looked just right. At the top of the hour, the three each opened paper number one.

After the instructions to open at 2 p.m., were two words, written with pencil on the white paper.

"Listen carefully!"

Far down the beach Bruce looked up sharply. From her sunny rock, Annie smiled. The skipper wondered what their response might be. The instructions said simply, "Listen carefully."

Bruce tried to focus on the sounds coming to him. He could hear a chainsaw across the harbor, probably someone cutting firewood. He could hear a distant aircraft. It was probably a small floatplane headed for one of the outer islands. He listened. The faint sound of music came from the resort pub, actually only the bass rhythm of the music. He tried to listen… for what? He could hear the light breeze stirring the tree-bows overhead, waves lapped lightly along the beach. The tide was low, but still going out, he thought. Listen, for what?

Minutes passed slowly. Bruce became aware of what he wasn't hearing. There were no traffic sounds, no sirens or emergency vehicles. He could not hear a voice, from anyone. He listened so intently he became aware of the light ringing in his ears. It was pretty darned quiet on his part of the beach. Listen, for what?

Annie also heard the chainsaw, and the aircraft. She listened to the gentle sounds of lapping waves, and the rustle of leaves in the trees behind her. Diving birds were her attention for a while. They arched their necks as they plunged beneath the surface. As closely as she could listen, however, they made no sound. Two seagulls at the far end of the harbor were bickering over a snack. She became aware of the vast quiet of the bay. No boats were moving; just clouds coasting silently across her afternoon sky, their mirrored reflection on the water. It was all so big. In the quiet, she realized the enormous world she was sharing with others. She wasn't aware when it happened, only that eventually she realized her mind was not racing, not careening from thought to thought. She felt serene. Was that the word? Yes, her mind was serenely resting.

The skipper knew that an hour of listening is a challenge. We are not wired to be that still for that long. But he listened. He thought of music, the sounds that people make moving about, the sounds of the boat, the dock, and the noises that comfort him and remind him that his world is normal. In this un-normal quiet, he heard faint sounds of workers across the bay, and back at the resort. He listened carefully to the melody of a small bird, singing in the bushes near the beach. It repeated its plaintive song several times before falling still, like the rest of the world around it. The gulls were a quarrelling distraction. He pondered the thought that perhaps silence was the natural state of the world, that howling winds and crashing seas, screaming gulls and noisy humans are simply interlopers into the higher domain of stillness. As the minutes passed, he felt strangely disconnected from his world, and strangely small in its enormity. The minutes passed as he listened.

Their instructions were to open the next piece of paper at three o'clock. All three checked their watch repeatedly, to be punctual. In a distant union, they read the words on the second paper.

"Reach Back."

Bruce at first thought it might be some sort of yoga exercise. He stretched his hands far behind his back, pivoting from side to side. He understood that this was no physical challenge, but a time to recall. "Reach back to what?" he pondered. He thought of the folks in his office, their easy banter and efficient teamwork. He dwelt for a bit on his days in college, the studies, the sports, the friends. He became aware that he was recalling happy or pleasant memories. He thought of his family, divided by divorce, yet strangely intact. The people he loved truly loved him. There was no void where family should be. His thoughts deepened until he focused on, "except for my grandfather. I miss him a lot, and wish I could have known him better. I can still remember the smell of his Bay Rum aftershave." Bruce smiled a contented memory. He remembered the dinners at grandpa's house, always lavish with several desserts. He remembered the sound of his laughter, and his deep singing voice.

The tide was low slack, the beach expanded to its shiny wet fullness. Occasionally a squirt of water would mark a butter clam near the surface. Bruce remembered when his grandfather took him clamming at the ocean. They were after Razor clams, succulent and scarce. They would track the out-going waves, seeking a telltale hole. When he spotted one, his grandfather would position himself between the hole and the waves, and with his long curved shovel, dig as fast as he could. Bruce recalled the catching bag, which always seemed proudly full. He remembered the satisfied smile of a full limit of clams, and the promise of yet another dinner.

The people of his past had each donated a quality that combined to make him the person he was today. As he reached back, he became increasingly aware of how blessed he was, and how rich.

Annie reread the words, "Reach Back." She felt some amusement, and some frustration. She wanted to reach ahead, to grasp the future, to deal with the possibilities and potential that she was convinced awaited her. At least she wanted to reach the full of this present day, to stay immersed in its richness. How could she reach back for a full hour? "Back to what," she asked herself. She thought of her apartment, which reminded her of her dorm room at school. Then, without much invitation she remembered her home in Portland. It was simple, the home of plain people. She could recall the carefully chosen colors in her mother's design, the meticulous yard in her dad's care. She could still see her old room, which her sister assured her was unchanged since she left for school. Thinking of her little sister left a sweet trace on the reflection. Strangely, she felt a surge of confidence and positive joy. These were the people from whom she came, the foundation stones from which she was built. These were her people, simple, yes, but creative, uneducated, but artistic, blue-collar, yet loving, kind, and oh so happy. Yes, they made a wonderful loving home, and she was part of it. She promised herself to call them as soon as she got back. It had been far too long.

The skipper had written those words on the paper, so it was no surprise to him. He knew that he would reach back to some reflections on the churches he had served. He could remember faces, both laity and clergy, and rooms, and experiences that had been terrific. He could also remember the times with the bishop, and the bitterness he still felt over that exchange. "Reach back," to what, to the attack, to the loss, or to what he still had?

He focused on the happy memories of the family when the kids were young. If he had it to do over, he would have worked less, and played so much more with them. He wasn't sure they really knew him as a person. He would have involved himself more. He reached back to seminary, recalling the exhilaration of thinking beyond his expectations, of exploring new regions of ideas, with unimaginably gifted men and women. He reached back to his home church as a young man when the pastor had sat with him one rainy afternoon and pondered the possibility of ordained ministry. He had felt "called," and when he took the first tentative step, there seemed to be a divine affirmation that invited another step. Gifts, graces, skills, and talents beyond his own seemed to be poured out upon him. He was convinced that he had been blessed by incredible opportunity. As he reached back, tiny moments of power, little flashes of strength poured into him. It was an altogether positive hour, too soon over.

The trio checked their watches. It was four o'clock; time for the next sheet of paper.

Bruce was thinking that he liked this easy afternoon exercise, until he read the three words of the third sheet. They simply commanded,

"Reexamine your motives!"

His first reaction was purely defensive. "There is nothing wrong with my motives," he thought. "I want to be successful – who doesn't? I want to have a little recognition –nothing wrong with that. I want some security with a person I love – everybody wants that. Why not?"

"Maybe," said a small voice somewhere in his conscience, "maybe those motives aren't really good enough. Maybe that's why my train keeps falling off the track. Maybe that's why I feel like I'm going in circles instead of somewhere." Bruce listened to the small voice as he picked up a piece of driftwood.

In the past, whenever his work went well, there had always been something spontaneous about it, something uncontrived, something free, because he was doing what he loved to do. But lately, especially with the thought of Annie added, it had felt more forced, calculated, competent, but dead. Why? He studied the wood in his hands. Perhaps because in both his job, and the plans, he had been looking beyond to the rewards he hoped to receive. Both the work and the relationship had ceased to be an end in itself and had become a means – to make money, to have a partner, to pay bills, to acquire new status. The sense of giving something special through work, of helping people, of making a real contribution to the world, in short, all the reasons he had gone into the job in the first place, had been lost in a frantic and futile clutch for something else. He dropped the stick in the sand.

As Annie read those three words, she had an immediate question. "Had the skipper wondered about her reason for coming on this trip? Did he suspect that she was trying to reappraise her relationship with Bruce, maybe maneuver him into something much more?" She reread the words.

"Why was she on this trip," she asked herself. "Was the future with Bruce the central issue for her right now?" She pondered the various aspects of her world. She loved her job, had great friends, was making more money than she knew what to do with, and had a great family. She had a marvelous life! "Yup, the relationship is the issue!" "Reexamine your motives," meant that she needed to ask herself those 'why' questions. "Why did she love Bruce?" "Why did she want so much more?" "Why did she want to spend the rest of her life with him?" Because he was a joy to be with, the best friend she could imagine, and he loved her. Because she trusted him, loved to talk with him, play with him, grow with him, respected his ideas and knew that he would love her always. Her conclusion was that they would have a wonderful life together, with adventure, security and prestige. She grimaced a bit thinking such a selfish thought. Then with a fresh clarity, the rest of her thought emerged. Because they would have a family together, and erase the memory of the child she didn't have. She sat up straight on her rocky lookout.

The idea slammed into her consciousness. She was conflicted over their future because she was unclear about the motive for it. If her motive was wrong, nothing could be right. You just can't get to right from such a wrong base. It was a truth as reliable as gravity. She knew in her heart that if she acted out of love, and love only, the problems with their future planning would disappear. As long as she was trying to use it as a means to a personal end, those problems would persist. Like Dr. Phil says, "If you keep doin' what you've been doin', you'll keep getting what you've been getting."

The skipper smiled as he looked at his sheet of paper. "Reexamine your motives," he had written those darned words. But at the moment, he couldn't remember why he had chosen those particular ones. The motive for being on this trip was pretty clear: he wanted to help the kids, and it was an enjoyable way to spend some time with Bruce. The motive for his job was also pretty clear: he wanted to help folks move beyond conflict to positive resolutions, and he could earn a decent living doing it. "Reexamine your motives," the words were sort of haunting.

He wondered about the biography of his life. What are the operative motives? If someone who knew him quite well were to write his personal history, what would they say? What are the activities that receive most of his time and attention? Isn't that a way to look at motives? Who are the people he plays with? What gives him joy, meaning, or challenge?

The skipper continued to wonder what his biographer would say about the Christian life specifically. How tenacious did he hold certain doctrines and principles? Was he faithful in church attendance or support? What were the satisfying positions he held in the church organization? Did he have a meaningful prayer life? How effective did he relay the message of faith? Was his motive to be a servant, or to be served? Somehow the entire hour slid by without coming to any conclusions about the reexamination of his motives, and not once did he think about his quitting the ministry.

By five o'clock, the eastern clouds were taking on a pink and purple blush. It was time to open the fourth and final piece of paper.

Bruce read the words on his paper, and smiled broadly. He thought, "It sounds like something dad would have us do."

Annie climbed off her rock and walked out onto

the wet sand at the edge of the bay. She reread the six words.

The skipper watched the reaction of his crew. He thought about his response to the afternoon. It was a good process, even if he had little time to develop it. (1) Listen carefully to calm a frantic mind, to slow it down, to shift the focus from inner problems to outer power. (2) Reach back to capitalize on the fact that our mind can hold but one idea focus at a time. We blot out present worry when we touch the happiness of the past. (3) Reexamination of motives was the core of the afternoon. This was a challenge to bring motives into alignment with capabilities, and conscience.

Now, number four:

Write your troubles on the sand.

He reached down and picked up a fragment of a seashell, then kneeling under the vault of a spring sky, he wrote several words on the sand. As he stood to examine his work, a knowing smile melted the lines on his face. He stepped back to read the words one last time. The tide was quietly, but oh so surely coming back in, erasing those troubles forever.

"I don't know why you asked that special question, then" Annie was smiling, as usual, as they sat at the corner table in the hotel dining room. Only two other tables were in use. They had freedom to continue the conversation that had gone on since returning from the beach. "I just felt like I must have said something to show you what I needed to ask. How did you know that my motive was a problem?" Her bearing was casual, but her focus was direct.

The skipper repeated himself. "Seriously, I had no idea how you would hear the question, or what it might relate to in each of us. I could have just as easily asked, 'What's going on with you right now?' Or I could have said, 'What makes you tick?' The result is what counts. It sounds like you had an insight."

They had been at the table for almost two hours. The last rays of afternoon had worked their way up the face of the rock outcropping that bordered the marina. Shadows of evening crept from the far side shore until they finally captured the harbor, lights coming on like diamonds in the twilight. Annie's earlier excitement was somewhat abated, but not much.

"It just seems to me that you have been listening to my thoughts!" She was repeating herself also. "I feel like I understand what has been going wrong with all my plans, maybe with a lot more." Her elbows were on the table so she could lean closer to her dinner partners.

Bruce had been pretty quiet since their beach walk. That in itself was not too different. Now, however, he interjected, "Well, it sort of worked for me too." When Annie looked directly at him, he added, "I think I know why I've been less than helpful with future plans. I think I have been concentrating on what changes are going to happen." That quirky smile creased his lips, "You know, after…" Somehow it was difficult for him to finish the thought.

Annie gave him a teasingly radiant smile.

"No I don't mean that kind of happen." He tried to correct the course of his suggestion. "I'm thinking about more bills, or a house, or something else." Obviously he was struggling to get around his thought. "Your place is little, so is mine. They're O.K. for one, but we'd have to find a new place for two of us. I've been thinking about the changes in time commitments, the gym, the guys. You know, changes." He paused unable to formalize the entire thought.

"Sounds like a case of cold feet." Annie's smile did not fade. "I've had them too."

"No, that's not what I mean." Bruce was careful to keep his response soft. "It's not cold feet. I guess I have had stuff out of sync, that's all. I've been looking past problems, trying to fix the future that may not even happen. I've been trying to apply business principles where they don't belong. I've anticipated the worst case scenario, which has made it happen in my head." He reached across the table for her hand. "I can't imagine a better life than one with you."

The skipper said to both of them, "That could make a girl feel absolutely giddy." Annie nodded her agreement, and Bruce looked at the tablecloth, unaccustomed to that level of frank affection.

Taking a large breath, he asked, "If we get it, you know, the forgiveness, the new start and everything, and we don't do anything about it, doesn't that mean the problem is deeper in us?" Bruce was again taking them to a new depth of discussion.

"You know, Bud, it might help if we speak in generalities, instead of about you or me." The skipper had been thinking about an analogy that could help focus this.

"Suppose, just for the sake of this conversation, that you have a bag of battery acid." Both of his listeners smiled, delighted with his wit and quick change of direction. "It might be a heavy bag, but nonetheless, it's going to be destroyed, sooner or later. Maybe it's the only way you can get the acid to your battery, which is in need. Maybe you're taking the acid to be safely disposed of in a recycling center. There could be some good reasons for it, probably more bad ones. But if you don't manage it soon, you will have a much bigger problem."

"Very definitely timely action is important when we know we have a problem. I've been thinking about your aunts," he continued. "Two of them have been very supportive about my marital change, and about my leaving the ministry. But one has been so upset she can scarcely talk to me. She has made every possible excuse not to be around me, to avoid me completely. It's almost like she is so furious about my divorce and loss of ordination, she has internalized it as her own. She is obviously confused."

A sad smile creased the skipper's face. "It's been nearly five years, and like acid, the problem is spreading to her kids. They have heard so many variations on the theme, they are pretty uncomfortable around me. She would rather not attend family functions if I'm going to be there. The bag is being dissolved."

Annie asked a question she thought she knew the answer to, "Was she real close to your former?"

"She was," he agreed. "For a while they were like sisters, maybe even closer than she was to her own sisters. And maybe that could be the root of the problem. If she accepts my divorce, she'll have to admit that her relationship with Mary is radically changed. And maybe, if she accepts my leaving the ministry, she'll have to admit that she took pride in sharing my status. You know, 'My brother is a big-time United Methodist pastor.'" His voice mocked the sentence with comic pride. "Her denial is an attempt to control an uncontrollable event. Maybe she even thinks that by denying it she is maintaining a possibility that the entire episode is reversible."

The skipper chuckled dryly. "Try on that logic: she's staying angry at me for my own good." After a small pause, he went on, "She loves me. She's keeping some sick sense of hope alive by holding a grudge. She thinks she can make it right again! Yikes, that really is stinkin' thinkin'!"

"That's like avoiding a promotion and possible reassingment, thinking I'm doing something positive about my living situation." Bruce was fairly certain he had come to an understanding about his contribution to their problem.

"Or hurrying into one in the hopes of replacing a lost baby." Annie's sincerity was as clear as Bruce's insight, and as pure. The table was quiet, exploring the depths of possibility held in the vastness of the dark harbor.

Sensing the mood of the moment, the skipper said it was time for him to be heading back to the boat. They could take their time, if they wished. There were books to read, and plans to make. He really did need to put the waypoints into the GPS for tomorrow's journey to Maple Bay. During the evening, clouds had thickened. If the barometer was lower, they might be in for some rain. At any rate he would see them back aboard *Dreamer.*

Bruce asked Annie if she would like to talk about the afternoon. It seemed they both had some fresh insight to share. Maybe they could find a corner table at the pub.

It was well after midnight when the skipper heard the hatch- cover slide open quietly. The boat scarcely moved as the crew found their way to their bunks.

Notebook entries were made by each member of the crew:

Annie wrote: He didn't actually ask me, like a proposal. He said, 'would you like us to be married?' Well, I just really want to hear him ask. Of course we have had that moment before, but this still seems like a struggle. It feels good to talk about, but he is being so vague. I truly believe this is right. We need to stop allowing our personal history to define our future! I think we truly could be married, and that thrills me. I'm so happy!

Before anything like that happens, however, I'm going to do two or three things. I'm going to volunteer some time at Planned Parenthood. I'm going to send some money to the Children's Society; that will help an adoption process. Third, I'm going to find a church where I can belong, where I can be accepted, and loved like Bruce loves me. I am going to convince my heart what my head knows: that my abortion is past tense, healed, and forgiven.

She studied that last sentence carefully before she put her notebook away, and turned off the light.

Bruce wrote: My Gosh, she does love me. We've been a couple for quite a while, but this is different. She is more beautiful than ever before. I want to touch her, feel her breath on my face. I want to talk with her about everything. It feels like I can't be around her enough. Even now I miss her, and wish it were already morning.

I think she will ask me about marriage, if I don't get the job done. I know now that we both want to talk about it, and it will happen if I stop doing the Charlie Brown wishy-washy thing.

Annie, you are my treasure tonight. That means that I am enough in love with you not to see anything imperfect, not to believe anything uncomplimentary, and not to think any thoughts that might discredit you. That's why you are a treasure! Tonight I am aware of perfection in an imperfect world. I realize there is someone who must not be changed or altered, and cannot be improved. To say that you are a perfect treasure is as profoundly as I can say this: I love you just the way you are!

The skipper's entry recapped the day: Restitution is doing something significant enough to convince yourself that the breach is mended; the tear is sown back together. It need not be quid pro quo as long as it is authentic contrition. If in your heart you are truly sorry, your heart will not allow a modest attempt at restitution. It will require an absolute effort.

Listen…Reach back…. Reevaluate your motives…

Layer by layer, the past is…. (He switched to an attempt at poetry:)

> Layer by layer the past is peeled away,
> The hurts and fears, the hopes and tears,
> The failures, successes, and abysmal messes,
> Lord, you lift them like aging rose petals,
> from a bouquet of doom,
> discarding the loss, and saving the bloom.
> Oh, like Love, You save the best, and overlook the rest! Amen.

I truly believe that something important is happening here. The words of Hammarskjold are recalled, "I don't know Who – or What – put the question , I don't know when it was asked. I don't remember answering. But at some moment I did answer 'Yes' to Someone – or Something. From that hour, I was certain that existence is meaningful and that therefore, my life, my self-surrender, had a goal."

Can my ministry be restored? Can my life have rich meaning and purpose? Is there a goal? The most obscene word I can imagine in this moment is "no!" There is an increasingly negative action when that word is said just a bit to life, the life says, "NO!" in return, but in greater measure. Each day dawns with similarity – just another ordinary moment. Yet in these ordinary hours or minutes of this ordinary beginning there is a life-changing, heart-warming, love-creating opportunity, to which I may whisper either, "yes'" or "no!"

Ten years from now I will wonder at the opportunities I rejected rather than the risks I took. The risks will appear mundane, and the missed opportunities monumental. Here is the essence of the waste of life: love we have not shared, talents we have not used, risks not taken for fear of pain, real or emotional, all of which is the lewd application of "NO" to fulfillment. Tomorrow I will awaken with a "yes!"

Before sleep claimed him completely, light rain began to tap on the boat-top. How pleasant to be snug and secure. Oh, how good the night!

CHAPTER SIX:
MAPLE BAY,
VANCOUVER ISLAND, B. C.
Regain your feeling of safety and control

"O.k. Bruce, you can release the spring line. We're on our way." The skipper had released the stern line. With no breeze at all *Dreamer* eased back out into the harbor, then began a gentle turn toward the open water. They etched a graceful crease on the still surface of the bay, which was speckled with the continuing spring shower.

Annie, cuddled in her usual corner of the cockpit, was wrapped in a warm jacket. "How far is it to Maple Bay," she asked with a smile. "I feel like the child who asks, 'Are we there yet?'" They had discussed their destination over an early breakfast at the hotel dining room.

The skipper watched her sip coffee from her paper cup. "About twenty-two miles. But we are going to be playing with the tide I'm afraid. We should be able to be there in three hours, but the last four or five miles go through the Sansum Narrows, which I hope we reach at low slack. But if we are fighting the tide, that might take some extra time. We should be there for a late lunch at worst." He appreciated her quick smile and that head nod that said she understood. She pulled her feet in more tightly under her jacket, and seemed resigned to a quiet morning. Bruce finished securing the lines, and joined them, finding his own coffee cup.

The trio reflected the quietness of the morning as they made the westerly turn outside the harbor. Ahead the open water of Swanson Channel seemed calm, with not a hint of the powerful tide sweeping beneath it. The dodger provided shelter from the light rain, and the engine offered enough ambient heat to keep them from the morning chill. Altogether it was a peaceful beginning to the day.

Annie was the first to try to open a conversation. "Norm, do you believe in dreams?" She wanted to use a more formal title for him, and had thought about "skipper," or "Mr. O'Banyon," even "dad," like Bruce did. She made a quick decision to stick with the too familiar because it was a little better than most other options.

It made the skipper smile too. "It depends on what you mean by 'believe in.'" He looked at her expression to see if there might be a telltale hint at where the question would lead them. I believe we all do dream. And I believe that sometimes dreams are assisted by some of the bad snack choices I make just before bedtime. What do you have in mind?" It probably wasn't the best question he could ask, just the first one that came to mind.

"Well I just wondered if sometimes dreams help us see what's about to happen." Her shy smile suggested an honest question.

"One of my best friends, Dr. Sommers from the UW, has talked to me quite a bit about dreams. He says that we all dream every night, and dream quite a bit actually. There are two major parts of our sleep."

Before he could finish the thought, Bruce chuckled, "Yeah, long, and longer! I especially like the second part." Annie shushed him, and asked the skipper to continue. She really was interested.

"There are two parts of our sleep," the skipper said again. "The shallow part, or "Rapid Eye Movement" (REM) and the deeper more restful regenerative part which is called "Slow Wave." He looked at her until she gave that little head nod.

"He says that we go through cycles of REM then Slow Wave back to REM several times during the night. The deep sleep is when we regenerate our body, and it is in that shallow sleep that we dream, and probably remember only the final moments before waking."

"But I don't dream every night." Annie didn't mean for her reply to sound like an argument, even though it might have been. "I did have a really long dream last night. It seemed to last for hours."

Bruce still felt playful. "I hope it was a spicy R-rated one, featuring me as the leading man." His chuckle still suggested a light-hearted affection.

"Knock it off," she said with mock anger. "On this trip it is going to be G-rated at best." It was the sort of banter that best friends can share.

The skipper decided to get back to his thought-track. "Dr. Sommers does say that we are sexually aroused several times, every night." That should get their attention, he thought. "Think of your brain as a super Pentium processor that is constantly spinning out thoughts, like 'what do I hear, feel, or smell?' When we sleep, we have a filter sort of function that blocks all of that, so we can actually relax and rest. Emergency messages can still get through to wake us, but generally the activity of our processor is below our conscious level. Dreams are the random activity that we catch as we are awakening from sleep." That seemed like a fair recollection of the information he had heard.

"Then you probably don't think that our dreams can teach us new stuff, or warn us of the future, do you?" Her question was tinged with a feeling of disappointment.

"Do you mean are they extrasensory, or clairvoyant?"

"Yeah," she thought about it for a moment. "I think some of my dreams sort of show me an experience I've never had before, and maybe something that could happen in the future." Her sincerity was obvious.

"I'll bet there are a lot of folks who hold that belief," the skipper smiled. "And probably a lot that don't." He looked at their course. By now they were well out into the channel, ahead was the imposing slope of Salt Spring Island. "I think the important thing is your feelings when you remember a dream. When you awaken, are you sad about your dreams, are you anxious, or happy?"

He went on, "I can remember an anxiety dream that I had over and over for years. It always followed the same scenario. I was the pastor of a very large church, which was filled with worshippers. A large choir was ready to enter, ushers were seating the last few spaces, while I, confused and unprepared, stood there in a dirty T-shirt, unshaved and completely bewildered. I would awaken with a sense of foreboding, somehow doubting all the work I had put in to prepare myself for the real church service. I just called it my 'anxiety dream'." He gave her a smile that invited some response.

"Yuck!" she grimaced. "That sounds like one of those nightmares that makes you glad it's morning, and time to wake up."

Bruce wanted into the discussion. "I've had a dream where I'm playing basketball. The game is tied with only a few seconds left to play, and there are all sorts of people on the court. I can't get through to even try a shot. Do you think I should call that a frustration dream?" He seemed genuine in his question.

"Is that how you felt when you woke up, and remembered the dream?"

"Yeah, frustrated, angry, and blocked from every angle."

Annie thought for a few moments before saying, "Seems like there could be a message in there, don't you think?" She looked from Bruce to the skipper. "Maybe that has something to do with our future, and it's trying to tell us something." She wanted to put a little more urgency into her question.

"I think it might have about as much of a message as snoring does. You know, there is sound coming out of his mouth, but not much content." The skipper grinned at his own humor.

Annie persisted. "Then you don't think there is depth or meaning to our dreams?" She seemed almost disappointed.

"Remember now," he began carefully. "I'm not trained, or even very well read in the subject of dream interpretation. I do believe that how you feel when you wake from a dream says a lot about your general outlook or attitude. Dreams of dread, or horror might leave you shaken with a feeling of foreboding. Playful dreams or happy dreams might have just the opposite effect. Some people dream that they can fly, and are exhilarated by it. But I think the source of your dreams is random and accidental activity of your free-wheeling unconscious thoughts."

Bruce asked a question while Annie was forming her own. "Do you still have those church dreams? Where you're out of control?"

The skipper shook his head. With that warm smile he said, "Not any more, especially since I no longer preach."

Annie was ready. "Then maybe they were connected," she said almost triumphantly. "You don't have them anymore because you don't need them!"

"I don't think I ever needed anxiety. I can't imagine anyone does. Remember, 'anx' is the German word for illness, and most doctors say that three quarters of the patients they see are suffering only anxiety related illnesses."

"But I can tell you how I used those dreams, when they did occur." He paused to think how best to say the thought. "I consciously put them in a category of humor. When I was awake enough, I'd simply see them as a preposterous joke. I'm never in a torn T-shirt, never unshaven in public. I spent hours in preparation for leading worship, and was proud of the sermons. I thought of the years of training and experience that could only be called excellent. By focusing on the positive, I used those silly dreams to frame a picture of success and satisfaction." The tide was still ebbing, and the southerly drift was trying to push them off course. The skipper gave just a bit more starboard rudder.

Annie wanted a good grasp on the concept, so she asked, "Didn't you say that our feelings come from our thoughts? Now it sounds like you are saying that it's just the other way around. Do you mean that it works both ways?" She seemed in a tangle of understanding.

"They are tied together," the skipper tried to explain. "Think about patriotism and flag-waving. Sometimes it's a noble feeling that promotes warm thoughts of our history. Sometimes it's a well thought understanding of how our government works, and the due process of justice. There may not be much feeling there until you think how much of the world doesn't know that sort of freedom. Our thoughts can lead our feelings, and vice versa. In the same way you can think about romance." He would have continued except a long look between his listeners was concluded with a wink and a smile.

Bruce said, "Yeah, we have been thinking about romance, and feeling pretty good about it." Annie nodded in happy agreement. "Maybe it's the fact that we never took this kind of special time to think about us, and maybe it's your help so far." He paused wanting to say rationally what could be blurted into the morning. "Annie and I are really sure… pretty sure… We want to do it right."

"That's fantastic, guys!" the skipper exclaimed. "I know that you are being very careful…"

Before he could say any more, Annie asked, "Are we supposed to get your blessing first?" There was a coy shyness that the skipper hadn't seen in her eyes.

"If so, you have it, of course." Then thinking just a bit more he asked back, "How about your father, Annie. Will he want to give a blessing before you make too many plans?"

"I don't know." She was honestly a bit perplexed not having a clear answer. "He,... actually they, aren't much on formality. I don't think that they would care one way or the other." The smile faded just a bit. "We just know that it feels right, for once."

Bruce was smiling broadly too. "Maybe we've given it enough thought to cause good feelings, or enough good feelings to clarify our thoughts."

They were well across the channel, drawing just off the north side of Moresby Island. The skipper thought of another way to tie up this conversation. "If we have been talking about recovery from some event, we can't imagine a thoughtless solution, nor can we accept one without emotion, just cold or lifeless. It really needs to be a balance between the two. Don't you agree?"

They both gave that head nod, which was by now familiar. The rain had nearly stopped, but the clouds were still heavy, holding onto the very top of Salt Spring Island.

Annie stretched her feet out from under her, grimacing with a bit of stiffness. "Do you think I could have another try at the helm?" She hadn't been this bold before, but it seemed a perfect way to end a major moment. "I promise not to run us into any more rocks." There was that twinkle again!

Appreciating her initiative, the skipper explained that their course would carry them around the island just off their starboard bow. "Stay about two hundred meters from the shore." When Annie looked at him for more information, he added, "About two football fields." She nodded, so in his official old navy voice, the skipper called, "Officer Pearce has the helm; the skipper is in the saloon for tea." Golly, life on a boat is fun! As he went below, they could hear the retreating refrain, "Oh a sailor's life's for me!"

It was more than an hour before the skipper returned to the cockpit. Bruce and Annie were busy examining an opened chart. Bruce grinned in relief. "We were just about to come down to ask about directions." Pointing off the port bow, he asked, "Is that Cowichan Bay, or is it the narrows?"

The skipper took a quick look all the way around, glanced at the chart on Bruce's lap, and then pointed a bit more to starboard. "You are perfectly correct. It is Cowichan, and the narrows are just around the corner. Pretty soon we're going to see another of those rock walls that we get to weave through." He took another sweeping look around them. There were no other pleasure boats in sight. "I'll take the wheel for a while."

Annie gave a quick salute followed by a curtsy. "Aye, Aye Cap'n." She hadn't wanted to tell everyone that she was ready for a potty break anyway.

Patches of kelp along the south end of Salt Spring Island suggested the tide was low. Rocks along the shore showed the wet line where the tide had been high just a while ago.

"Wow, it's beautiful here!" Bruce was aware of some blue patches off to the west. "It's still Canada, isn't it dad?" The rocky shore seemed to plunge deeply into the dark water.

"Yup, 'tis. Vancouver Island is the land on the port side. And Salt Spring Island is this tall rascal that we are getting around." The skipper reflected for just a moment. "Except for just a few buildings in sight, and of course the Canadian ferries that we have seen this morning, these islands are relatively the same as they were over two hundred years ago when Captain Vancouver was exploring. I can't imagine how confusing it would be to find the way through all these narrow twisting channels for the first time." They both studied the passing scenery.

Finally Bruce quipped, "Yeah, about as hard as planning a proposal, I think." His big smile reflected his attempt at humor.

From inside the boat a small voice could be heard, "I heard that, and you're in trouble, Bub!" *Dreamer* rumbled on across a smooth surface, leaving a lasting wake, which disrupted the reflection of trees and rocks. The narrowing channel brought the shoreline increasingly near, giving the look of added depth to the water.

When Annie returned to the cockpit she had pulled her hair back into a short ponytail, and traded her jacket for a sweatshirt. She looked at the shores on both sides of the boat coming closer. "Is this why they call it the Narrows?"

The skipper so enjoyed her wit and memory for details. "Yup, it is. But we still have a ways to go before we are in the real close stuff. It's still around the corner." He pointed ahead with a curving motion to his hand. "This was a pretty violent area for the settlers. If you want to hear a ghost story sometime, ask me about old Tzuhalem, who was so fierce, his own people exiled him to live in the mountain caves. In fact, that peak, right over there is Mt. Tzuhalem on the charts." Bruce bent over the chart to find the corroborating information. "He was eventually slain, trying to steal a wife from one of the nearby islands. They say that an autopsy later showed that his heart was as small as a salmon's."

Annie growled, "You're just making that up! I fell for those tales when I was a little girl, but you can't fool me now." She was firm in her denial.

"In this case," the skipper replied, "the tale is true, and a matter of local history. The bay and town site were named by the Hudson Bay Company in the 1850s." Bruce shrugged, unable to help her or add to the story.

As *Dreamer* began a gentle turn to starboard, Bruce

continued to study the chart. Finally he asked, "Can you pick out a rocky island near the shore? The chart says it is called 'Burial Island!'" His voice broke in a giggle.

"Oh come on!" Annie wanted to sound incredulous. "That's just wrong! You guys are just playing with me." Her smile however, suggested that this sort of play was welcome in this morning.

"Well, you look at the chart then," Bruce said in equal mock defiance. "I'm just reading what it says here."

The water was so still at low slack that *Dreamer* left a long visible wake as it carved between Sansum Point and Bold Bluff, which make up the Narrows.

It was just a few minutes before noon when the crew stepped onto the fuel dock at Bird's Eye Cove in Maple Bay. The passage had been perfectly smooth, and well timed. The tide was beginning to come back in.

The skipper asked the attendant about the large number of folks they had seen on their way into the bay. "Are they after clams, or oysters?" he wondered.

"No, they are the kids from the coastal people's schools, most of them Cowichan. They're cleaning up the beaches and shores as part of their spring festival. I thought they were juvies until I saw how many of them are here." The young man gave an unconcerned shrug.

Before they got their visitor's moorage, the skipper asked, "Aren't the Cowichans the tribe that makes those heavy woolen sweaters?"

"Sure are. They're as warm as a heavy jacket, and

nearly waterproof. They make caps to go with them. I think their store is in Duncan, but you can find them all over." He assigned them a moorage space, then asked, "Anything more this morning?"

"Can you tell us if there is a trail or a path out to the beach where they're cleaning up?" The skipper looked as his crew. "Don't you think it could be fun to join them?"

By the time *Dreamer* was securely moored and they had walked to the top of the dock, Bruce had tried unsuccessfully three times to promote burgers and beers before they made it out to the beach.

A short walk along the shoreline trail brought them to a wide beach where twenty or thirty youngsters were scurrying around in the driftwood. A young teacher, wrapped in one of those woolen sweaters, was monitoring the activity, calling out instructions to one or another of the workers. "That's too big for us to get in the bag, Robert. Just drag it up to the trail. We'll bring the truck down." "Frank, knock it off. You haven't put three things in that bag since lunch." "Monique, you're loafing again." "Come on guys, we've got a world to clean up."

She had a round face with black hair pulled back by silver combs, smooth skin and jet black eyes. Much shorter than Annie, she was in perpetual motion. "Can I help you?" she asked as the trio stepped out onto the beach beside her.

The skipper spoke first. "We saw you all out here and

came to lend a hand." He didn't want to say that they were just curious and wanted to watch.

Her eyes sparkled in surprise. "There is more than enough trash to go around. Grab a bag if you want to, and put as much junk in as you can." She pointed to a pile of black plastic sacks.

Bruce was quick to pick up one, and suggest that if he held it for Annie, they could work as a team. The skipper took his out toward the front of the driftwood line. For almost an hour they foraged, dug pieces of plastic from under the logs, old beer cans out of the sand, hunks of Styrofoam, rags, and found more trash than they expected.

"Walter, you're not moving very fast. Come on, we have a world to clean up!" Several of the nearby children murmured, "Come on, come on!"

Their bags were nearly full of trash when they heard the teacher call the students to the top of the beach. It was time for them to return to their school, time to go home. Bruce said, "Of all the possible things that could happen today, I had no idea I'd be cleaning a beach with a bunch of kids." Annie answered by saying, "After all that sitting this morning doesn't it feel good to stretch and move around?"

The plastic bags were being collected in a growing mound. "The truck will be here in a while to pick up this stuff for the landfill." The teacher was intent on thanking the unexpected guests to her work party. "You helped out a lot. What brought you to us today?" Her eyes studied each of them, remaining on Annie. "You're not from our island, are you?"

Annie felt obliged to be the spokesperson. "No, we just came into the marina on a boat. We saw you on our way in, and thought we'd see what was going on." Her eyes looked at the pile of trash. There was a large wad of nylon net, with two dead cormorant bodies, several oily gallon containers, a large part of a boat bow, a plastic cooler, even some paint cans.

Looking at the teacher, she said, "I'm amazed at all of this." Her hand swept over the mound. "You folks picked all of this off just this one beach, and just this morning."

"Yes, and there are many more beaches just like it up and down the island." There was a confidence, a quiet contentment that brightened the teacher's face. "We have been learning how to clean our world. The students have found that it is a collective effort." Her glance traced a couple of the students who had been less than energetic about the task. "And it can happen one beach at a time. If we will each do our part, in time, our world will be respectable again." One of the boys found that the cormorant feathers were retrievable.

The teacher scolded him. "Orti, what are you doing?"

"Just collecting some feathers for my brother." He held up a fist full of black feathers. "I'm going to tell him that they are raven feathers. He'll think they are way cool."

The teacher explained to Annie, "The First People believed that the most sacred of all the animals of our world was the raven. When the Creator wanted to visit this world, he would disguise himself as one. Even today, in most of our art, the raven is revered." Annie found in the open honest face a warmth that she admired, and envied a bit.

Annie extended her hand. "I'm Ann Pearce, and this is my fiancé Bruce, (it was really fun to say that even though it was a bit of a fib,) and his father Dr. Norman O'Banyon. We're from Seattle." The teacher accepted her handshake, and replied, "I'm Theresa Gilbert. My home is the Cowichan School."

Surprised, Annie quickly asked, "You live at the school?"

"Yes. It is more of a community center, with a fine apartment that is part of the contract. It is very convenient." Her smile was contagious. "We don't get much snow here, so I never get the excuse of a 'snow-day' for being late to class." Even her laughter was charming.

Annie finally asked a serious question. "I heard you say several times that we have a world to clean, instead of a beach. Is that part of a program, or a slogan?"

"No, it's the truth of it. We have a world to clean up, and it will only happen if we do it a beach at a time. No one else may want to help us, so we must work hard." Turning toward the mound of sacks, she added, "Look at this big pile! There is at least one of those on every beach, all around our world."

Annie said, "And your workers are children. So much more could be done if the adults helped." She was becoming an activist.

"That's true. If we had more strong workers, we could get the job done sooner, and perhaps better. We are all we have right now. We take time out of school to help the students prepare for our spring earth honoring festival."

"They get credit then for this work?" Annie was very interested.

Theresa smiled. "That implies we work our schools like your public schools. There are no credits for this work, but immense benefits. These students have learned the value of a clean beach today, and the negative effects of littering. Those are lessons that will last for a long time. In many ways, they will never be the same because of what they learned today." There was no malice in her next words. "I'm interested in teaching lasting life lessons, rather than credits to graduate."

"My grandmother once told me that almost everything might be cleaned. You can sweep the house, wash the dishes, rake the yard, wash the clothes, clean the beach, and clear the land. But you cannot wash the water! We call ourselves coastal people because of our connection to the sea. It can feed and clothe us, but we, in return, must be its caretaker. That's a life lesson these students are learning a little at a time." She seemed to realize that she was speaking much too passionately for these visitors.

Smiling warmly, she apologized, "Forgive me. We

were talking about picking trash off this beach." She looked at the sand, took a deep breath and went on, "Thank you for helping us. I think you set such a good example that even our slackers were inspired to pitch in." She again held out her hand.

Annie clasped it in both her hands. "I'd like to stay in touch with you, if that's possible. Do you have an email address?" Annie held her hand until Theresa produced a business card. They both were smiling, but only one in friendship, the other was merely polite.

(Addendum 2:)

Both Annie and Bruce tried unsuccessfully to reach tgilbert@cowichancouncil.net. But the experience on the beach was so motivating to Annie that when she returned to her office, she organized a team of beach-cleaners. To date they have had a positive effect on Golden Gardens, Redondo Beach, and the Arboretum.

By the time they were back to the marina, the sound of hamburgers and beer was a supper suggestion rather than lunch. They had a lot to talk about.

"I just can't get over how great Theresa was out there with those kids." Annie's smile was soft and warm. "She had a confidence that I envy. I've been thinking about it, and wonder if I could handle that chore that well." Her ponytail flipped from side to side.

They were seated in the waning afternoon sun,

sheltered by a plastic windscreen and warmed by a reflection heater that made the deck setting very pleasant. The burgers had been consumed ravenously, and a second round of Molson was easing them into an important conversation.

Bruce nodded, "I noticed that too. She seemed to be having a good time, but was in complete control of those kids." Looking at his dad, he asked, "Don't you think it's a struggle for all of us to find confidence? Aren't we all just a little intimidated by life?"

"Well Bud, I'm not sure I'd call it intimidation, or just plain discomfort. We are bombarded by so many challenges to solve, and new situations with which to cope, it's no wonder that we are frequently shaken. Our own sense of happiness, our sense of meaning is often linked to our trust, or assurance, or confidence."

Annie added, "She was like a calm center to a storm of activity. I just really admired her, and wonder if that is something that is learned, or was she just born with it?" There wasn't the slightest hint of disrespect implied by her question.

"I think it is something that we learn, and keep on developing as we get better at it." The skipper was thinking of a scriptural setting.

"If I remember correctly, the word confidence can be divided into two older words, 'con' which means 'with,' and 'fidere', which means 'faith.' To be confident means to face life with faith!" He made sure that they both followed. "I think Theresa had faith in herself, faith in her students, and maybe most important, faith in the rightness of what they were doing."

"Then you think anyone can get confidence?" Annie asked the question that Bruce was about to voice. "Just anyone can be confident?"

"Have we got time for a Bible study?" the skipper asked. "I can feel this turning into a major discussion."

Bruce grinned at Annie. "My calendar is clear for the rest of the afternoon, how about yours?" She giggled and nodded her head.

"O.K." the skipper began. He had written some notes on a napkin. "I think there are at least five steps in this crash course on confidence." He smiled a satisfaction with the beginning. "The setting is the Garden of Gethsemane on the night of Jesus' arrest. John tells us that Jesus knew all that was about to happen to him. When the crowd came after him, he stepped forward. That is step number one; stand up, step forward, don't try to run or hide. Seize the initiative to face what must be faced."

"In my mind's eye I can make a movie scene out of this, seeing the mob of lights moving into the garden, hearing the curses and threats. I know that Jesus could have escaped, could have melted into the shadows and gotten away. But he chose to step forward. It is vitally important to decide ahead of time that we are not going to be intimidated into fear by every problem that comes along. We have his courage to stand up to life, to our difficulties, to our heartaches, and assume a posture of certainty and strength."

"And that leads to the second step. We can, because we know that he is with us, that we are never abandoned or left alone, we can" he repeated, "affirm our identity. Jesus did that. Instead of the mob questioning him, he asked 'whom do you seek?' They answered, 'Jesus of Nazareth.' He said simply, 'I am he.' John tells us that his accusers cringed and fell to the ground."

The skipper looked around the deck, glad for their privacy and comfort. "I think I might have said, 'you just missed him. He went that way.' Or 'Good, I'll help you find him.' But Jesus affirmed his identity. 'I am he.'"

"Do you remember the words God spoke to Moses in the Exodus story?" When both Bruce and Annie shook their heads, he explained, "God called Moses to go to Egypt to free the Hebrew people who were enslaved there. When Moses claimed he didn't know God's name, the answer came to him, 'I am who I am!' That was the name that would liberate and deliver from bondage, the name of the God who cannot be defined, explained, packaged or ultimately defeated: 'I Am'."

"Here is the source of power of our affirmation. Here is the place we discover who we are. Jesus reveals to us the name, the nature, and the reality of the unknowable. He reveals God as Abba, which in Hebrew meant something like 'daddy.' Jesus prays for us, and what a wonderful prayer. He prays that the love with which God has loved him may be in us, and God may live in us. And most important, when you know the truth of that prayer, alive within the depths of your own life, you can stand and say, 'I am a child of God!' The destructive powers of this earth cannot overcome that!"

"I read about a college girl who had just become a Christian. She was attacked one night by a man who intended to rape her. He threatened her life if she did not submit to him. She looked into his face and answered, 'I am a child of God. I belong to Him. You can't do that. Leave me alone!' And he did! Step number two is: affirm your identity. Say it, or sing it, or shout it, but certainly believe it. I am a child of God!"

"The third step in the crash course is: put away the sword. This truly is the affirmation of nonviolence. The gospel writers all agree the scene was chaotic, nearly comic as the slave of the high priest is the only one wounded. Luke, the physician, remembers how Jesus takes even this dramatic moment to pause and heal the injured man. Put your sword away."

"When we face life's most challenging times, we may feel under attack, and our first impulse is either to run, or to fight back. Someone has said that in this day and age if the meek are going to inherit the earth, they need to be a lot more aggressive. Our response to problems is often to flex our muscles, to counterattack, or at least to get even. The problem is usually the same; we miss our target and wound poor Malchus the slave, or the children, or some other innocent by-stander. We see it all the time. Someone takes out the sword and accidents happen, the innocent pay the high price of violence. Jesus said 'Put away your sword.'"

The sun was making its way through the broken overcast. Finally there was color and springtime glory. After a big breath, the skipper went on. "The fourth step is the other side of non-violence: confront with care. Jesus did not respond with a threat of violence, but he did respond. He was not some spineless defeatist that just folded up. He faced the high priest, and the soldiers, and Pilate himself. When the high priest questions Jesus about his disciples and his teachings, Jesus turns the questions around. He confronts the high priest by asking, 'Why do you ask me. Ask those who heard me, what I said to them. They know what I said.' He refused to be intimidated by the pressures of political or religious leaders."

"Then an officer stepped forward and struck Jesus across the face, saying, 'is that how you answer the high priest?' And once again Jesus refused to be intimidated. He did not wilt. Rather he said, 'If I have spoken wrongly, bear witness to the wrong; but if I have spoken rightly, why do you strike me?' Jesus taught us to have the courage to confront – not to be pushed around by someone in power or authority. But the confrontation is always caring. It is not destructive. It raises the right questions. Put away the sword, but practice caring, confident confrontation."

Neither of his listeners showed disinterest, so the

skipper concluded, "The fifth step is to live, visualizing God's inner strength. When Jesus was before Pilate, surrounded by symbols of Roman authority and power, he wasn't fooled by the display. He announced, 'My kingship is not of this world; if my kingship were of this world, my servants would fight, that I might not be handed over to the Jews.' ...'For this I was born, and for this I have come into the world, to bear witness to the truth. Everyone who is of the truth hears my voice.' To which poor Pilate can only respond, 'What is truth?'"

"This final step is to begin to visualize as clearly and distinctly as possible the results of that confident faith at work in your life. What difference would it make if you really believed that Jesus was born to bear witness to the truth to you? Get a clear mental image of yourself responding as a believer of that truth. You actually can live into the image of a new future with confidence. God is giving us, right now, strength to defeat our fears. He is giving us the confidence we need to meet any challenge, to clean any beach, even our world." The skipper felt like he had just finished a sermon, a pretty effective one at that.

Annie had been listening so carefully she had forgotten to write down the five steps. "Can you tell me those steps again so I can put them in my notebook?"

The skipper slid his napkin over so that she could read along. Step forward; two, affirm your identity; three, put your sword away; four, confront with caring; and five, live from God's inner power." The long shadows of late afternoon were claiming the deck.

Bruce and Annie decided to walk back to the beach before returning to the boat. The skipper said he had lots of reading to do. Darkness settled softly into the cove. There were, eventually, a couple games of Hearts, Fan-tan, and a rowdy game of Cheat Casino. The subject finally turned to the plans of the next day.

Bruce asked, "Are we heading back tomorrow?" It was an unwelcome thought to each of them.

"Sort of," the skipper answered. "We'll leave as early as possible to ride the ebbing tide south. We can have the best part of the day in Victoria. There is a ton to do there, if we have wrapped up our work on the boat."

Annie asked, "Do you mean if we've worked through the agendas that brought us here?" She had an easy and lovely smile.

The skipper chuckled, "That would be an accomplishment, wouldn't it?" Then after a sigh, he added, "But tomorrow is Thursday, and we've been at this for almost a week. Even God rested, some."

Bruce also heaved a big sigh. "It's been the fastest week I can remember, and the best by far." Annie joined in his appraisal.

"Well, let's see what the last three days bring. I'm thinking that a few hours in Victoria are not enough. So we might stay on the Wharf Dock for two nights and slide back to Seattle on the afternoon tide, which might put us in late Sunday. At least it is a rough plan." With nodding heads of agreement, the skipper bid them goodnight, thinking, "Who knows what the next few days will bring?"

Notebooks:

Annie wrote: I seem to have so much energy! It feels like I'm super-charged! I could say that it's because I'm getting lots of rest, eating better than usual, but it feels deeper than that. I think there is a new source of energy that I'm enjoying. Maybe I'm not thinking about work, or any other distraction. Maybe this is what happens when a person focuses on just one activity at a time. I just know that I feel invincible! Wow! That's the first time I ever said that about me! I feel happy, in love, and filled with possibilities.

If you had plenty of energy and opportunity, to do anything you wanted, what would you do? I think I'm going to work on cleaning my world!

Bruce wrote: What's the old German quote? "Ve gets too shoon oldt, und too late shmart!" That's how I feel about dad tonight. I just finished Luskin's book. It was a formal repetition of the things dad has been saying all week long. We can't be negatively critical and positively affirming at the same time. (No matter how funny it may sound at the moment, it is still negative.) We cannot hold opposing feelings simultaneously about someone special to us, so the need to affirm is primary in all our communications.

Luskin says we find long-term healing in long-term commitments because we look beyond the current moment or situation. The long look frees us from thoughts of revenge or retaliation. It promotes healthy interaction between people, groups, even nations.

I surely do think a lot about a long-term commitment with Annie. She is on my mind, and in my heart, every waking moment, and it is much more wholesome than lust. If I thought I loved her before this trip, I was only aware of the visible part of the iceberg. She is so witty, so gentle, so thoughtful, so... kind. I just love her completely. I feel like a schoolboy again. Is this the healing that forgiveness brings?

Norm wrote:

It seems to me we have been through most of the processes. In the first, or injury stage, there were phases: 1.) The initial assault, with its loss of control or safety, 2.) The flood of emotions, shame and guilt, 3.) Denial, discouragement, maybe even depression were part of the reliving and retelling of it.

In the reflection stage there were more phases: 1.) Grieving the loss, 2.) Discovering our own participation by expanding the assault story, 3.) Identifying personal snags that made it unlikely to forgive.

Finally, we got into an insight stage where we: 1.)

Used our insight, and thought to see the picture clearly. 2.) Prayed and meditated upon our dilemma, 3.) Added a new gratitude dimension, 4.) Began to focus on the future by reminding ourselves that the world would be improved if we could forgive.

Now the hard part begins! We must be in the beginning of the application stage where we 1.) Completely renounce our anger or resentment, 2.) Help others in their efforts to live in mercy, 3.) Design a lasting plan for mercy to flow into our relationships, 4.) Know recovery as no more pain, and no desire to retell the account.

I'm thinking of forgiveness as the transference of mercy from person to person. It is like an electrical circuit. When connections are complete, a surge of electrical energy is possible. In the case of forgiveness, mercy is the energy that surges through the circuit.

CHAPTER SEVEN:
VICTORIA,
VANCOUVER B.C.

Focus on the future; create a positive spiritual perspective

The skipper turned on his bunk light to check the time. It was still dark, but time to be up and about. The day was calling him to action. Quietly he shaved, combed his hair, and buttoned a favorite blue flannel shirt. It was time to wake the rest of the crew.

When he opened his cabin door, however, he found them reading at the salon table. They both smiled prankishly. Bruce was the first to speak, "You said you wanted to leave as early as possible." Giving a quick grin at Annie, he went on, "She knocked on my door fifteen minutes ago. I think she's going to be a diehard boater for sure."

Annie nearly giggled. "I couldn't sleep. It feels like I'm all wound up. Today just seemed too important to stay under the covers any longer." She looked affectionately from the skipper to Bruce.

"Well, let's go up to the Boat House and see if the grill is open. They have a terrific breakfast, if you're brave enough to try it." The skipper headed for the companionway hatch. Outside a low overcast muted the first attempts of dawn.

In less than an hour they were back aboard, getting ready to be underway. Annie exclaimed, "I can't believe how large those portions were, and I can't believe I actually tried to eat the entire thing. Did they call that a Fried Pile? It had potatoes and onions, bacon, garlic and green peppers in it. I think there might have been some seaweed! I can't believe how good it was!" She was still feeling that strange new invigoration. "What can I do to help?"

"The tide is at full ebb, which is going our way," the skipper explained. "I think we're going to be on the diesel most or all the way. Jeepers tells me its thirty-three miles to Victoria. If we can do eight knots on the engine and get an additional three from the tide, we can be there before noon." Looking around the salon to make sure everything was stowed and sea ready, he advised them, "I'll take the first helm. It's pretty chilly this morning. If you two would like to stay down here where it's toasty, you can spell me off in an hour or so. O.K?" Within a few minutes, *Dreamer* was backing out of the marina slip, and negotiating the narrow channel toward the mouth of Bird's Eye Cove. They were heading south, toward Seattle and the end of their journey.

The skipper was startled just a few minutes later to hear the cabin hatch slide open. Both Bruce and Annie were bundled in Gore-Tex jackets. She also had her bunk blanket that was soon wrapped snugly around her legs, feet tucked in their usual cozy way. Bruce was carrying two cups of steaming tea.

"Annie asked me to explain the tide business," he began sheepishly. "It seems to be really important from our first day out. Now, we both are asking you to explain what seems to happen regularly each day. I thought I understood, until I tried to put it in words." His smile was boyish and appealing. "I told her that sometimes it's in and sometimes out. She asked me where it went when it is out." His shoulders shrugged his confusion.

The skipper took a grateful sip of hot tea. "To begin such a large subject, you must remember that the earth's surface is two-thirds water, which is subject to the gravitational pull of both the moon and sun. If you think globally, the change is miniscule. The attracted surface of the ocean doesn't bulge so much as it gives a tiny swell in the middle. But each day here at latitude 48 North, the tiny change in the middle turns into about 15 feet of water in and out twice a day. The major high and low tides are affected by the moon, and the minor by the sun. There is slack about thirty minutes in between tides when the incoming, or flooding tide is nearly full, and changing to ebbing, or out-going. Another slack happens when the low tide is making up its mind to start back in. Just think about how much volume must come in through the Strait to fill Puget Sound, which is one hundred thirty miles long and almost twenty miles wide in some places. That's an enormous amount of water in and out twice daily."

He took another sip of tea before continuing. "The tides are less dramatic near the equator. I think we had eighteen inches of change in the Virgin Islands. Then in Anchorage, I've heard their tides are twenty feet!"

Bruce was impressed. "Wow! I never thought of tides as having that much power, since they make so little fuss, just going back and forth."

Dreamer was just making the southern turn to clear the narrows.

"Actually, Bruce," the skipper began a discussion that would last much longer than their journey, "The tides are only indications of the powerful effect of the gravities of our own planet, the moon and sun. Like a complex watch, these forces are in constant balance and adjustment."

"Then why don't they have that effect on us, dad?" Bruce's question was sincere, not for a second argumentative. "It seems logical that we, being mostly fluid, would weigh more at high tide than at low." Grinning impishly he added, "We could jump higher, or run faster, when we were at low tide. Or maybe we should all just crowd together at high tide." It was fun morning banter.

"I know that you are just kidding." The skipper was relaxed in this close conversation. "In comparison to the vastness of the ocean, our water content is too slight to be on the scale. Gravity, however, does have a huge affect on us. It keeps us fairly secure when a huge centrifugal force would fling us far out into space."

Annie squinted her confusion, while Bruce answered, "You mean the fact that we are spinning on our axis, right?"

"Yeah, if the planet is nearly twenty five thousand miles around, at the equator we must be traveling over a thousand miles per hour to do one revolution in 24 hours. But what is even more impressive, is that we are on an orbit around the sun which will take us 575 million miles in one year, or an average speed of 18.5 miles every second! At this very moment powerful forces are at work on us because we are going 66,600 miles per hour. To put that in perspective, when you see the new quarter moon rising, we were just there an hour ago! Yikes!" He added the exclamation to make his point. "There are very powerful natural forces at work on us right at this moment." In the distance the skipper could see a Canadian ferryboat on its way out of Swartz Bay. They were making excellent time.

"You know dad, I have trouble thinking about forces or powers around me that I cannot sense or measure. I'm not arguing with Mr. Newton's apple. I'm just saying that my brain is less abstract than some to get around notions like velocity and momentum that are undetectable." The grin had faded to a serious expression. Bruce was wrestling with a spiritual discovery.

"You mean it has to be weighed or calibrated for you to take it seriously?"

"Naw. I know love doesn't weigh a thing, or memories, or laughter. But the scientist in me knows that power can be put on a schematic. The thought of mass in motion at such a high velocity is a new notion for me."

The skipper was studying their course. Little Piers Island was now evident, marking their transit through Colburne Passage. Annie followed his gaze, and asked, "Is there a channel through there?"

"Yup, it's just a matter of trust." Looking carefully at Bruce he reconnected with their conversation. "Bud, there are lots of different powers at work on us, and in us that probably befuddle the best scientists. That leads me to suggest we talk about God's Spirit, the gifts of which are many and powerful, and the fruit of which is the very best experience we can have."

Annie immediately sat up. "I was sort of interested in tides, but you have my complete attention now. Is this something we can talk about now?" She seemed to be holding her breath waiting for the answer.

"Well of course we can," the skipper said quickly. Then looking at Bruce, he added, "If all of us want to be in the conversation."

"Hey! Count me in," Bruce answered. "Remember, I'm the power guy. That's my field. Of course we usually speak of micro-volts instead of eternal power." He chuckled at his own humor. Since the boatyard episode, his attitude had gotten sweeter, and noticeably happier.

The skipper took a sweeping look all around them for other traffic. Once again, they were practically alone on their way into Swartz Bay. The overcast sky had lowered and darkened with the early morning, and scarcely a ripple of wind marred the smooth reflection of the passage.

"It's a huge conversation first of all," the skipper began. When both Annie and Bruce assured him that they had no other scheduled obligations, he began. "Let's think about this together." He took a deep breath because he understood what an important discussion was beginning. "For the sake of this discussion, let's use the word 'ministry' for doing all the kind, just, merciful, compassionate deeds we can imagine."

Before he could go on, Bruce said, "You're not talking about Church work are you?"

"I am not," the skipper said confidently. "Jesus said that others would know that we are his disciples, which means student, if we have love for one another. So ministry is all the projects, big and small we can do for each other in love." As Annie and Bruce grinned at each other, he added, "Not that kind of love, although I suppose it is a good place to start."

"In the Greek language, there are four different words for 'love.' The first is *eros* from which we get the word erotic. It is passionate love or affection, it is gender sensitive." He enjoyed his wit. "The second is *philia*, like Philadelphia. It represents brotherly love. Love of country, school loyalty, great friendships all relate to this form of love. *Storge* is love of family, our kith and kin that is blood love. It has been said that we get to choose our friends, but we are stuck with *storge*. *Agape* love is total, absolute, unconditional love. That's the way God loves us."

"Now, if we have any of that sort of love we could say that we are doing ministry. We are having love for one another, and that, in the New Testament terms is ministry. And here's where it gets a bit complex. If we think God gives us gifts to complete projects, we miss the point. God gives us projects to complete us, and equips us with the gifts to accomplish that. And," he took a deep breath, "we all have different project opportunities, so we each have a different mix of gifts."

Before Annie could ask, Bruce broke in. "Wait, wait! I don't understand. Do you mean that we are custom-made ministers?"

A kind expression from the skipper accompanied his response. "I said this was complex. Let me try to make it a little more understandable." Again he paused to frame the right words.

"Being a gracious host or hostess is easy when we are entertaining family, but when we are welcoming a stranger into our home because they need shelter or nourishment, that's loving in a ministry way, called hospitality. When we teach someone who is less familiar with the gospel story, (Annie pointed to herself) that's loving in a ministry way. When you encourage someone who is feeling weak or despondent, that is loving in a ministry way, and God helps us develop those skills, through the Spirit. In the New Testament, Paul identifies more than two dozen different forms of loving in a ministry way. He calls them gifts of the Spirit"

Annie shook her head. "I'm not understanding the concept here. Do you mean they were like holy men or women? Or were they like missionaries or pastors?" She was trying to get the idea clearly in mind.

"Well yes, they were," the skipper nodded. "But remember, this was before any sort of organized Church. They were missionaries in that they were going into a world with a startlingly new message of God's love, and the word 'pastor ' means shepherd, which they were trying to be to the new converts." He took a big breath with a grin. "And no they weren't. They were just ordinary believers who were willing to accept extra-ordinary projects. Paul's instructions and explanations were general in nature, trying to help people understand the concept of an active God, assisting in the development of individuals and communities."

Bruce also wore a frown, trying to stay up with the conversation. "That sounds pretty evangelic. Is that the word? Or should I say fundamental?"

"Like so many words, it is up to the person just what the meaning might be. Yes, it is evangelic, which means it is in keeping with the Good News of the gospel, and it is fundamental in that it is basic belief content. There are, to be sure, ways of using those words, which are more extreme, and frequently abrasive."

Without waiting for the questioning to develop further, he went on. "In the New Testament, these several personal characteristics are given to ordinary people to conduct the work of the faith. In time administrators were needed, so that became understood as a spiritual gift, given by God, as was knowledge, wisdom, teaching, prayer, even humor."

"No way," Bruce interjected. "How could that be a gift from God?"

"I think it's in Galatians 5 or again in Corinthians 12, that Paul talks about the ability to bring laughter and joy to situations and relationships to relieve tension, anxiety, or conflicts, and to heal and free emotions and energies needed for effective ministries."

"Who knew?" Annie giggled her delight. "Who had a clue that religion could have anything to do with humor? I certainly didn't! That sounds like some kind of miracle to me."

"Miracles are on Paul's list of gifts too," the skipper

continued. Believers are given the ability to do powerful works that transcend our perception of natural laws, and means to free individuals from conditions that restrict needed ministries. Who knew, indeed?" His affection was evident to both of his listeners. "But remember, the tasks were given to fulfill or complete the individual, not just to get tasks done."

They were passing the Canadian ferry terminal at Swartz Bay, making sure there was plenty of seaway for safety. Overhead the morning gloom seemed to deepen even more.

"The thing that I have said to the churches, when we talk about this subject, is that God doesn't wait until someone with the appropriate skill set comes along to do desired ministry. God simply and profoundly gives the gifts needed to accomplish the work, because that's how people grow spiritually."

Once again Bruce interjected, "Dad, do you believe that you received special gifts, then?" It was a sincere question that helped clear up some of the confusion.

"Yes, I definitely do. But remember, those gifts we've been talking about were given before there was a formal status of clergy. I think that is how my 'call into ministry' was understood in the first place. I had some great friends in the Church who urged me to consider going to seminary, but only after early experiences of devotion and service."

"I can remember how violently my knees trembled

and my hands shook when I read scripture in a Sunday morning service. It was not my shining talent that they saw, but God's merciful gifts at work in me. Courage is another of those gifts to get the person completed."

Annie asked, almost breathlessly, "Did you do miracles?"

The skipper chuckled, "In a way. I wrote several sermons without being thrown out of the pulpit. I found I had a gift for preaching that was a little instructional, or teaching, it was a little motivating or encouraging, it was biblically accurate, it helped people feel better about themselves and their world. A blend that was welcomed in every congregation I cared for. And it always reminded them that they were eternally cherished, and of significance. I think that was something of a miracle. It also helped that I frequently followed pastors who were less trained or prepared."

"But dad," Bruce needed clarification, " if God wants the work done, why wouldn't all pastors have those gifts?"

"There you have the right question, Bud. The gifts are given, or offered might be more accurate. There are countless opportunities for doing tasks of love that go unnoticed. It is up to each of us to be receptive, just as we were in receiving forgiveness. If we don't recognize or receive the gifts, they cannot be employed. Just like many people failed to recognize the beautiful sunset last evening, or the look of affection in the eyes of their loved ones this morning, gifts can easily go unaccepted."

"Hold on for a second." He gave all his attention to a narrow passage between drying rocks. "This part is just a little tricky. I'd hate to scrape the paint." *Dreamer* gracefully swept through the narrow opening into a wide-open channel. "Sydney is just off our starboard bow, and Vancouver Island is pretty populated from here on south to Victoria." They admired a number of large homes with groomed lawns right down to the water's edge.

"O.K., we've got about another hour to get around James Island, which is a marine park, and avoid Little Zero Rock. I think the tide will be going to low slack about there, so it will be easy to see. Who wants to steer?" Neither Bruce nor Annie volunteered.

"Dad it's not that we don't want to. I think we are too into the discussion. Can we be listeners for a little while more?" There was such sincerity that the skipper felt a warm wave of affection for them both.

"Slackers!" the skipper said mischievously. "You'll pay with shortened rations, no rum, and the beatings will continue until your attitudes improve!" They all chuckled.

"There is a ton more to this discussion, and I would encourage you to plan to study more of it when we get home. I'd be more than happy to help. The point that I want to get to this morning (he checked his watch) is not about the gifts of the Spirit, but the fruit of that holy and present Spirit in your lives. Remember, God is in the business of completing individuals, not just getting a lot of holy business done." Once again Bruce and Annie exchanged confused shrugs.

"As God is in residence within a person, there is an increase of several wonderful characteristics, called the fruit of the Spirit. They are described in Galatians 5: 22-23. There are three sets of three for easy recollection. Love, Joy, and Peace are the first. Patience Kindness, and Goodness are the second three. Faithfulness, Gentleness, and Self-control are the final three. Paul says, 'If we live by the Spirit, let us walk by the Spirit. Let us have no self-conceit, no provoking of one another, no envy of one another.'"

Annie said softly, "I'm familiar with those words, but can you help me understand what they might mean in 'the Spirit'?"

"I can only try," he replied. "We can take them slowly, one at a time." Pausing to make sure they were both ready, he said, "Love seems pretty obvious, but it means much more than a tender emotion. This fruit is an act of will that reaches out. You might say it is an increasing concern for others, day by day, month by month. In marriage love is a refreshing care for each other. In the world around us it is increasingly seeing the wounded, lost, or disadvantaged people as an opportunity to assist. O.K. with that?" They both were writing in their notebooks. Without looking up, they both nodded.

"Joy is a wonderful New Testament word '*macharios*' which means a deep confidence and optimism, unshaken in difficult times, and completely self-contained. In marriage there can be an increasing season of gladness between you, marked by laughter and an eagerness to be together." He smiled as they wrote rapidly. "Ready?" They both nodded again, without looking up from their work.

"Peace is the fruit of calmness and inner guidance, even when things seem to be going wrong. The word 'shalom' doesn't relate to tranquility so much as the very highest good that could come to this particular moment. So the third fruit is an increasing calmness in your hearts, home and life, a growing awareness of God bringing out the very best." They both seemed to write more, even as the skipper asked, "Ready to go on?"

"Patience is a tough one. It means an endurance in the face of frustration or hardship without thoughts of anger or revenge. Patience is not seeking revenge, or not even wanting it. Patience in marriage means that there is an increasing stretch in your attitudes toward others, more flexibility toward those with whom we share our time." Bruce was hurriedly writing 'flex-ability.'

After a sweeping look for any close traffic, the skipper went on. "Kindness is one of the most important words we can use for each other. It could mean tenderness, courtesy, or even compassion. In marriage, kindness is a growing self-honesty, which causes us to care more for others. It's the 'walking in another's shoes' sort of thing." The cockpit was busily quiet while they wrote in their notebooks.

"Goodness is another big New Testament word. It can mean generosity, or giving to those in need without thought of reward. In marriage, goodness means you seek to be a blessing more and more to each other. You are better people than you were a year ago. Does that make sense?" Bruce held up his hand, pausing the skipper until he could finish writing another sentence. Finally he said "O.K."

"Faithfulness relates not only to our fidelity, although it is definitely a matter of dependability in all our relationships, faithfulness means that your fears are on the decline. (He put emphasis on the word for effect.) Think about it! Doubts are not the opposite of faith. In fact, some doubts lead to a stronger faith as we work through them. The opposite of faith is fear. The more we have a trusting obedience to God, our fears will more and more evaporate." His listeners were hurriedly writing; like court reporters, they were trying to capture every word. He waited until they were ready for him to go on.

"Gentleness is simply quiet strength born out of modesty, without defensiveness or arrogance. In marriage, gentleness is being increasingly thoughtful, or more courteous, softer in our touch, emotionally, physically, or spiritually. As we see others as more precious, we value, and protect them more. Does that make sense to you?" Both Bruce and Annie looked up with a quick smile.

"Finally, the ninth fruit of the Spirit is self-control, which means moderation and balance in one's personal life. To be sure it does not mean denying ourselves from the good things that have been labeled in the past as luxuries or privileges. It does mean, in marriage, that we are more in charge of our emotions. We can claim them as appropriate." As the two were finishing their notebooks, the skipper concluded, "There they are, a tree full of fruit: love, joy, peace... patience, kindness, goodness, ... faithfulness, gentleness, and self-control. I can think of no clearer definition of characteristics of a spiritually well person."

"Wow," Annie began. "How can I... what do we need to do ... I really want my life to look like that. What can I do to begin?" She was sitting on the edge of the cockpit very straight.

"I think you simply let God bless you." The skipper said slowly, "You simply start believing as much as you can that God loves you, and wants to use your life as a blessing to others. You may begin by seeing opportunities for service as ways in which God is trying to complete you." The skipper was once again aware of the depth of her green eyes. "It is the next step after receiving God's forgiveness. Now receive God's loving gifts, and the fruit of the Spirit that accompany them."

Bruce moved very close to Annie. "It seems so huge, like an amazing puzzle," he said. "Where do we start?"

"Remember those rating scales you did several days ago?" the skipper asked. "On a scale of one to ten, ten being maximum, how would you rate your desire to live a vital, dynamic faith? How would you rate your partner's willingness? When it comes to mercy, grace, and forgiveness, rate yourself, then your partner." The channel ahead of them was opening to Haro Strait, wide and free of traffic. "Now compare your answers to see how well you interpret each other's openness to growth." Both Bruce and Annie bent in quiet conversation. The diesel engine throbbed powerfully below them.

"Before I go below for a potty break, here's the assignment for the morning," the skipper finally said. "Take a look at the list of nine fruit of the Spirit. Choose one that you would like to emphasize for the next month. There is no specific order, none are primary, all of them are essential, and you both don't need to agree on the same one. It may be kindness or self-control. It may be joy or patience. Just choose one to concentrate your growth efforts for the next month. Write the word somewhere that you will be reminded daily. Pray for more of it in your life. See what opportunities develop." They both hurriedly wrote a few more lines in their notebooks.

"I'll steer," Bruce said at last. "It looks like a wide open course."

The skipper said, "The course is about 145 on the compass." Then pointing just off the starboard bow, he added, "That's Little Zero Rock, which must be avoided. Just stay to the east of it and we'll be fine. I'm going to see about another cup of tea, after a more compelling appointment." Everyone chuckled as the skipper hurried below.

"Junior officer O'Banyon has the helm!" Bruce growled in his cockney voice, since no one else would call the helm change. A light rain began to fall, speckling the still surface around them.

"Sweetie," Annie began quietly. "Do you understand all that about the Spirit?" She glanced at the companionway to be sure that the skipper was not within earshot. "I want to believe it, but I must have missed most of what he told us." She twisted uncomfortably. "Do you get it?"

"Well, I've heard a lot of those conversations and sermons my whole life," Bruce replied. "But I think that's the first time he has explained it that carefully. It made some sense, didn't it?"

"You weasel," she smirked. "You didn't get it either, did you? You're just trying to make me think that you did." She beamed a radiant look of affection at him that warmed the soggy morning.

"What I am aware of," Bruce refused to respond to her calling him a weasel, "is my need for some really serious bible study, and a place where we can explore this more. I can hardly believe that such an important topic has been in front of me for all this time and I didn't know it. But it explains why religion has been boring to me. I've always thought of it as a historic sort of thing that happened way back in Jerusalem. To think that there are personal gifts, personal benefits from the faith that makes us more fit for living with others. That just changes everything!" He wished he could return a portion of the joy he found in her eyes.

"Well, let's ask him to help us when we get back. If he won't teach us, maybe he can show us where someone else will." Her smile didn't fade. "Hey, which one of the nine fruits did you pick to emphasize for the next month?" Her smile became mischievous. "That sounds fun, doesn't it? 'Which fruit did you pick?' Why, I picked some peaches, cherries and a big box of patience." They both giggled at her humor.

Bruce thought for a moment, then answered, "It's a little bit like asking which one do we feel we most lack, isn't it?" He pondered a bit more. "It's like asking, 'am I less kind than joyful?' Or, 'am I less loving than good?' I don't think I can answer that question." He had a small frown.

"No, that's not how I heard it. It's like the glass that's either half empty, or half full. Imagine going to the gym and having your trainer ask you, 'Which muscle group do we need to work on, abs or quads?' It's not that you are less of anything, but would you like to be more of something." Her exclamation point was a quick bob of her head, which sent morning curls out of place.

"Hmm," Bruce smiled. "When you put it like that, I can tell you that I was most interested in the last one, the self-control one. Being more in charge of my emotions, whether at work or at home, just sounds so good to me. I think I have gotten lost in the negative stuff before, and let my emotions guide me. Yup, I want to pick a peck of self-control!"

Annie was scooting aft to be closer to Bruce. "Me too. I'd like to have more self-control, but I think goodness was the word that caught my attention. I think I could be more generous, and a better person than I was a year ago. A crate of goodness will be a wonderful pick for me." They both laughed softly.

"Honey, (he loved to call her endearments) if you get any gooder, I'm a sunk duck for sure. I'm already head over heels in love with you. If you get any gooder, I'm completely a basket case." They were still chuckling when the skipper peeked out of the salon to ask if he could bring anyone a cup of tea. They both declined.

"But dad, you can take a look at that boat over by the rock. I think the guy is waving to us." Bruce pointed off the starboard bow. "At first I thought he was fishing. I don't think the boat is moving. But he just started waving that cloth like he was trying to get our attention."

The skipper moved to the nav-station where the VHF radio was already on channel 16, the emergency channel. "Little Zero Rock fisherman, this is sailboat *Dreamer*, over." He opened the transmitter to listen for a response. He could only hear other faint traffic noise. "Little Zero Rock fisherman, this is sailboat *Dreamer*, over." He paused again to listen. After two more tries, the skipper went into the cockpit to assess the situation.

The tide was low slack. The rain had increased to a steady drizzle. With low visibility he guessed they must be at least a mile away from the fellow, who continued to wave.

"O.K. Bud," the skipper said as he took the wheel. "I'll take a look. You two might want to get something warm to drink if you're chilly." The dodger did give surprising comfort and protection from the rain. Without checking if they were still listening, he said, "If we see or hear any emergency, we are bound by the rules of the road to respond." *Dreamer's* bow was swinging toward the small boat, and finally the figure stopped waving the cloth, although he was still standing.

When they had closed to about 200 meters, Bruce went out on the bow. It was clear that this fishing boat had seen better days. It was 17 or 18 feet long, probably trailerable, and the canvas was torn in several places, worn in several more. There was only one person on board.

When the distance was near enough to hail the man, Bruce called, "You havin' trouble?"

The man answered, "Oh Jeez, I think she died, 'eh?" *Dreamer* came to a stop about twenty feet off the disabled boat's beam. "She just damned died, you know. I think the ol' generator's fried, but everything's cooked. I got no power, no radio, not even any damned oars, 'eh?" He rubbed his cap off his head in frustration. "Can you give me a jumper, or an extra battery?" It was an excessive request born out of his need to get the boat started again.

The skipper shook his head. "But I can give you a tow into Oak Bay. That's about five miles isn't it?" It seemed the only reasonable solution short of trying to repair the old boat here. "Have you got a dock line or two?" When the man produced a short frayed rope, the skipper directed Bruce to the forward deck locker where he would find two long lines. Within moments Bruce was back in the cockpit with the braided Dacron lines. "Now, fasten one to each aft mooring cleat, make sure you pass them in under our lifeline, make a loop on the end, and I'll get close enough to pass the lines over to make a tow." Speaking loudly to the stranded boater, he said, "Hook them both to your bow cleat and we'll be in Oak Bay in less than an hour." Gladly the man acknowledged the information.

"Beats the hell out of tryin' to drift there," he said with relief, and just a faint bit of humor. Then loud enough to be heard clearly, he said, "You're the first ones to stop, all day. I been out here since last night. Plenty of boats came by, but none stopped to help. Hell, they could've at least called in a distress to the Coast Guard for me." He looked tired and cold.

The skipper called to him, "Have you had anything to eat this morning?" When the man shook his head, the skipper directed Annie to make up a big cup of tea, and look for any loose food. "You know, cookies, pastry, the things Bruce likes." They all grinned.

"Bruce, get us a couple of fenders, so I can ease alongside." When Bruce asked if that meant 'bumpers', the skipper gave him a thumbs up signal. The whole process only took four or five minutes. The distressed boater was on his way to safety.

It was just 10:20 as they eased out of Oak Bay. The marina folks had been helpful, waiting for them to arrive, and securing the disabled boat. The weary man had quickly called his worried wife, then, profusely thanked the crew for helping him. "Jeez, you're one in a million, even for Yanks, you're right fine folks." He had carefully given a handshake to each member of the crew. "Bet you weren't counting on savin' my dirty ol' hide, 'eh?" His gratitude balanced any offense his language might have made. "God bless America, 'eh?" The morning rain was getting heavier, closing in around them like a soggy curtain. The crew acknowledged that they were glad to be of assistance, then swung *Dreamer's* bow back toward the open water beyond the harbor's entrance.

The skipper re-engaged the morning's conversation with an observation. "I am convinced that God did not intentionally disable that boat just for us. It does stand to make a good point, however. Our discussion about the Holy Spirit can find an illustration here. Most people have a faith like that old boat. They are not sinking, are not in any immediate danger, but they are not doing what they were meant to do. They are not going anywhere without power. God has a way of helping us find our best in each and every situation: fruit and gifts, gifts and fruit."

"You know," Annie began with her typical grin. "I've been aware of a very happy feeling since we helped him. I was happy already this morning, but this seems deeper, or stronger, or maybe it's just that it's not about me for once." She looked at both the skipper and Bruce. "I'm proud that we were the ones who stopped to help him."

Bruce was nodding agreement. "I was a little worried that he might have some sinister plans to get us at first. Didn't you love his crude talk? He was a pure fisherman." He thought for a moment. "Do you think that Simon Peter might have been something like that?" It was a moment of theological reflection uncommon to Bruce.

Even with their interruption, they were still approaching Victoria's harbor entrance by noon. Their conversations had ranged from the old boater to possible sources of bible study, to the possibility of some more time aboard *Dreamer* this summer. Annie was especially interested in that topic. There was little traffic in the approach to the harbor, just one more turn and they would be able to peer into a very sheltered harbor.

The skipper was studying their course carefully. "We are allowed only on the south side of the channel."

Before he could explain, Bruce asked, "You mean they drive on the same side as we do?"

"No, Bud," the skipper enjoyed the question. "That makes sense to me, but both inbound and outbound boats share this half of the channel. Air traffic gets the other half." Even before he finished his sentence a blue and white Canada Air seaplane coasted directly over their mast and landed a hundred meters ahead of them.

"Holy cow!" Bruce was alarmed. "That was close! Is it safe for us to be in here?"

"Relax, brother. Everyone knows the rules, and those pilots are good. We will see them coming and going all through the daylight hours, it's just part of the color of this place. I don't think there has ever been an accident." They slid past the huge stern of a docked cruise ship, so massive in its patient waiting for a fresh load of tourists. Ahead there was an array of docks and marinas. With one more turn at the inner marker, they enjoyed the inner harbor even through the gray rain.

Dreamer slowed to barely maintain steerage as they gazed at the parliament building, and the stately Empress Hotel. The inner harbor was its usual hectic collection of seaplanes, harbor tugs and tourist boats, each respecting the presence of the others, yet all bound for a different destination. A Red Ball ferry, the *Coho*, sounded its horn to disembark for the Strait of Juan de Fuca crossing to Port Angeles. There were too many delights to look at all at once.

Nearby, the Wharf Street dock offered a selection of slips. After another slow circle of the inner harbor, the skipper chose an inside moorage to reduce bow waves from passing vessels, and as far away from the main dock as possible to protect their privacy. "We'll do a port side tie-up, Bruce." Before he could add more, his deck hands were on their way out of the cockpit to get bumpers and lines ready. He smiled as he thought there could hardly be a more enjoyable way to enter port. A trained and motivated crew made such a grand difference.

Just a few minutes later, they were snug under the dodger, sipping hot tea. Annie was in her customary corner spot, curled under a warm blanket. "I've heard you use the phrase 'spiritual formation'," she began simply. "Can you tell me what that means? It sounds pretty formal." Rain was a steady patter on the canvas top.

The skipper took a customary deep breath. This would be a tough task. "Well, think about it. The process is often slow, becoming the sort of believer we are challenged to become. If I try to put into words a definition, I'd say that spiritual formation is a dynamic process of receiving through faith, and appropriating through action, commitment, and discipline, the living Christ into our lives." His eyes were steady as he looked into hers. "The purpose of the formation is that our life will conform to and manifest the reality of that presence in the world." He was still for a moment as he reflected on his definition. "Christ fully within me, and within the world," he repeated.

Bruce asked, "Is that from scripture, dad?"

"The concept is there, I believe, but not those specific words. In Colossians 1:27, Paul says, 'the secret is simply this: Christ in you!' Or the words of Jesus put it this way according to J. B. Phillips, 'I am the vine itself; you are the branches. It is the man who shares my life and whose life I share who proves fruitful. For the plain fact is, that apart from me you can do nothing at all'."

Bruce frowned. "That sounds pretty negative, doesn't

it? I mean, I think we can do quite a bit on our own." He looked at Annie with affection.

"It is simple, but not simplistic," the skipper replied. "Jesus came for one purpose, and one purpose alone: to bring himself to us, and in bringing himself, to bring God. To be sure there was much accomplished outside that core reality. However, each lesson or miracle points to the fact that not only does he justify us by providing full pardon for our sins, he indwells us to give us the power to be and do all those things God intends us to be and do. That is crucial, but not complete until we realize it in our life."

Annie's puzzled look hadn't changed. "I sort of understand what you're saying. But how would that look in real life?" She thought for a moment, "I don't mean that the other isn't real." She stammered to silence.

The skipper simply said, "I know what you mean."

"Let me tell you about a retreat conference I was asked to attend, to teach a class on spiritual healing. I was using a book written by a Canadian medical doctor, Hans Selye, as I remember it was *The Stress of Life and Stress Without Distress*. His research was mainly in the science of biochemistry. Still, he discovered that positive emotions, which we have been calling 'mercy', attitudes such as gratitude, praise, forgiveness, and joy, are health-enhancing factors. Likewise, negative emotions, which we have been calling 'malice,' such as resentment, anger, jealousy, or fear, have a debilitating and disease-inducing effect on the body."

"There was a young woman in attendance who was suffering from rheumatoid arthritis, and some other complications. She wore a back brace and had to take considerable sedatives for pain control. I had not known her before and only became aware of her suffering from some of the other women in her small table group."

"In retrospect, I believe that I was there because Christ was at work in me, and through me. On the second day, I asked her about her feelings. I think that because I was genuinely concerned for her, and had no other ulterior motive, there was a miracle of the spirit. A meeting happened, and I was only present. I only asked a few questions for clarification about the time and circumstances of her suffering when it all came pouring out. She shared a malignant resentment and unresolved guilt that was poisoning her entire being."

"As a teenager, she had been active in her church youth group, played the piano for worship and had been on two youth mission experiences. The summer before she entered college, she was in the church, practicing her music. The new pastor made a sexually explicit suggestion, which stunned, and confused her. Her parents were active in the church and had been responsible for the choice of this new clergy. She felt trapped. There was no one with whom she could share her disillusionment and hurt, lest the congregation be divided, splintered by his betrayal, and her father's leadership discredited. She felt defenseless, trapped, and betrayed. Her resentment and bitterness closed her off from others and finally cultivated an almost toxic distrust of clergy. That's when the pains began."

"I told her that I could understand her fear, and shared her anger over an unscrupulous leader. But how could she believe me, a clergyman, in saying that not all were corrupt? I did tell her that I knew that God loved her, and intended much more for her than pain, disability, and discomfort, that music and praise were still in her life."

"Then I asked her if she could hold my hand. That was the awful degree to which her bitter distrust had grown. I don't know why that was the question, except that it must have been a divine meeting. She almost flinched when her hand rested on mine. I told her that the past was robbing her of the love, peace, and joy Christ was offering. I asked her if I could pray for the pastor who had offended her. First she shook her head; then when I asked again, she nodded, tears streaming down her cheeks."

The skipper reflected a moment before concluding his memory. "The conference concluded with a communion service, a time to recommit our lives to Christ. She was there, in the front row. I decided to phrase the prayer in such a way that the conference would not understand the story of her bitterness, yet she would know that the prayer was specifically for her. I asked the group to pray general prayers for their families and friends, those distressed by grief, by discomfort, for those in stressful marriages, for those who were seeking a new path, a new job. We prayed for the leadership of our nation, for those in the church who have the heavy burden of responsibility."

"Then I asked them to repeat after me, 'Lord, forgive the one who has hurt me.' Her head jerked up as she looked at me, but her lips did not form the words. I repeated, 'Lord, forgive the one who has hurt me.' She shook her head. I went to her side, placed my arm around her and said, 'Lord, forgive the one who has hurt me.' Then it came – her own prayer: 'Lord forgive the one who has hurt me so deeply.' Her body relaxed, and together we prayed the rest of the prayer of commitment, concluding with the Lord's Prayer. She received the bread and cup with a fresh confidence and strength."

"Think about it," the skipper said in a way they were beginning to anticipate. "It was only because I had been blessed that I could be a blessing, only because Christ had healed me that I could be a channel of healing to her. Because of his indwelling in me, he could be effective in the world around me. That is spiritual formation."

"Several months later I was called to lead another healing conference by the folks who had invited me to the first one. 'You won't believe the dramatic changes in that woman's life,' they said. 'She is free from her back-brace, free of medications. She is active again in the church. It's a real miracle.' I believe that is true." The skipper looked at the rain pelting the water around the boat.

"Hey," he said vigorously, "I'm way ready for lunch. How about you guys?"

Annie protested, "Wait, I want to know more about her. How is she now?"

The skipper gave a little shrug. "I couldn't say. I haven't seen her since that communion service. Remember, our growth is a matter of being faithful wherever we are, the rest is up to God."

Looking at the rain again, he asked, "You guys ready for lunch?" When they both nodded in agreement, he went on "I know a place just up the hill at Trounce Alley. They do a platter of tapas. You know, those yummy little samples of good stuff."

Annie was stretching out from under her blanket. Bruce quipped, "That sounds like something out of Harry Potter: Trounce Alley! Do we get our wands there?" His humor was in good repair.

"I'll make you a deal, Bud. I'll buy lunch, and if you like it, you can get dinner." They all grinned at the ruse.

Annie paused. "I'm still not quite clear about this 'indwelling' of the spirit. Could you just explain a little more?" She squirmed in a little wave of embarrassment. "It's something I would really like to know," she said in a soft voice.

"In seminary," the skipper began as though there had never been a suggestion to find some lunch. "I had a pastoral care professor who introduced us to a Dr. Loring T. Swaim, who was faculty at Harvard Medical School. Along with treating his patients with the latest medical and physical therapies, he prescribed spiritual therapy for those who were receptive and willing. He offered five spiritual laws that lead to improved health and wholeness. They are opportunities for the advance of the indwelling spirit. If I remember correctly, they are:"

"The Law of Love: 'This is my commandment, that you love one another as I have loved you. Greater love has no one than this, that a person lay down his or her life for a friend.' (John 15:12 – 13)

The Law of Apology: 'So if you are offering your gift at the altar, and there remember that your brother has something against you, leave your gift there before the altar and go; first be reconciled to your brother, and then come and offer your gift.' (Matthew 5:23 - 24)

The Law of Change: 'You hypocrite, first take the log out of your own eye, and then you will see clearly to take the speck out of your brother's eye.' (Matthew 7:5)

The Law Concerning Fault Finding: 'Judge not, that you be not judged.' (Matthew 7:1) 'So whatever you wish that others would do to you, do so for them; for this is the law and the prophets.' (Matthew 7:12)

The Law of Forgiveness: 'For if you forgive others their trespasses, your heavenly father also will forgive you; but if you do not forgive others their trespasses, neither will your Father forgive your trespasses.'" (Matthew 6:14)

"He felt strongly that if a person would reflect upon those laws, hidden sources of discomfort, even disease, at least some blocks to wholeness might become apparent. We can only work on what we understand. I think he had something good to offer." The skipper looked from Annie to Bruce. When neither of them said anything, he concluded, "O.K. then, let's go eat!"

As they trudged off the dock, wrapped in their Gortex rain-gear, Annie pondered to herself, "It has to be more difficult than that!"

As they made their way up the street, they were surprised at the light traffic. The rain was keeping shoppers under cover, even on this normally busy Friday afternoon. "Hey, look a Christmas store, in May!" Across the street an Irish specialty store caught Bruce's eye. "Have you seen a tartan plaid for the O'Banyon's?" "Look at all these tea pots! What a great china shop. I'd like to come back here later!" Each block had an abundance of promise. Finally, they came to Trounce Alley.

To their surprise, there was a twenty-minute wait to be seated. Obviously, lunch is an indoor activity on a rainy Friday afternoon. The place was packed, which was also an indicator of good food. By the time the crew looked at the menu, tapas samples were not substantial enough. The boys went for hearty beef sandwiches with stout beer, and Annie opted for the stew in a bread-bowl. It was delicious!

The meal was nearly complete when Annie's hand brushed a wet umbrella, concealed behind the corner curtain. "Hey, someone left an umbrella!" It was large, red, and looked brand new. As she brushed back the curtain to get a better look, she noticed a small leather purse on the floor beside it. "And they forgot a purse, too." She signaled the waitperson to reveal her discovery.

"We've been really busy today," the young woman began. Her weary shrug indicated a disinterest in a time consuming detail. "There was a mom and a couple of kids here, and there was a family with a little girl. We could put the purse up at the register; but the umbrella is from the Marriott. They have those big red ones for their guests." She was hoping they would take this inconvenience away.

Annie asked, without looking at the other two at her table, "How far is the Marriott? I'll take it there. After all, I found it." The logic may have been flawed, but the intent was pure.

The crew had been talking about the use of the remainder of the afternoon. The skipper had made a shopping suggestion that had sounded like great fun. Everyone had enough money to do this little scavenger exercise. They agreed to buy five items each, one for every one of their senses. No more than ten dollars per item could be spent. They agreed to meet back on the boat in two hours and exchange, sort of, their mystery gifts. Annie assured them that she could return the purse and umbrella without jeopardizing her shopping time. After synchronizing their watches, they each went in a different direction.

Norm headed for the Bay, whose full name was Hudson Bay Trading Company, which was far more romantic. It was a four-story mall, a full block square, of shops and stores. He would find lots of treasures there. Bruce had spotted some interesting shops on the way up from the wharf, and Annie was grateful for the umbrella as she made the short walk to the hotel. The new Marriott hotel was directly behind the Empress from the harbor. There was no mistaking its splendid exterior.

As she approached the counter, she was greeted by a happy smile. "Did you find a little girl's purse?"

Annie was caught a bit off balance. "Yes, I did. But how did you know?"

"You are under our umbrella, and not a guest with us, and you have two purses in your hand." The smile grew to a full chuckle. "We can look in it, but I can tell you it belongs to room 717. I can take it up, unless you'd rather." Something about knowing that it belonged to a little girl caused Annie to want to complete the task.

"I'll be happy to take it up," she said. "And we'll split the reward, O.K.?" Her humor was contagious.

An attractive woman with green eyes opened the door at Annie's knock. A puzzled expression left her face, as soon as she saw the purse in her hand. "You found it!" was her greeting. "Jenny, your purse came home." Hurried footsteps signaled an excited young girl. "Come in, and thank you all at once," the happy woman said to Annie. "We couldn't remember all the places we were shopping and browsing this morning. We were afraid we might not find it in a busy place like this. I'm Kathy Swanson, by the way. This is Jenny."

Jumping up from the couch, where he had been watching a televised golf match, an eager son said, "Wow, you found her purse! Cool!"

The mom smiled at his exuberance, "And this is my son Scott."

Annie introduced herself, and explained that she was on a boat in the harbor with her fiancé and his dad.

Eager little fingers were opening the purse. "Mom, it's all here, the money, and the tickets, and my presents, and everything." Delighted eyes scanned Annie in gratitude. Happy hands held hers, bidding her to enter the room so she could be shown the treasures returned.

Annie explained where and how she had found the purse. She couldn't explain why helping a child was so very important to her right now.

Jenny sat down on the floor, pouring out the contents between her feet. There was a surprising amount of dollars, which were explained as birthday gifts from her grandmother, and from her father, who had not lived with them for a long time. There was a ticket to the Museum of Labor and Industry across the street from the hotel, another bundle of tickets for the aquarium, and a voucher for the double-decker bus tour, and a handful of coins. There were silver hair clips, and a butterfly necklace. It was a surprising cache for a small girl. "Oh thank you, thank you! I didn't think I'd ever see my Sunday school cross again." She held up a little silver cross on a fragile chain. "My teacher gave it to me to remind me about Easter."

"That's funny," Annie said with a wisp of a smile. "I had a dream about a cross last night. I hadn't remembered it until just now." Jenny was too busy sifting through a handful of cards and papers from the bottom of her purse. There was really no reason for Annie to stay. As she rose to leave, Kathy offered her a folded twenty-dollar bill.

"We'd like to thank you for going out of your way to do such a kind thing." When Annie declined the gift, she was surprised to receive a warm hug, even with damp raingear. "I want my kids to know that there really are honest people in this world. I'd like to thank you for helping me show them. Isn't there something we could do?" Her request was genuine, and unnecessary.

"Maybe we'll see you at supper, or lunch somewhere along the way. It would be nice to share a meal." Annie was unsure how that would work, but it felt right to say.

"We'll be downstairs at 6 o'clock. The dining room is never busy that early." They were making their way to the door.

"Bye Jenny. Take care of your purse. Bye Scott." He waved back from the golf match. As she said, "Have a great afternoon," to Kathy, there was another grateful hug. She hurried back into the shops and busy stores, remembering that she had five gifts to purchase. Never far from her consciousness, however, was the thought of that sweet little girl, and her lost purse, that was found.

Annie was the first one back to the boat, although she could see the skipper coming from the other direction, hunched over in the afternoon rain. When he looked up, she waved happily. Bruce came along within a few minutes, and Annie had to repeat her Good Samaritan story.

When the teapot was heated, they sat in the cozy salon, listening to the rain on the deck. The skipper unveiled his idea: "O.K. I think this will work. We'll wrap our gifts in this old grocery sack paper, then, one sense at a time, have a blind drawing. We'll roll a dice, odds lets you keep your own gift, even, lets you trade." Bruce needed a bit more explanation. "If you roll a 1, 3, or 5, you keep the gift you purchased. If you roll a 2, 4, or 6, you get to trade with either of the other two, your choice." Bruce nodded his head in understanding, a big smile spreading across his face.

"So, I get to exchange those cheap things I bought for the really good stuff you guys got, is that it?"

"Yeah, Bud." The skipper's smile was no less playful. "And I think I'm the only one here who knows where the Thrift store is located. They had genuine treasures there." After just a moment's hesitation, he asked "O.K. which one goes first?"

Annie blurted out, "Taste!" Each placed their wrapped gift in the bag. To their delight, they had all purchased chocolate in one form or another. The boys each rolled odds. Annie's four let her trade with Bruce. "Hey, this could be fun!"

Smell brought another similar response from them all. Each had found a cologne or fragrance that was pleasant. The dice turned up two trades this time, and so no one had their original purchase.

Touch was an interesting mix. Annie had found a charming hand warmer that she privately hoped to keep. The skipper had found a set of juggling balls that were suede covered and colorful. Bruce hoped that he rolled an even so he could trade. He had purchased a tartan plaid scarf that he hoped his dad would appreciate. After only a bit of negotiation, each had the gift that most pleased them.

The sound gifts were interesting. The skipper had found a Celtic CD, which he thought was quite cool. Annie had a small brass bell that had a clear sweet tone, and reminded her of the "Ding, ding, ding", crossing in the fog. Bruce had a toy, that when dropped made a shattering sound similar to breaking glass, although there was, of course, no damage. The negotiations were more heated, but finally, each had their preferred gift.

The final gift in the scavenger shopping list was sight, something to see. Annie had purchased a fantastic picture of an eagle soaring over an evergreen forest. The skipper had found an interesting crystal that sent sunshine into a myriad of rainbows dancing on the bulkhead. Bruce hesitated to reveal his purchase. "I broke the rules a little," he apologized. "I went a little over my limit, and I really want to trade. Do I still need to roll anyway?"

"Well, let's see, what you have." The skipper enjoyed the game. "Then we'll know how to bargain."

Bruce revealed a tiny gold cross on a delicate gold chain. At first glance the design seemed to be simple. But closer inspection showed detail that added depth and power. It was totally lovely, and everyone in the salon knew for whom he had purchased it.

"Oh Bruce," she said softly. "That is just the most beautiful cross I have ever seen!" Tears formed in her eyes. "That's the most wonderful thing you could ever do! You just don't know…" A tiny shudder ended her words. She moved to give him a huge hug.

Then she told them of her dream last night. "I had the most lovely dream. I think I can remember it, but I think it gets mixed up with our conversation about the indwelling Christ, and little Jenny's Sunday school teacher." Her voice was returning to normal, but tears still shone in her eyes. She straightened her back, and took a deep breath.

"I dreamt that I was at the Last Supper with Jesus and all the disciples, just like the big painting. There was candlelight, and we knew how holy the moment was. Lots of food was on the table. Before he gave us the bread and the cup, Jesus gave us all a cross pin, and said that it didn't mean much right now, but in just a few days it would have more meaning than anything we could imagine. It would become a priceless treasure to us. He wanted us to never forget the meaning of the cross, to remember it every time we wore the pin." She caught her breath. "Isn't it weird that Jenny's teacher gave the class a cross to wear and told them to remember Easter, and I had that dream the day before you gave me such a splendid gift?" She drew in a deep trembling breath. "My mind is all jumbled up with such good feelings." She smiled toward the skipper, then turned toward the man who had become more than precious to her. "Thank you, Bruce!" She gazed at the cross again. "Thank you, from the bottom of my heart!" She slid over to him again, and kissed him long and lovingly. The boat was still, barely a movement, and hardly a sound. Outside, the rain had stopped in the early evening twilight.

After a pleasant moment to savor the scene, the skipper got up and put his hand on Bruce's shoulder. "Good job, partner. I'm proud of you." He reached across to touch Annie's shoulder as well. "You are a pure joy, by golly!" There were tears in his eyes, too. "I think I'll do some heavy reading before supper." He headed toward his stateroom.

"Skipper," Annie said softly. "I think you said if we liked lunch, we could pay for supper. Wasn't that what you said?" Her voice became a bit firmer. "I think it's my turn to buy. What would you say to dinner at the Marriott? I heard it was good, and not crowded if we go early, like maybe 6 o'clock?" At the moment, there was no definite plan behind her suggestion. That would come later.

An hour later, as he returned to the salon, Bruce greeted the skipper with a broad smile. "Wow, dad, you look fantastic! We just have these play clothes." The skipper was wearing white Dockers slacks, with a white turtleneck under his navy blue blazer.

"Thanks. I've kept this on the boat for an occasional dinner at the marina. It seemed like the best choice for an evening when Annie's buying." They all laughed at his shift from the spotlight. "Let's leave a couple of lamps on, just in case it's dark when we come back."

As they made their way up from the dock, and around the stately Empress hotel, the three chatted about the excitement Victoria offered visitors who were there for the first or fifth time. There was a growing crowd of shoppers, carefully making their way to the inviting shops. Best of all, the streets, still wet from the afternoon rain, reflected a radiant hint of sunset colors, breaking through the clouds. There was a tangible promise to the evening.

The lobby of the Marriott radiated warmth, from the chandeliers to the large fireplace, and happy reception staff, its newness evident in gracious detail. The skipper excused himself to "wash up" before finding the dining room. Annie suggested that she would make sure they had an available table for them.

Moments later, as the skipper was rounding the corner on his way to the dining room, a pleasant voice asked him, "Excuse me. Could you tell me about tickets for the Butchart Gardens?" His attention was caught by a lovely lady with green eyes, a hint of dimples, and a radiant smile.

"Excuse me?" was his initial response. "May I help you?" Her gaze seemed to tangle his thought process.

"I'd like to make arrangements for the three of us to go to the Butchart Gardens in the morning," she answered brightly. "Could you arrange for the tickets, and tell me the time we catch the bus?" Her face was framed with soft auburn curls. The smile didn't dim a bit, and there were tiny laugh-lines at the corners of her eyes. It was an enjoyably confusing moment that was clarified by her next question. "You are the concierge, aren't you?"

Chuckling, the skipper finally understood, and answered, "No. No, I'm not, I'm sorry to say. I was just making my way to the dining room. But I will help you find the person you need, if you like."

"Oh I am so sorry! I thought you were... The concierge's desk is right here... You look so official, I jumped to a conclusion. Silly me!" There was a comfortable grace about her, even in an unlikely situation. At that moment a young woman stepped behind the counter and asked, "How can I help you?" She was wearing a name badge with "concierge" clearly engraved. With a musical lilt to her voice the woman began to explain her confused moment.

Seeing the situation resolved, the skipper said cheerily, "Enjoy the gardens," as he turned again toward the dining room. For just a moment he wished that he could have been more helpful.

There were several empty tables available as the skipper looked across the dining room for his dinner mates. To his surprise, he found them sitting with two children, happily chatting. Annie saw him walk in, and waved him to the table. "This is Jenny, the owner of the lost purse this afternoon," she announced proudly. "I was just showing her my new cross." However the skipper had anticipated the evening, this was surely an unexpected turn.

Bruce added to the introductions. "This happy guy is Scott, who loves the Mariners. He plays in Little League, and thinks he might be a first baseman someday." A bright smile accompanied the young man's "hello." He even held out his hand to give a formal greeting.

"Their mom will be right back," Annie said in answer to the skipper's look around the dining room. "This is Jenny's first trip out of Seattle."

"We're even out of the United States," Scott said with earnest conviction. "I've been to the ocean before, and even California." The twinkle in his eye suggested a buoyant humor, and eagerness to be in a conversation with new friends.

Jenny added, "Our dad lives there, I think. We haven't seen him since we were little." When Scott gave her a warning look, she quickly changed the subject. "We are on our first vacation together, 'cause Scott won the science fair."

"Yeah," Scott broke in. "And it had to rain! Bummer. We had to stay in our room all afternoon." The grin on his face belied any harsh feelings.

"You won the science fair? Way to go Scott! But just think," Annie said with a little giggle, (was she beginning to talk like the skipper?), "If it hadn't rained, I wouldn't have known where to return the purse, because the big red umbrella was with it. And if you weren't in your room, I wouldn't have had a chance to meet you two." Giving Jenny a one armed hug, she said happily, "I'm really glad it rained today. I got to meet my little 'sister of the cross'."

Jenny hugged her back, saying, "Now I have a big brother, and a big sister!"

"Hey," a familiar voice spoke from behind them, "that sounds like a pretty important conversation." It was the attractive lady with green eyes from the lobby, who had been on the skipper's mind since their chance encounter. "It looks like my table has grown."

"Hi Kathy!" Annie stood up to hug her. "We saw the kids, and thought we'd say 'Hi'." Her obvious delight was contagious. "Let me introduce you to the rest of the crew. This is Bruce, my…" she hesitated before saying, "fiancé." After they shook hands, Annie said, "And this is our skipper, Norm, Bruce's dad." Both Kathy and Norm burst into laughter, before they shook hands. Now it was Annie's turn to be confused.

Kathy explained, "I mistook him for the concierge,

in the lobby, and asked him if he could get us tickets to the Buchart gardens." Then assessing his attire, she asked, "Well, doesn't he look like a person with all the answers?" They all laughed at her humor.

Annie answered before the skipper could quip back. "You can't believe how much he has helped me find answers this week. He was on his way to a fun vacation when the two of us hitch hiked along. He has been such a big help to us, working out personal plans and really good stuff."

Annie suddenly realized her exuberance during the introduction. She worried that she had gone a bit too far, so tried to clarify her statement about the skipper. "He's a retired pastor, and has been super helpful." Feeling herself getting in deeper where she didn't want to be in the first place, she quickly said, "We'd better find a table, and let you enjoy your supper." Her wane smile was more from embarrassment than politeness.

"I have a better idea," Kathy said, coming to Annie's aid. "Why don't we find a larger table for all of us? You said you were on a boat together? I'd love to hear about it." She was already signaling her intent to the hostess. "We want to hear about your trip." Jenny, who was holding on to Annie's hand, nodded vigorously.

The evening passed too swiftly for all of them. The conversations ranged from baseball and the Mariners, (Scott thought he would shave his head like Jay Buner for back-to-school next September. His mom just shook her head.), to Sunday school, (Jenny was thrilled to be able to tell her teacher about the sisters of the cross story.) The new pastor of their church was too stuffy. He didn't do much with the children, just the choir. Annie and Kathy chatted about work. Kathy was happy in the HR department of Starbucks, and yes, they did sell over three hundred million pounds of coffee last year, and yes, their business plan envisioned more stores than McDonalds. The skipper mostly listened, and asked an occasional question. Annie confided that she had been on a fast track since graduating from the U, passing several of her peers. Software design was a tenuous career, with obvious rewards and grave challenges, but after this past week, she was sure that she could handle anything that came her way. It always seemed to come back to this past week.

As the desserts were being finished, Kathy asked the skipper, "Can you tell me about the material you all have been using on your trip?" Her green eyes were warm and quite lovely. "It sounds like a motivation seminar." She could have gone on, but she paused, waiting for an answer.

He gave a little shrug, almost shy. "I don't know how to describe what we've been up to, exactly," he began. "I guess I would say that we have been exploring some of the forgotten good stuff that has been buried under the junk we have accumulated." It was a difficult question to answer, or avoid.

"Annie told me that you are a mediation counselor.

Does that have something to do with the material you've been using?" Her sincere desire to understand more about them was easy to see, and pleasant to receive.

The skipper smiled, "We have been sharing some thoughts of a number of different authors on the subject of forgiveness, and reflecting on a lot of the New Testament material. I know that sounds like a seminary rather than a seminar…"

"Everyone has issues," Annie interrupted. She wanted to give him some happy praise. "Norm has been a wonderful guide, helping us sort out solutions to some of the weightier ones we have, that have been obstacles to us." Her smile toward the skipper was radiant. "And," she took a deep breath, "he made up a bunch of application exercises. We filled a bay with luminaries, wrote our worries in the sand, helped clean up a beach with a bunch of island kids, and went on a shopping adventure. That's how Bruce gave me this cross." Once again her eyes filled with emotion. "I can't remember being this happy."

Kathy reached across the table to pat the skipper's arm. "Wow, that's a great endorsement. I hope you can publish that. Because if you could package something that helpful, it would sell better than slow roasted house blend." Her playfulness was careful not to minimize the importance of what Annie had said. "How can a girl with issues sign up for the next session?" Their shared chuckle released any tension that might have been growing. She finally took her hand away from his arm.

"At least I'll keep a notebook with good notes," the skipper replied lightly, "for the next session." Easy laughter allowed him to ask a new question, even though he could still feel the warmth of her hand. "Did you manage to get tickets for the gardens tomorrow?"

"Yes, I did, once I chatted with the real concierge." Her chuckle was soft and rich. "We're scheduled to catch the 9:30 bus, right in front of the Empress." She paused as though thinking through her next statement. "She did warn us, however, that it is a bit early for the dahlias and roses. But the azaleas and rhododendrons are beautiful right now, and the Japanese garden is worth the trip by itself. Would you like to join us?" The question was unexpected to them all.

Jenny's voice was the first to respond, "Yes, do, please!"

Annie could see that both Bruce and the skipper were thinking about the right way to answer, which would need to be courteous and careful. "I think that would be great," she said quickly. "as long as it doesn't interfere with the skipper's plans for our day." She thought that would take care of the essential considerations.

"Actually," the skipper replied, "the gardens are on my list of possible things to do or see. We could also consider a couple of stately churches, or Beacon Hill Park seen from a carriage."

"Could we see your boat?" asked Scott. He had been pretty quiet for the last several minutes. "I've never been on a sailboat, have I mom?" His grin was innocent and contagious.

"Let's take one adventure at a time, O.K.?" she joined his grin. "I think by the time we get back from the gardens, our day will be pretty full."

"That's what the skipper told us at the beginning of our trip," Annie said earnestly. "He said that we didn't know what was coming to us, but our task was to position ourselves so that we could see it and receive it when it happened." Her satisfied smile indicated that she had been listening carefully.

The skipper looked at his watch, a sure indication that the hour was late. "I know I am in trouble when people start to quote me." Looking at Annie he asked, "Are you sure I said that?"

Before she could respond, Scott said, "My coach says the same thing." He gave a quick nod of his head, slid off his chair to take a bent knee stance and thump his fist into his left hand like a first baseman's mitt. Squaring his shoulders, he announced proudly, "Before a first baseman can catch it, he has to po-si-tion himself in front of the ball! Then he's ready for anything!" They all laughed with his enthusiasm.

Annie was quick to pick up the check when the server brought it to the table. Kathy argued that it should go on their room account. Annie answered, "This is my opportunity to show the skipper that I am a dependable crewwoman. I agreed to do supper tonight, and I am honored to do it!"

"Then maybe I can get lunch tomorrow," Kathy suggested. "I feel like I should be in this mix somehow."

"I'll tell you what," the skipper finally said. "We'll think about this on the way back to *Dreamer*. We need to go right past the tourist information place. If they are still open, we'll see if there is room on the bus for us too, O.K.?" It was moved, seconded and passed unanimously.

Notebooks:

Annie wrote: I'm amazed at all that can be compressed into any one day. We started in Maple Bay, gorging on a fisherman's breakfast. Then there was the long journey with the discussion of the Holy Spirit, the rescue of the old guy and his old boat, Jenny's purse, my wonderful cross, dinner with new friends and now the quietness of the boat with plans for tomorrow. It is really more than this girl can grasp. It is like I'm dancing from mountaintop to mountaintop. We're on mountaintop time, which has more in each minute, and more minutes in each hour. I'm not sure what to make of all of it except this: each day has all sorts of possibilities in it. Usually, I get caught up in what to wear, traffic, my desk, phone, email, meetings, none of which are mountaintop stuff to me. I think I have been feeling so invigorated because I'm just dealing with treasure. I'm happier, more alive than I can ever remember being. I'm in love with Bruce, our future, our dreams,

… it's all about our, not mine. Maybe that is why I'm so happy! I'm on mountaintop time! Sweet! Excellent!

Bruce wrote: I think I'm having an adult vacation, or something. Usually I'm concerned about activities and attractions; I wonder about the new sensations or discoveries I might make, what new sights I might see. Now I am discovering new depth in me, and amazing insights with Annie! I'm even more amazed at my dad. I think I have moved into a new region of relationship with them both. It's like I'm meeting him for the first time. He is funny and serious, informed and searching. I have never known him to be unkind, but that is different than this kind, kind, kind man. He seems like my best friend, my professor and counselor, my coach and dad, all rolled together. I have known Annie for a long while, but never on this level. Suddenly she is a part of every thought. She is darling, attractive, interesting, clever. I'm in love with my best friend!

I think I had better do a better job at telling them both how much I appreciate this fantastic trip! I would be lying if I said it was anything less than life changing. I wonder if Annie feels the same way. I'll bet she does. I wonder how dad is feeling about this trip. Does he miss not going up to Desolation Sound, or not being on a solo journey? Naw! He really likes having us along to listen and learn. I think he is in his perfect element. But I also wonder if there are times when he is lonely. I thought he brightened up a bunch at dinner. (Reminder: ask Annie what she thinks about this.)

Rank yourself from one to ten on everything: 10, 10, 10, 10. Now rank your willingness to grow: 10, 10, 10, 10!

Norm wrote: We have only two more days! If tomorrow goes as planned we'll have very little time for discussions or notebooks. Perhaps I should concentrate on what happens after we get back to Seattle. Right now that seems a long way off. Their hearts are right, and pretty excited about all we have covered.

(He thought for several minutes before continuing.) It really is a process. I must remember that! I do not need to feel any urgency or anxiety about their progress, as long as we just keep working at it. Seattle is not the destination. We've made great progress, and still have a discussion about prayer for the trip back. Then, I think we can make plans to get some other folks involved. (He started a list of possible resource people for them. Several more minutes passed before he added this entry.)

I can still feel the warmth of her hand on my arm! I wonder if that is a sign of how lonely my life has become. Every day I am surrounded by people, but I can't recall their touch. Perhaps she touched a switch that has been turned off for a long while. I think I had better be very cautious, and aware of how much I liked that. It almost makes me smile… What do I mean almost?

He turned off his lights, still pondering the questions he had raised about his own heart.

It was a little after two in the afternoon, when the six of them trooped down the dock. Warm sunlight dodged around puffy clouds. Their voices were happy, like folks following an adventure.

"That was all together lovely," Kathy said with the same enthusiasm she had felt for the entire trip. "I can't choose which my favorites were, the baskets were so bright and colorful, and the huge Rhodies were taller than any I have ever seen."

"I liked the koi pond," Scott broke in.

"The whole Japanese garden was my favorite," Jenny added. "Those were very old trees, and still pretty tiny."

"I still have trouble believing our bus broke down," Bruce said with a wry smile.

Kathy was the first to respond. "I know! When the big bang happened, I thought we had blown a tire. But then it just jerked to a stop. Can you believe how upset some of the passengers got at the driver? They acted like it was his fault, or something." Turning to the skipper, she added, "You seemed to understand right away that it was a mechanical problem."

"My first thought," he replied, "was that we had hit something in the road. The sound seemed to come from underneath the bus. But I wasn't sure. I was pretty sure there was no immediate danger, though."

Annie quipped, "Is that why you made a joke? 'I just hate it when that happens to me!' Isn't that what you said?" Her eyes twinkled with the idea of humor at the moment of a crisis.

"Old guys and old buses run a definite risk," the skipper chuckled.

More than one voice protested his use of the "old" word.

"But when we bounced to a stop, I was pretty sure the problem was the drive shaft," the skipper said seriously. "We weren't going anywhere for a while, so why not enjoy where we were? I think it's Dr. Phil who says, 'When you choose the behavior, you choose the consequences.' We wanted to spend a leisurely morning, and we were in the Canadian countryside." He gave a shrug to emphasize his point. "I thought it was a grand morning." As a continuation to the thought he said, "Fun game of twenty questions you started, Kathy!"

"I was just following your lead," she answered with that happy grin. "But how did you know that the delay was going to work out so well for us?" Her green eyes studied his face again.

"At first I was just hoping," the skipper smiled. "But it only seems reasonable that the company that is working hard to get and keep the tourist's trust, wouldn't allow this to be a major day-wrecking inconvenience. They would want to do something to keep us sort of happy. I just wanted us in a 'po-si-tion' to receive it. And we did!" They all chuckled at his use of Scott's word.

Bruce got into the conversation. "But my gosh," his voice was filled with surprise, "giving us vouchers to high tea at the Buchart Gardens restaurant is quite a lot for just an hour's delay on the bus. Didn't it take about that long for the other bus to get out to us?"

"Yeah, about an hour, maybe a little less. But I'll bet that we remember what a good thing happened to us on the way out to the gardens, rather than the bus breakdown. It probably didn't cost the bus company menu prices, but they accomplished their goal. They brought back very happy customers." The skipper gave a little snort, "Shoot, the passengers on all the buses that didn't have an emergency this morning, are wishing that they were on ours." Everyone joined in the humor of his observation.

Jenny broke into the reflections, "Mom, can you make those cucumber sandwiches when we get home?"

Before she could answer, Scott added to the question, "Yeah, and without crusts?" Again, the laughter was unanimous. Attitude makes all the difference in the world!

They made their way down the dock, still talking about the adventures of the morning, with occasional exclamations about the beautiful boats that were moored, awaiting visitors.

Finally, Annie could point out *Dreamer*. With obvious pride, she announced, "Here's our home away from home!" Carefully, she made sure everyone had soft soled shoes before she asked the skipper, "Permission to step aboard, skipper?" It was only a courtesy, yet one that conveyed respect and tradition.

He answered, "Granted!" Then, looking at Bruce, he continued, "While you show them below, I'll check the oil, and light the fire. We do want to get on the slant, don't we?"

Scott answered with raw enthusiasm, "You mean we get to go for a sailboat ride, too?" His question was directed toward Kathy. All eyes turned her way to see her response.

"Well, do we have enough time? Is it too much trouble? I don't know what to do." She shrugged her shoulders. "It would be easier to say 'No,' but I'm not sure we'll have another chance." Her smile was a bit embarrassed mixed with genuine interest. "Skipper, would it be too much trouble?" The others were already aboard.

"It would be our pleasure to take a tiny stroll outside the harbor. And it would be no trouble at all." Letting his voice take on the gravel of a pirate, he added, "Arr matey, we was born for sea duty, we was!"

As Annie helped Kathy aboard, she said proudly, "I know just where to sit to stay out of the way. Let's take a quick look below first, and leave the rest up to the boys."

The following minutes were filled with "OOOs" and "AAHHS" of appreciation of the style and space of the boat's interior. When the skipper started the diesel, the cabin was aware of the power at their disposal. Bruce trotted up the dock to inform the harbormaster of their intent to sail for a few minutes. They would leave their bumpers attached to the dock cleats to reserve their space.

"I just love their sailor talk," Annie confided to Kathy. "They are pretending this is an old ship of the line, and they are casting off for some pirate cruise." Letting her smile grow, she said, loud enough for both guys to hear, "It's alright if you don't understand what is being said. They repeat it in English, and then explain." When the skipper said to Bruce, "O.K. you can cast off the spring line... now the bow... I've got the stern," she turned to Kathy and said, "See what I mean?" Both women giggled at her joke.

The graceful boat eased out of the marina, made a slow pass through the inner harbor, before they found their traffic lane outbound toward the sea. It seemed effortless to the folks seated in the cockpit.

When they were at the outer buoy, the skipper took a sweeping look around to make sure they were out of traffic, before saying to Bruce, "Mr. O'Banyon, would ye haul the main, please." Annie just looked at Kathy, nodded and smiled.

They sailed toward Race Rocks, back in along the shore, and then out toward the channel marker. By the time the skipper was asking Bruce to roll up the sails, everyone aboard had a fresh, pleasant understanding of how a sailboat works, and Scott had been delighted to steer, although Jenny declined. It was a most enjoyable introductory experience. Late afternoon sunrays were slanting under the western clouds.

The skipper was thinking about the next phase of the day. "It may be way out of line for me to suggest that we could have your company for dinner too, after such a fun day. But you do need to eat supper somewhere, how about with us?" His gaze was on Kathy, of course. "I'm thinking it would be enjoyable to see if there is a table at the Blue Crab. It's the dining room at the Sheraton." He waited, expecting a polite or reasonable decline. All eyes again turned toward Kathy, to see her response.

"Well, I don't think…I don't see…" There was a pause. "I can't imagine a nicer end to a marvelous day. But I insist on picking up the check. O.K?" Her eyes seemed to have an inner light.

"If you insist, we can split it. But that's my last offer," the skipper said with conviction, as though the discussion had been going the other way. Without waiting for her rebuttal, he asked Bruce to go below and give the restaurant a call to see if reservations were even possible. "You'll find the number in the cruising guide for Victoria." The skipper thought to himself, "That went exceptionally well!"

Kathy said to Annie, "I'm really not dressed for

a dinner out, my face isn't done." It sounded like the beginning of a list of obstacles.

Annie whispered reassuringly, "We're on vacation. I don't have anything else to wear, and if you'd like to freshen your face, I've noticed that we have about the same color of eyes. I'll bet my stuff will look really good with your complexion." The bonds of friendship run deep, and can grow in a day.

Bruce's head popped out of the companionway. "Six o'clock O.K? It's either that or 8:45."

Quickly the consensus was reached that 6:00 was the crew's favorite time to dine. "We have a nice trend going here," Annie observed. They were well into the inner harbor approach.

"You know what?' the skipper asked. "We could go from our dock right to the restaurant, if we use one of those little water taxis."

Bruce asked, "You mean one of those little round water bug sort of things that have been zipping all over?"

"I do, in fact. They ferry folks all over the inner harbor. It would only cost a couple of loonies, but how fun would that be. It would be a Victoria experience, 'eh?" the skipper said with conviction.

"I'll need to check my circuit breakers if I have much more of a Victoria experience," Kathy said with a twinkle. "This is so over the top of anything that I could have imagined."

"Me too," Jenny chimed. "And I don't even know what the top is."

Scott had been thinking about the water taxi. "What's a loonie?"

"Canada doesn't use a bill for one dollar," the skipper answered. "They have a one dollar coin called a 'loonie', with a picture of the Loon on it, and a two dollar coin called a toonie."

"There sure is a lot of fun stuff to learn in Canada, isn't there?" Scott's eyebrows arched in a query.

Both Bruce and the skipper answered immediately, "Lots!" They watched the Parliament building slide past, and made the turn toward the Wharf Docks.

By the time the server lit the candles on their table the harbor was full of twinkling reflections. The meal had been wonderful, and their conversations had been wide-ranging, from schools attended to favorite vacations. They had talked about their families, their pets, and their pet projects. Kathy especially liked volunteering at the kids' school, her flower gardens, and singing in the choir. Sooner or later, the topic of the church had to come up.

"Yes I loved being a pastor," the skipper said softly. "In all of the churches that I served, there was a sense of accomplishment and joy."

"Were they big churches?" Kathy asked. "Sometimes I think smaller churches are able to keep that close feeling easier."

The skipper reflected a moment before answering.

"Yeah, Kelso was pretty good size, with a fun staff in the education and youth areas. It also had a thriving preschool during the week." He smiled sadly. "Issaquah was growing like mad; you know the right place and time. Then the bishop and I had a conflict." Once again he smiled. "Do you remember the line from 'Man of La Mancha', where Poncho says 'whether the rock hits the pitcher, or the pitcher hits the rock, it's going to be hard on the pitcher?' It works that way with the bishop as well. Whether he was right or not, he was always the bishop."

The skipper didn't know how much of his history he should share with this delightful dinner partner. Taking courage, he began, "When I asked not to be assigned to another broken congregation, he said there were very few options for me. I was eventually assigned to a tiny entry-level church with minimum salary. Most of my peers saw it as major career failure. I saw it as the moment to try something other than parish work." The skipper wanted to be honest, without dragging out a lot of old scars.

"Do you like mediation work?" Kathy asked sincerely.

"I think it is a different way to help people who are stuck in conflict. But it doesn't take the place of being a pastor." The skipper was aware of the gorgeous setting, and the lovely lady with whom he was sharing this gentle evening.

"Do you miss it?" Kathy's question was soft and sincere. The conversation had become very two-sided, with the others listening.

"Sometimes I miss it a lot, you know around the high festivals of Christmas or Easter. I miss being in on the planning for great music or drama." He thought for a moment. "But I get over that, because I don't think I was defined by the ministry. I could probably still be doing that in some church, at some level, if I chose. I always have the choice."

Kathy pursed her lips, and gave a little sigh. "I was defined by being a homemaker and a mom, and I loved it. Greg wasn't much of a dad when Scott was born. I think he was more inconvenienced than anything else. But when Jenny was born, he just left us. There must have been some other things going on with him. He moved to California, and we haven't heard much from him for years."

Annie interjected, "Does he help with child support?" It was one of those questions that was really none of her business, except it had to do with the on-going responsibility of a parent.

"No, he left me the house, and all the bills. He was supposed to do his part, but it didn't quite work out that way. In eight years there have been some thin times, for sure. It's good to have a supportive family nearby. And I am very grateful to be working for a fantastic company. We've done O.K." Her smile was authentic. "Lately he's sent some presents to the kids. Maybe he's growing up."

Annie was still thinking about a father who would so abandon his family. "Aren't you very angry at him?" She looked with admiration at the two children who were lost in their own projects at the table.

"No, not angry anymore." Kathy looked at her children with gratitude. "But from time to time, I really need your refresher course in forgiveness." She thought about how the rest of her answer would sound in this situation. "The worst part is that it has kept me from thinking that I could share my life with anyone else." She chuckled at the sardonic thought, attempting to change the subject. "This is the closest thing to a date I've had in a decade." It was too sad to be humorous, and too true to be ignored. A plan began to take shape for Annie.

"How about meeting me for a lunch when we get home, or maybe a dinner? I would love to have some time to talk," Annie was carefully studying Kathy's face. "I'd like to share some of the really helpful things I've learned in the last few days. I'll bet they could be helpful to you, too."

"Well sure," Kathy replied brightly. Then looking at Bruce, then the skipper, and back to Annie, she said, "You know the really refreshing thing about the time we have spent together is the affirmation I have felt from you three. There hasn't been a moment of judgment, or awkward questions. It has been a refreshing experience."

Annie was eager to demonstrate some of her new attitude. "One thing I have learned this week is that there is no room in a happy heart for unhappy criticism. Our finest response is always going to be one of gratitude, which causes me again to say, 'Thank you, skipper', for another larger than life day! Oh, my gosh, the bus ride, the gardens, the high tea, and the ride on Dreamer, and now this amazing meal. Thank you for it all!" She reached over and gave him a big hug.

"Can I say that you are more than welcome," he replied. "It has been a very memorable day for me as well." The skipper felt the conversation drawing to a close, but wanted to make one last lingering suggestion. "We could take a water taxi back to the Empress dock, which would be pretty speedy; or we could walk the four or five blocks to the Marriott at our own pace.

Bruce was the first to answer. "I think there is an ice cream shop on the way. Who's up for second desserts?"

The stroll was leisurely and sweet, oh so sweet.

They said their "farewells" in the Marriott lobby. There was a round of "thank you," and then another. Jenny wanted to hug Annie once more as her "sister of the cross." The skipper had told them that they would be leaving about 7:00 o'clock, just before low tide. It would be a pretty long ride back to Seattle. Yes, they would watch for the Clipper, and yes, they would stay in touch. One last hug, Oh, good the night!

Notebooks:

Annie wrote: Nine nights ago I was terrified with the prospects of being on a boat with Bruce's dad. I was lost in the feelings of self-incrimination. I was floundering in a sea of negative memories. Night by night, like layers of an onion being peeled away, those terrible feelings have been removed. My heart is filled with happiness. She scribbled out the word happiness and in its place wrote, BLESSINGS!

The skipper says we are all supposed to feel this way all the time. Get out! How could I get any work done without feeling panic over schedules, or competition with other designers? What would it be like if I actually respected the people I work with, or applauded their achievements. What would it be like if I was less aware of quotas and more aware of production successes? I am eager for each new day because I know that something wonderful is going to happen... like the bus breaking... like finding a lost purse... like meeting such a sweet new friend.

There has been a quiet revolution going on inside of me. It's like the fear and anxiety are being replaced by positive moments of discovery that chain together to make a day just like today. Awesome! I can only imagine what one more day might bring. It will probably be what I po-si-tion myself to receive. If this is what he meant when he said we would have the fruit of the spirit, I want much more of it. I want it for Bruce, and my family. I want it for the skipper. If my life can be this much happier, can his?

Yup, quite a quiet revolution...blessings!

Bruce wrote:

I think it came together for me when the bus broke down. My first reaction was frustration and anger. I thought about being mad at the driver, or the company for putting us on such frail equipment. But then, when dad and Kathy started playing games, and having such a good time, I realized that the circumstances only are the showcase for the importance we place in it. I saw him change the attitude of most of the folks around us, simply by reminding them that we were still having fun. No one believed, at first, that it would all work out as cool as it did. Can you believe it? We got courtesy high tea for our inconvenience. No wonder he had such a big smile on his face! We weren't inconvenienced at all. If the bus hadn't come when it did, I think he would have arranged a hike to the winery just up the road. He said to us earlier that it doesn't matter what happens, it's how we respond to it. I saw the truth of that today. I know I will become a better person if I can integrate that into my life.

From now on, when something happens that might seem bad, I'm going to count backwards from five to think of ways I might reverse the experience. I can't believe that everything will work out like today. But, why not give it a chance, or at least try to find that optimistic ray of hope. If it doesn't make it better, at least it won't make it worse.

When I see how much influence a positive, proactive attitude has on a situation, I know Annie and I have no significant reason to put off our wedding. I want to ask her right now... well maybe tomorrow... or when we get back to Seattle. I'm so sure she will say, "Yes!" and mean it.

Norm wrote:

"Life is what happens while we are making preparations for something else."

Life is a series of little things, or little moments. The truth is, they aren't little! I wish I could remember where that came from. It certainly applies to this day. I thought I had a pretty good lesson plan going. We have accomplished about all that I had hoped. Today was going to be a casual day of reflection. Instead, it was a day of discovery, surprise, and a tremendous joy.

I am surprised by Kathy and her family. How could anyone have foreseen the chance meeting? I am surprised to be so welcomed into her schedule, and so delighted to share her time. She redefined a hug for me today. It was more than a 'farewell' it was 'I like you, and hope that you like me.' I do, a lot!

The joy I sense is in Bruce and Annie. They have completely come alive during this trip. It must be more than just getting away from their jobs. I think it is more than just being on the boat for a week. The truth is, I think much of what we have been discussing is sinking in. I'll be surprised if we get back to Seattle without some sort of wedding plans. That makes me very happy.

These are magical years, therefore magical days,

therefore magical moments, which we can share. I have been so focused on Bruce and Annie I haven't given a lot of evaluation to my own future. I think it is time to reassess, and set some fresh goals. What would I like to be doing a year from now, or five years? Who would I like to be with? What accomplishments will I hold as my best effort? If I knew that I couldn't fail, what would I begin tonight?

Darkness claimed Dreamer's staterooms, each filled with quiet thoughts, and unclaimed questions.

CHAPTER EIGHT, SEATTLE:

Prayer is the conclusion, and beginning.

The Wharf Street Grill lights came on as the crew made their way up the dock. A small group of fellow boaters pushed their way into the welcoming aroma of coffee and pastry. Even in the pre-dawn shadows, it was easy to see that this would be a busy place as the morning came to life.

When they finally had steaming cups in front of them, Bruce asked in a partial whisper, "What did you think of her?" A playful grin hinted a shared secret.

"Think of whom?" the skipper answered with a puzzled expression.

"You are so bogus!" Bruce snorted. "We've been talking a lot about them. And you know that we are talking about Kathy and the kids. Don't you wish they were going back to Seattle with us?" He shared a little wink with Annie.

"Nope. I haven't given them a thought this morning. Have you had time to look at the menu?" He seemed to be fully absorbed in the breakfast selections.

"You are so bogus! We saw the way she hugged you last night. That wasn't someone you don't think about!" It was fun morning banter. "BOGUS!"

"O.K. Maybe I have thought a little bit about her … them. But I'm more concerned about getting started for Seattle. Weather span says we might only have light winds from the northwest. We may need to diesel home, and with little wind, we could run into some fog."

Annie's attention was on full alert with the word,"fog." "You mean we might need to ring the bell again?" The prospects suddenly dimmed her eagerness for this final day.

"I don't think it will be that thick," the skipper answered. "But we will need to depend on Jeepers to show us the way, and the radar on the big boats that might be in the shipping channel." After a reassuring smile, he started to say that there was nothing to be concerned about, when the server came to their table for the order.

As soon as the orders were taken, Bruce leaned over toward the skipper and whispered, "Bogus! You were just trying to change the subject. I'll bet she has been on your mind a lot since yesterday." He paused, not sure whether he could jest more. "Frankly, I thought she was marvelous. What a sense of humor, and her wit is almost as sharp as yours. I really like the lady."

A moment of quiet held the table before the skipper replied, "Yeah, I do too."

A few minutes later, the crew, filled with blue berry pancakes and fried eggs, made their way back toward the dock. A light morning fog was being illuminated by the first efforts of sunrise.

"We have time for a potty stop, and then I think we need to get that big ol' boat off the dock," the skipper said with a touch of nostalgia. "I think the last leg of our trip needs an early start."

"Shall we just meet back at the boat?" Annie asked.

Bruce couldn't pass the opportunity for a bit of morning humor. "Yeah, I'll bet you still want to visit that Christmas store. They're not open on Sunday morning." He gave her shoulder a little bump.

"I'll bet they will be," she shot back at him. "Besides, I still have some loonies I need to spend."

"I'll bet we come back here before the summer's over," the skipper said with a bit of a twinkle. "We may still have lots of unfinished business. I'll see you on the boat."

There was very little activity on the inner harbor as *Dreamer* eased out of the marina, just two or three other yachts heading out toward open water.

Suddenly, Bruce asked, "Hey, who's that on the Empress dock?" He pointed off the port bow.

Annie said excitedly, "It's Kathy and the kids."

Indeed it was! They were waving and jumping up and down. In their hands were white cloths, like hotel towels. The skipper eased the bow over toward them a bit. The crew could hear them calling out, "Goodbye, goodbye! Thank you! We'll see you in Seattle, Bye!" They looked like they had just rolled out of their beds to give a big send-off. "Bye, Bye! Thanks for everything!"

The crew joined in the parting celebration. "Bye! See you in Seattle!" They all waved back.

"How cool was that?" Bruce asked. Annie had tears in her eyes.

By the time they were at the outer buoy, it was clear they would have no wind to sail for a while. The fog limited visibility to about a quarter mile, which eliminated Annie's anxiety about ringing the bell all morning. The water surface in the Strait was as smooth as a lake, with a calm sheen. It was even too early for the gulls to be active.

"I'll tell you what," the skipper began, "if you want to read, or catch up on your notebooks, I think I need to be on the helm. After a while, if you want to continue our conversation, you could bring me a cup of tea. O.K?" *Dreamer* was slicing a clean wake across the glassy surface, the strong diesel powering them easily east by southeast, directly toward Seattle. The GPS indicated the course setting to their next waypoint, a mile north of Port Townsend.

It was only a few minutes later when Bruce's smiling face came up the companionway. "We thought this might be a good time to start, since we are both pretty interested to hear what your plan for the day might be." In his hand were two steaming mugs of tea.

Annie followed him into the cockpit, and took her usual corner spot, tucking her feet under her bunk blanket. "I'm all set too," she announced cheerily. "But I can't imagine what could be added to make the trip any more complete."

Bruce agreed, and wanted to add his gratitude. "We have been talking about what an outrageous week this has been. We are both very grateful that you allowed us to be here, with you." It was as much emotion as he could express without losing control of his voice. "Thanks dad! Thanks for everything. I want to pay for the fuel fill-up when we get home." It was just another way to say it.

The skipper smiled warmly. "You are both welcome. It has been a much better experience than any of us expected."

"I think the moment brings us to the topic for the morning, because when we are forgiven, gratitude is the logical emotion. Having been made right with God, with others, and ourselves, we want to stay right. Gratitude is one of the ways we accomplish that, so I thought our final discussion would be about prayer."

Both Bruce and Annie looked at him with expectation. Finally Bruce asked, "Is there something special we should say, or some special way we should start praying? It seems to me I have had prayers all my life." Again, there was nothing but searching in his voice.

"You know, Bud, I'll bet there is more diversity in the Christian faith over prayer than any other single thing. What it is, and what it does seems so divergent to many. How we should pray has been a topic since Jesus first taught his disciples, which is a great place for us to start." He swept his gaze all around to check for any other boats. There were none in sight.

"Let's begin with the obvious: prayer is a conscious connection with an Almighty and grace-giving God. We may have a host of reasons why we do it, but it is first and foremost, an effort on our part to be near, connected to, or in the presence of the Almighty, who we genuinely believe, loves us." He paused to watch their pens at work in their notebooks. "The disciples had witnessed Jesus seeking time to be in prayer. He prayed before the great signs and miracles; he prayed before key decisions were made. He seemed to draw power and focus from those times of prayer, so they asked him to teach them to pray also."

"To some people being connected to God may seem like an absurd notion. God is, after all, holy and eternal, and we are limited and finite. How in the world could we connect?"

"But until 1844," he continued, "Samuel Morse couldn't convince the congress that messages could be sent across a wire. It was just an absurd notion. How ridiculous the idea sounded that the human voice could be carried the same way, until Alexander Graham Bell demonstrated that it actually could. At one time or another, ideas like fiber optics, laser communication, or satellite up-links have been unbelievable. So the obvious beginning point is that we have fantastic communication possibilities, many of which have not been revealed. I think that it is so amazing that we can go down to the cell phone in the salon, and call Fiji, or Tokyo, or New York. We can dial 911 and get help any time we need it. I have heard that today there are nearly a half billion telephones in the world. We can be connected to any of them. We can also be connected to God."

"I'm really glad that the disciples asked Jesus to teach them to pray. They didn't ask for preaching tips, or success formulas, or religious secrets. They asked him to teach them to pray. They sensed that if he had experienced its power, they could too. If he had lived it, they might as well. Could he share it with them? 'Lord, teach us to pray,' they asked."

"Jesus began by announcing a liberating communication possibility. He taught them to approach prayer with confidence. He said, 'ask, and it will be given you; seek and you will find; knock and it will be opened to you, for everyone who asks receives, and he who seeks finds, and to him who knocks it will be opened.' That's a triple promise. In the Hebrew pattern, a repetition like that is the same as saying, 'it's really, really, really true!' Jesus wanted them to begin with confidence. God would hear their prayer. They really could connect."

"The nature or character of God was revealed by many of the parables and stories, but principally He is revealed when Jesus tells them to call him 'Father' or 'Abba', which means 'dad' or daddy.' Regrettably many people want to limit the nature of God to the images they have of their own father. It was however, a word Jesus carefully chose to suggest the very nature of One who cares unquestioningly, One who protects, helps, soothes, comforts us, and nurtures absolutely. And it was a word that had never been used in relationship to God. Nowhere in all of Rabbinic literature, is there anything that corresponds to Jesus' use of the personal pronoun 'my father' or 'our father.' He was teaching something shockingly new."

The skipper waited until their pens were still, before he continued. "Can you sense the confidence that he must have conveyed to them? This prayer is so special that in the early church, only the confirmed members could pray it. They thought that spectators and inquirers weren't ready for its power or mystery. It was called the 'believer's prayer.' It begins with confidence."

"Then, in the second place, we go forward with gratitude. We are included in the mystery of it, for we are invited along. Jesus had every right to say, 'my father,' for he is the Son of God, the Messiah. But in this we are welcomed to stand with him, in the place of holy closeness and to pray, 'our Abba.' We go forward with gratitude because a new way of praying is being born, a new prayer reality. It is so simple we might miss it. From the lips of Jesus we receive a Christian mantra, an ancient Aramaic word, 'Abba!' The whole point of which is that we sense a growing closeness, a holy connection to God."

"The challenge for us today is…" the skipper would have gone on had not Bruce interrupted.

"But dad, how about 'thine is the kingdom. Or 'give us this day'? There is so much more to the prayer." The intensity of his question demonstrated his involvement in the topic.

"Of course there is. It could take years of study and still not reveal all the inspiration in this prayer," the skipper affirmed. "God's name, or nature, will be hallowed, his Kingdom will come, and the future does belong to him. Out of God's goodness we are given daily bread, which is the work of a creative providential Father. Our sins are forgiven, which is the work of a redeeming Father on our past. And the Work of a Holy Spiritual Father releases us from bitterness and prevents future sins by enabling us to forgive others. That is the triune nature of God involved with our past, present and future needs. He delivers us from the power of temptation, from the threat of evil, and from death itself. No wonder the early church added the benediction of kingdom, power, and glory. This great God that Jesus revealed to us, and connected us to, is 'Abba.' Our Father." For several minutes the only sound on the boat was the throb of the engine.

Finally, the skipper began again. "This is a perfect time and place to talk about prayer. Can you see anything but water out here?" His hand swept around them.

Both Bruce and Annie pivoted around. There was nothing to see except sea and fog; wane morning sunlight struggled through.

"Here's my point, then. We know that the Strait is only sixteen miles wide, so beyond our available evidence we believe there is a larger reality, Victoria behind us, Port Angeles over there to the right, Hurricane Ridge beyond it, Port Townsend ahead of us. We would call that a belief system based on experience, and physical evidence like charts. We are chugging ahead, full of confidence that we will not fall off the edge." He smiled at the humor of his model. "Now, we know there was a time in human history when sailors actually believed there was an edge that they could fall from. That was their operating reality, and it limited their vision and filled them with fear." They listened to the sound of an approaching powerboat, its engines rumbling in the soft veil of fog. Finally, it came into distant view, a couple hundred meters to starboard, hurried past, and disappeared again from their sight.

"Suppose that ancient primitive view of the world is a model," the skipper reconnected their discussion, "for the way we have been living, day after day, from a belief system based on personal experience, and flawed evidence that says, 'you're unhappy, sinful, or undependable.' Suppose that all of your life you had been told you were inferior, dense, awkward, sinful, or," looking at Annie, "not fit to be a wife or mother." The words struck her like a physical blow. The waves from the passing cruiser rocked *Dreamer* from side to side.

The skipper slowed the diesel, took it out of gear, pressed the engine kill switch, and turned the rudder hard to port. Instantly *Dreamer* swung around on its momentum. It made a full circle and part of another before floating aimlessly, silently to a dead stop. Save for the faint glimmer of sunlight, it would be difficult to know any direction for sure.

"Don't worry," the skipper assured them. "'Jeepers' knows where we are, and where our proper course is. But for sake of this discussion, wouldn't you feel more secure if there was a very large, safe dock right next us, a dock where we could be securely moored?" Both his listeners nodded their heads. "Of course we all would. So for instruction's sake, let's imagine that we are the sailboat, God is the dock, and prayer is the mooring line that holds us safe and secure. If the dock is over there," he pointed off to the port side, "we don't ask the dock to come alongside of us. We move to the dock. If the dock is out there," he swept his hand toward the bow, "it is our task to position ourselves next to the dock." The happy thought reminded him that he could have used Scott's "po-si-tion."

"Jesus gave us a new belief system for prayer by giving us a radical new understanding of the nature of both ourselves, as a loved and valued person, and the nature of God, whom he called 'Abba.' He literally gave us a new reality in which to live. So with confidence and gratitude, we can be safe and secure, even in the midst of challenge or sadness. Our task is to want to be tied to the dock. It is essentially a choice for us."

"Isn't that only obvious?" asked Annie. "Doesn't everyone want that?" Her question came from a heart still trembling.

"Look at us. We're floating around free. We're on our own. We're having the time of our life," the skipper answered. "Aren't those the standard excuses we hear from folks who are far from the dock? The temptations may appear lucrative, or pleasurable, or more stimulating than anything you've ever known. There are millions of reasons why folks choose not to be tied to the dock, yet evidence shows that they are not very fulfilled, nor aware of dangers that might be closing in on them." Both Annie and Bruce turned to look at the soft drape of fog, and listened for any telltale engine sounds. Only the empty Strait sighed to them.

"We've all heard the old statement, 'I'll believe it when I see it,' haven't we?" the skipper went on at last. "I think that, at least from the standpoint of prayer, is just backwards. Instead, we might come to see it, when we believe it. The more you think about it, we can create any sort of world we choose, if we truly believe in it. Our belief system allows us, maybe even forces us, to live according to it."

"Case in point," he said with a grin, "you both went to school believing that you were going to excel because you had been in the upper percentile of your high school classes. Right?" They both agreed. "And you did achieve even more than you hoped. But can you imagine how difficult it would have been for you if you had come from an abusive home, or one financially deprived, or one of illiteracy, or maybe if you'd had a history of drug arrests, court encounters, or even jail records? The probability of your success would be doubtful at best because it would have come from a problematic, flawed belief system. The belief system we hold shapes our reality; it makes our world." *Dreamer* continued to drift on the tide.

"It sounds to me like you are saying that there are optional realities available to us, more than one." Bruce was wrestling with a philosophical problem.

"That is exactly what I'm saying. Of course the world is real, and what happens on, and to it is real, but even those major things are optional at some level. I am saying that we create our own world. If we choose to have a world that is made in God's image, in Christ's image, then we tie to the dock and hold on as securely as we can... with prayer. Do you want to live in the world as a forgiven person? Then tie to the dock, and believe that you are forgiven! If you want to live in the world as a generous person, tie to the dock, and begin living as a generous person. If you want to be kind, compassionate, considerate, loving, tie to the dock, and see that world open to you. The belief system that you choose will generate the consequences." This was not an easy concept for any of them.

After a moment, the skipper tried to complete the thought. "Prayer is not a vehicle by which we get to modify the world to meet our personal needs, no matter how pure they might be. I've always marveled at people who scoffed at safety standards, and then, with thrilling eloquence and polished phrases, prayed for healing of their shattered bones; or people who knew the medical risks they were taking, but went ahead anyway; and then asked, with fervent passion, that the obvious consequences might be reversed. Jesus warned people who would build their house on sand, because the natural consequence was destruction."

"We get to live in the reality created by our faith system." He turned the key, starting the diesel again. "Prayer is the way we stay connected to God. It is the way we come to understand how the holiness of the God that Jesus revealed, and connected us to, can be present in us, in our world, and in those around us. Prayer does change our world because it changes our realization of it, and our po-si-tion to it." The bow swung around to port, then steadied on their course. They were on their way to Seattle, again.

"I think it was Evelyn Underhill who challenged us to 'focus on the bold affirmation that persons of prayer are children of God who are and know themselves to be in the depths of their souls attached to God, and are wholly guided by that creative spirit'. I think she was talking about a serious contemplative form of prayer. But one that helps us literally feel the presence of a loving, gracious, faith-filling God."

The skipper shrugged his shoulders to ease some of the tension that had been building during this lengthy conversation. "There's one more part of this that I think is essential. I'll just call it the 'increase and decrease of desire.' When you are praying, you are usually focusing on those things of significance to you, and wondering if they are in keeping with the will of God." When they looked at him with puzzled frowns, he explained. "When you are praying about a wedding, the when, where, if, all those pertinent questions, aren't you seeking God's will be done? When you are praying about the health of a colleague, or surgery for a family member, aren't you seeking the same thing? You can even pray about your jobs, or a church home, or buying a kitty." Bruce nodded with new understanding, and Annie chuckled at the thought of a kitty.

She said, "I'm not sure I have the grasp on this yet. Do you mean that my feelings are going to be like a barometer of God's will toward these things?"

"Not exactly," the skipper said with a growing grin.

"Let me change the model a little bit, sweetie," he said patiently. "Suppose you went to your grandmother's house for the weekend. You needed to talk to her about Bruce, and hear what she felt about your future. You know that she loves you. You admire her sweet spirit, and her abiding faith. You relax in the aroma of her kitchen, and are charmed by her favorite hymns. Together you chat about marriage in general, about the old days, about Bruce, about the future. She tells you that she has always been proud of you, and is confident that you will make a wise and careful choice in all these things. She assures you that you have the full support of your family, whatever your final decision might be. Let me ask you, how would you feel as you left her house?"

"Yeah, I see what you're saying. I'd feel really positive, refreshed, and she hadn't made any decision that I should make in the first place." New understanding lit Annie's smile. "I would have increased desire for those things because of her presence, not because she had given me her guidelines."

"I know this must sound really strange to you right now. So the only thing I can suggest is that you try it. While these matters are on your mind, go to a quiet place with no interruptions. Keep them on your mind, while for about ten or fifteen minutes, maybe more, you do all that you can to stay connected to God. I have found it helps to just say 'Abba,' or 'Lord.' That's my favorite word. Say the word, 'holy,' 'Savior,' 'Emmanuel,' or 'alleluia.' The point is to allow the focus of your prayer to be something other than the stream of words you would pour out to God to justify, or argue the case for your concern. Don't worry about any structure, or phrases. Just let your mind be focused on God. " The skipper could see the skeptical smile forming on Bruce's face.

"This is just an experiment, guys. Try it three times a day for a week, and see if there is any change in your feelings about the matters on your heart. Is there an increase of desire, or a decrease? Also be aware of any change you might feel in your own vitality, in personal attitude, energy level, or focus."

"Dad, this sounds sort of off the wall, don't you think?" Bruce was really struggling with the scientific self that he had carefully groomed.

"Yes it does, son." He rarely used the term any more. "The empirical method would tell you that there is no valid measuring level here. Try it anyway. Think of it as a spiritual break, like a kindergarten recess for your spirit. But let your prayer time be a priority for you to give it an honest try. Remember, you will see it if you believe it." Annie was carefully studying Bruce's face. "Can you do that?" The morning light seemed to be growing brighter; overhead there was a genuine hint of blue sky.

"Of course I can," Bruce answered with a firm voice. "Most of my life I have thought of prayers as something memorized, or part of the liturgy of the church. This is a whole new notion for me. I think I might be a little dubious, but what could it hurt to try. Right?" He looked at the skipper, then at Annie.

The skipper gave a grimace. "That is the attitude of, 'I'll believe it when I see it,' don't you think? Isn't that the attitude that you've had in the past? What I'm suggesting this morning, and maybe I haven't said it clearly enough, is that you make an intentional decision to shape a change in your life by reshaping your belief system, anything you want to become. Then, begin realizing that possibility of being the sort of person you were crafted, created, designed to become. God's pure plan for your life is the very best. Didn't we say that the meaning of 'peace,' or 'shalom,' is the highest good that God can provide? Let that pour into your life through prayer." The skipper felt he was close to a rare communication moment with Bruce.

"If it helps to make a procedural model, use these three ingredients: openness, stillness, and waiting. By openness, I mean readiness, even expectation. When we expect to be with God, we are ready to see divine inspiration, however it pleases God to be revealed. By stillness, I mean to keep out the clutter of noise or distractions by using our prayer word. It helps us center our attention on God by not thinking of words or phrases. And by waiting I mean to welcome God rather than trying to anticipate or force the moment. Remember, it is you who are moored to God, not the other way around."

"Hey," Annie said suddenly, pointing off the starboard

side, "isn't that land?" A distinct headland was appearing out of the fog.

"I do believe that is Point Wilson. Port Townsend is just around the corner," the skipper replied. "I'm grateful that Jeepers has brought us to our waypoint safe and sound, and the flooding tide has helped our speed a bunch." Looking carefully at both of his companions, the skipper asked, "Are you O.K. with all of this? Have I said too much about it, or…?" He let the question hang in the air.

Bruce was the first to say, "No, not too much at all. I want to hear much more about this, because I think you have only opened the Prayer 101 door." His voice was strong again, and his resolve was becoming evident. "I'd like very much to experience this. I want to be a person of faith. Maybe I should use your words, I choose to believe I can become a person of faith."

He would have said more, but the skipper asked him, "You believe, then, that you can have the God revealed through Jesus more in your life, more in your world?"

"I definitely do!" Bruce said with conviction. "Motivation is not my challenge, it is simply knowing what the first step might be." He loved the wrinkles at the corner of his dad's eyes. "It is not comfortable for me to think about such a new concept, but I am thrilled by the possibility."

"Well then, it seems like you have already begun, if you are really open to it. We are after all, people who believe in the process." The skipper's chuckle was warm and genuine. He was aware that the morning sun was burning away the fog.

Bruce shook his head slightly. "I thought my cup was full yesterday, and now I feel like more has been added. I want to say 'thank you,' again and again, for this amazing trip. You have helped me... us so much." Then, showing a genuine grasp of sensitive caring, he took a big breath and asked the skipper, "You've been on the helm for quite a while this morning. Would you like a break now, or should I come back in a few minutes?"

"The charts say that this is an area of tide rips," the skipper answered with a satisfied smile. "Thanks for the offer. I'll stay with it a while, then take you up on the break after you spend some time below." Both Bruce and Annie stretched their legs, ready to put this new information to work. As the steaming exhaust chimneys from the Port Townsend lumber mill slowly slid passed to starboard, the skipper watched the west-bound Victoria Clipper, a jet powered catamaran, pass to port on the far side of the channel, on its way to pick up some very special passengers. He smiled a happy satisfaction.

Nearly an hour later, he hurried down the companionway toward the head. "I was dancin' foot to foot," he said with a thin grin. It was obvious he was in a bit of a hurry.

"Hey, who's driving the boat?" Bruce asked.

As the door closed behind him the skipper said,

"It's O.K. I have the helm locked down on course. I'll hurry."

Bruce was making his way up to the steering station. Sure enough, the setscrew was tightened, keeping *Dreamer's* wheel on course. They were a couple of miles from the shore and no traffic in sight. It was as the skipper said, 'O.K.'

Moments later, when he returned, the skipper said, "That will teach me to have a second cup of tea." His grin, no longer urgent, suggested only humor.

"I'm sorry dad," Bruce began an apology. "We got so into our discussion that I lost track of time. I should have spelled you a long time ago." The three were back in the cockpit together.

"It was really my fault," Annie declared bravely. "We tried the prayer time, separate of course," she said as though there might have been some confusion. "I liked the idea of using the word, 'Emmanuel' because Amy Grant sings that Christmas song. I told Bruce the surprise for me was how quickly a quarter hour can go by when I just said over and over, 'Emmanuel.'"

She was nearly breathless with enthusiasm. "I don't think there was any flash of light, or deep insight. But I really do feel refreshed after that first time of prayer. It was... no, it is wonderful." She looked first at Bruce, then at the skipper. The boat was making great progress, just passing the east end of Marrowstone Island.

Bruce offered, "My choice was, 'Lord'." He smiled

knowing that his dad had suggested that as his favorite prayer word. "I think it is special that you use it, and because Jesus used it often. It does mean 'Master,' doesn't it dad?"

"It does!" The skipper thought about how much this young man had grown in just a week. "It is a title showing honor and majestic authority. Think about it, (his listeners both smiled at his use of the familiar phrase,) at the time of the first Easter, it was Thomas who said, 'My Lord, and my God,' when he saw the nail prints in Jesus' hands. By the time the New Testament was written, 'Jesus is Lord,' was a basic confession of faith." The skipper nodded proudly. "I think it is a perfect prayer word."

Not wanting to be left out of the conversation, Annie said, "If I remember correctly, 'Emmanuel' means, 'God with us,' doesn't it? I have heard that so many times in the Christmas readings." She was pretty confident that she was right, this time.

"That's exactly what it means. And how perfect for a prayer word: to say over and over again, 'God is with us.' It is a prophecy from Isaiah, made to king Ahaz, that if the nation would be faithful, there would be a savior born, and the government would be upon his shoulders." The skipper broke into the melody familiar as the Halleluiah chorus. "And in the Old Testament, it is spelled, 'Immanuel.'"

Bruce was quick to comment more. "I don't know if I was doing it right, but this is the first time I can think of that prayer was not a labor, and the minutes passed more quickly than I expected." Annie's curls gave that quick nod to show her agreement. "But I'm not sure if I would think of it as prayer, because I didn't say anything." Bruce's eyebrows arched to show his sincere probing.

"You didn't say anything specific, you mean. But did you sense that you and God were on the same plane? Did you feel in any way connected?" The skipper's blue eyes searched his son's face.

"Yeah, when you ask it that way, I did. I was thinking about all sorts of other things though, you know, how great this trip has been, how much we appreciate your work for us, how bright our future seems. There were tons of things that were going through my mind."

The skipper tried not to smile too largely with satisfaction. He didn't want to claim any of Bruce's success. He did say, "Bud that was what you were praying about, rather than trying to make fancy sentences, or worrying about semantics. Gratitude, praise, petitions are all components of authentic prayer. I'm proud that you grasp so much of the concept right away." He offered and exchanged a high five with him. "The other thing I want to suggest is that you make sure that this is a process. You might not have sensational insights immediately. But try to think about your general feeling about prayer. It seems to me that this has been a pretty O.K. experience for once. Do you agree?"

"Oh definitely!" he answered. "And if I think about

it, all those things seem more clear in my mind, like I sharpened the focus, or made them a little bit brighter on my screen." Bruce was looking at the shoreline far to port. "I'm anxious to have another try at it later. Does that sound like something I would have said a week ago? I don't think so!" His voice was playfully mocking.

"But how about all those people," Annie asked, "who want prayer before a meeting, or during a special worship experience, or…" she was having some challenge forming her question.

"How about prayer as most people think about it?" the skipper finished for her. "Do you think I am saying anything against how prayers are often shared or heard in church?" He shook his head. "I don't mean to take anything away from that activity at all. In fact, we can call those 'devotional' prayers, and just think how many I have used for us just this week! There are times when those shared prayers help focus, or inspire," he smiled weakly, "or inform folks. Some of the time those prayers are like sermons we listen to with our eyes closed, and some of the time they are like a laundry list of human complaints. Some of the time they are like the poetry other people write for us, or the words to a familiar old hymn that touches our hearts. We must assume that God, who knows our very heart, has at least a vague knowledge of our situation, and a notion of our needs. Our prayers are not an attempt to inform God. So they must be an effort to rally our efforts to do something about them."

"I have heard it said," the skipper concluded, "that we should pray as though everything is up to God. But we should work as though everything is up to us." He paused to point out Foul Weather Bluff, and the north end of Hood Canal.

"Aren't there some pastors, though," Annie asked seriously, "who just seem to have a special holiness when they pray? I can think of some Christmas services, where I was moved to tears by beautiful and often-repeated prayers."

"Sweetie, I hope I have not said one thing to take away that wonder." The skipper looked into her face with honest sincerity. "Prayers in public worship are a source of great faith." He took a deep breath, knowing how close he was to offending her spirit. "But Jesus also warned his disciples about those who prayed long, flowery, loud prayers that were designed to impress the listeners, and display the eloquence of the prayer. Jesus said that they had already received all that they would ever get from that sort of activity. I guess they were for show, rather than true connection to God, for display rather than devotion. Does that make sense in light of our previous discussion?"

From their port quarter they could hear the whine of a jet turbine. Most of the fog had burned away, which enabled them to see the classic union jack graphics on the side of the Victoria Clipper, on her way into Seattle.

"There go our friends," the skipper said with a wry smile. "They will be home hours ahead of us."

"Was that a prayer?" Annie asked. The tone was playful, but the meaning was serious.

"If you are asking whether I feel connected to God, the answer is, 'yes.' And if you are asking if I'm thinking about their comfort or safety, the answer is still, 'yes.' And if you are asking if I am praying for anything that is yet to happen…" he paused as though carefully choosing his words, "yeah, I guess that is sort of in there too." All three of them were somewhat surprised by the skipper's boyish response.

The skipper finally broke the comfortable quiet that had settled over the cockpit. "Hey, who's ready for some food, or at least something soothingly cool to drink?" He looked at his watch to confirm that, in fact, the morning was very nearly over. "As I see it," he began playfully, "there are three jobs. Someone needs to steer; someone needs to watch out for traffic, deadheads, or unknown disasters; and one needs to make sandwiches. I'm willing to do either of the last two." His pause conveyed the understanding that he was looking for volunteers.

Quick as a flash, Annie said, "I'll make sandwiches!" Giving Bruce a friendly jab in the ribs, she continued, "Looks like it's your turn to drive, big guy." Laughter filled their space, like bubbles around children at play. Minutes later she had a plate full of deviled ham sandwich quarters, a bowl of chips, and three chilled bottles of Molson Canadian. Sometime during the laughter and reflection, they each realized that this was to be their final meal on the journey.

"Dad is that a Coast Guard station in front of us?" Bruce asked from the helm. They could see a small lighthouse and a huge radar antenna near the typical red orange coast guard buildings.

"It sure is," he replied. That's Point No Point."

Annie mused, "Most of the names around here are either Native American, or early explorers. Who was No Point?"

Before the skipper could answer, Bruce chuckled, "He was my professor in Comp Science. I never did know what he was talking about for sure." His humor drew smiles from the others.

Finally, the skipper answered. "It looks like a classic turning point because it seems to stick out into the Sound. Actually we will hold our course. It really isn't a point at all. Skunk Bay forms a receding shoreline to this west side; that's what gives us the impression of a point. Just as soon as we clear these trees, we'll be able to see the skyline of Seattle." The news was both welcome and nostalgic.

"Dad, would you mind taking the helm again?" Bruce realized the briefness of his duty. "I'd like to get something from my stateroom." His expression did not seem to be prankish.

The skipper's remark was, however. "Oh sure! He does a tiny bit of work, enjoys a beer, and now he wants a nap!" His gaze swept the area for traffic, just a couple of small fishing boats at the point and a smattering of fellow travelers on their way back home. There still was insufficient wind to put up the sails.

Annie was browsing through the pages of her notebook. "I'm still hooked on the idea of a world that is subject to our attitudes. That just flies in the face of everything I know to be true about reality." She looked at the skipper, hoping to reengage the discussion.

"I know what you mean," the skipper said at last. "When I was at Willamette, I loved the geology class. The challenge for me was the professor's insistence upon teaching us the concept of evolution, which was alien to my creationist belief. He continually had evidence of a geologic past that stretched way beyond the dimensions of scripture, evidence in the form of fossils that established a time line I couldn't debate. I found, to my surprise, that by integrating his view of the past with my understanding of scripture, I had a fresh idea of how God created. There was never a question of the truth of one or the other, but the shift of understanding that can happen when we shift our attitude." He was trying to say the same thing they had shared a couple of hours previously.

Annie pursed her lips and asked, "In my notes I wrote, 'the way we choose to see the world creates the world we see.' Did I write that correctly?" When he nodded, she asked again, "Are you saying that my interpretation or perception determines the shape and scope of what is created?" Tiny furrows creased her forehead.

"That is probably a stretch of what I had in mind." Then, trying to find a way to be clearer, he said, "Suppose that a firefighter in the midst of a forest fire, and a farmer in a field of ripe strawberries, were both doing their job in Yakima, when a great big rain storm swept through. The firefighter is gratefully saying 'thank God, the forest is saved!' while the farmer is saying sadly, 'an act of God washed away my crop, and destroyed my livelihood.' The way each of them chose to perceive the same rainstorm created their worldview. For one it was a blessing, for the other, a curse."

"I can think of an old story that may help me clear this bit for you. There once was an old Chinese farmer who had a son, and one old horse. One day the horse ran away and the neighbors gathered around to sympathize with him. 'Oh what terrible misfortune,' they said to him because his horse was most of his earthly wealth. But the farmer replied, 'who knows? Only the future can tell.' Sure enough the next day the horse returned to the barn, bringing with it an entire herd of wild horses. Now the neighbors gathered to proclaim his good fortune, for he was vastly advantaged. 'Oh how lucky you are,' they cried enviously. 'Who knows?' the farmer said. 'Only the future can tell.' Wouldn't you know, the very next day as he was trying to tame these wild horses the son was thrown to the ground and his leg was badly broken. Once again the neighbors came saying, 'Oh what misfortune! This is such a terrible thing, to have a crippled son.' You can guess the farmer's reply."

Annie nodded, "Who knows, only the future. Right?"

"Right you are," the skipper grinned. "And the very next day a great Chinese general came through the district conscripting young men into the army to go to war. Now the neighbors declared his good fortune for being able to keep his son at home, to which he gave the same reply. Did the concrete absolute world of that farmer change from situation to situation? One horse is after all one horse, or a herd is a herd. But his perception and understanding of that world was very flexible. The world he chose to see, created the world he could embrace."

"But skipper," Annie wanted to keep from arguing, "You are not saying that we can choose to be an optimist or a pessimist are you? That would color our view of the world around us."

"That might be part of it," the skipper agreed. "But it is more than just an interpretation. Each of us can in a simple way access an amazing advantage within ourselves once we come to believe that mercy is a choice, and malice is optional, and not inevitable. When we finally make up our..." He would have finished the sentence had Bruce's grinning face not appeared so suddenly in the companionway. He had a nervous expression the skipper hadn't seen for a long while.

"Sorry to have taken so long," Bruce said as he entered

the cockpit. "I had to pray for courage." His smile did not fade, nor did his nervousness.

Looking first at Annie, then the skipper, and back to Annie, he said, "I've been trying to find the right time and the right way to say this." He paused for a very deep breath. "Sweetheart, I love you. This week has been a time when I have seen just how much that love means to me." He removed a small velvet box from his pocket.

"I can't think of a better time or place than this to ask you if you'll marry me." Her tiny gasp was like a kiss. "I want to be your husband, forever. Will you be my bride?" He lowered himself to one knee and offered her a lovely diamond ring. The rumble of the diesel and the soft splash of the bow wave were the only sounds on the boat. "Honey, will you marry me?"

Tears filled her eyes as Annie said, "Oh Bruce, it's so perfect! Yes, I do love you, and…" she paused to quiet her trembling heart, "Yes, I want to be your wife. Yes," she said firmly, and finally, "I'll be honored to marry you." She leaned forward to receive his kiss.

The skipper, who had been holding his breath, cheered and clapped his hands, "Oh yeah! Way to go guys!" Then, leaving the helm for a moment, he came around to hug and congratulate them both.

After a minute or two of happy celebration, Bruce said to his dad, "I didn't ask you if I could do this. I assumed that this whole week has been a blessing from you. I really do love her." His nervousness was still spilling over in unrehearsed sentences.

"Of course you have my blessing. Your mom will be delighted, as will your sister. You didn't need to ask me, your heart was already telling you how right this is. Have you talked to Annie's folks?" When Bruce shook his head, the skipper said, "Sooner is better than later in this case. If they are traditional at all, they might think their blessing is important."

Annie was still smiling and looking at her ring. "They will probably wonder where the wedding will be and how much it will cost them. I don't think they have the idea of giving a blessing." The words were tainted with sadness but her smile remained radiant. "Bruce this is gorgeous. Tell me how you chose it, and when?" She raised her eyes to his.

"It has been a real challenge for me to keep this secret. I got it when I bought your cross. I think it might be an anniversary ring, with the three-diamond setting. I know this might be something that we should pick out together. The shopkeeper said we could exchange it, or if you want to go shopping for another, we can keep this for a future anniversary celebration. But I thought it might represent you, me, and the Spirit of God with us."

She looked lovingly at the ring for a long moment. "It's perfect!" she whispered. "I think I need to cry for a minute." She pulled her knees up, buried her face in her hands, and quietly sobbed.

Bruce looked anxiously toward the skipper, needing some guidance.

"Everything is just fine, Bud." The skipper reassured him. "You did good! That is a wonderful memory, in which I am delighted to be included. Everything is just fine!" He was quiet for a long moment, then said, "I am honored."

Annie wiped her eyes and blew her nose on a napkin. "Oh wow! In my little girl dreams I was always surprised by this moment. Now, it's better than I dreamed. Bruce, you are wonderful!' She reached for his hand.

"Skipper," she said tenderly, "I think I'm going to choose my world, a happy, healthy, faithful world. And I think I need to ask for your help." When their eyes met, she said, "Oh not in my choice. But, I am thinking that my parents might not be much help in seeing the possibilities for our wedding. Do you think that I might impose upon you more, to be our guide," she paused for a deep breath, "my guide?" Looking at Bruce for confirmation, she continued, "Can you help us plan a reasonable, small, or intimate wedding that won't be a big show? Can you make some suggestions that would keep it affordable? I think I'd like not to count on my parents' money, or their limitations." Thinking about that thought for just a minute, she said, "Who knows, it might be a time of growth for them too. Only the future knows." She trembled with delight.

The next hour and a half was spent in delighted

conversation about possible venues, formats, invitation lists, sequence of dinners, traditions, and happy laughter. The in-coming tide was at full slack when *Dreamer* finally eased into the Elliot Bay Marina. Mooring lines were secured, bags were packed, and a quick clean up made her ready for the next adventure.

As the three made their way up the dock, the skipper said, "You know, Maggie's at the Bluff," he pointed over to the marina-side restaurant, "makes a fantastic hamburger. I'll buy!" When Bruce and Annie looked at him, he added, "Well, it's a sort of an engagement party! Think about it! They have a chocolate brownie dessert called a 'shipwreck sundae' that is world famous, and will knock your socks off." Their laughter echoed through the marina.

Epilogue:

On Friday May 26, 2006 Annie and Bruce were married at St Andrew Presbyterian Church in Renton, Washington. Dr. Norman O'Banyon, being the interim pastor to the congregation, officiated. In the full wedding party, four attendants on each side, Scott Swanson was ring bearer and honorary best man. Jenny Swanson was flower girl and honorary maid of honor, being sister of the cross with the bride. In attendance, along with a full house of family, colleagues, school chums, and friends, was Kathy Swanson, who sat very close to the pastor at the reception. It may be time to plan another session aboard *Dreamer!*